COUSIN ASH

COUSIN ASH

S.E. SHEPHERD

This edition produced in Great Britain in 2022

by Hobeck Books Limited, Unit 14, Sugnall Business Centre, Sugnall, Stafford, Staffordshire, ST21 6NF

www.hobeck.net

Copyright © S.E. Shepherd 2022

This book is entirely a work of fiction. The names, characters and incidents portrayed in this novel are the work of the author's imagination. Any resemblance to actual persons (living or dead), events or localities is entirely coincidental.

S.E. Shepherd has asserted her right under the Copyright, Design and Patents Act 1988 to be identified as the author of this work.

All rights reserved. No parts of this book may be used or reproduced by any means, graphic, electronic, or mechanical, including photocopying, recording, taping or by any information storage retrieval system without the written permission of the copyright holder.

A CIP catalogue for this book is available from the British Library.

ISBN 978-1-913-793-81-4 (pbk)

ISBN 978-1-913-793-80-7 (ebook)

Cover design by Jayne Mapp Design

Printed and bound in Great Britain

❀ Created with Vellum

ARE YOU A THRILLER SEEKER?

Hobeck Books is an independent publisher of crime, thrillers and suspense fiction and we have one aim – to bring you the books you want to read.

For more details about our books, our authors and our plans, plus the chance to download free novellas, sign up for our newsletter at **www.hobeck.net**.

You can also find us on Twitter **@hobeckbooks** or on Facebook **www.facebook.com/hobeckbooks10**.

To Kim, Peter, Tracy, Karen, Dave and Julie – my cousins
As children our families were entwined, and we remember those days with nostalgia

NOTE FROM THE AUTHOR

In the UK, when a person has been missing for at least seven years and has not been heard from during that time by family members or any other interested party, there is a presumption of death.

People in the category presumed dead have been declared dead through legal process, in absence of a body. It is not definitely known whether the people in this category are actually dead, but for legal purposes their status as dead has been declared.

No one has heard from Cousin Ash for more than twelve years. Ash is in the category presumed dead.

PROLOGUE

ELIZA – 2010

'SCOTT!' *Eliza called her cousin's name, trying desperately to see anything in the impenetrable darkness.*

Ash was still screaming. Those horrifying wails that caused Eliza's blood to run cold, the cries moving further into the woods as every second passed.

'Help me. Where the hell are you?' Reaching behind her, Eliza placed her hands on the ground and pushed herself back up to standing, angrily kicking out at the root that had sent her flying. Reaching all around her, she tried to grab onto anything that might be a part of Scott. But there was nothing. He was gone.

Then, as abruptly as they'd started, Ash's screams stopped.

In that instant, Lullaby Woods became still.

Somehow, the silence was even more alarming than the previous cacophony of sound. In the dark, hushed woods, Eliza realised she was now totally alone. All her senses stifled. 'Scott, Ash – where are you?' She waited, still clutching at the air around her, her chest rising and falling with such ferocity she thought she might pass out. This was real fear.

Before, in their childhood game, she would love that moment when Uncle Robert gave the signal, and they all raced back through the woods to Auntie Miriam and the safety of the car. She would throw herself onto the back seat, feeling the adrenaline course through her veins. It was so exhilarating. But now, this absolute blackness and total absence of noise, save for her own heartbeat, this was not exhilarating. This was the most disturbed and lonely she had ever felt.

1
ELIZA – 2022

Eliza threw a stick and waited for Bear to return it. Picking it up, he made off across the park with it in his mouth.

'You're supposed to bring it back!' Eliza shouted after the disappearing pup. 'It's called fetch, not steal.'

She gave up. He just wasn't getting the idea. Never mind, the most important thing was that he got to have a good run about. Whatever had possessed her neighbour to choose a puppy that was half Newfoundland? He had boundless energy. Far more than Eliza at this ridiculous hour.

Bear returned. The stick was nowhere to be seen; it no doubt lay ripped to shreds on the grass. Eliza searched the ground. 'You want another one?'

Bear wagged his fat tail, loving the game.

As Eliza watched Bear bound off again, the latest stick hanging from his mouth, she experienced a swell of love for him. Offering to walk him had been a good idea. If nothing else, it meant she was forced to get out and get some fresh air herself, and at this time of day there was a nice cool breeze.

'Can you put your dog on a lead?' A woman with a small terrier was making her way across the park, shouting as she walked. She had on extremely sensible shoes and a well-worn, waxed jacket, and she had a face on her like everybody's least favourite headmistress. It was immediately obvious there was going to be trouble.

Eliza gritted her teeth. She had hoped that coming this early would mean there would be no other dogs here. Bear still needed to work on his manners when it came to greetings.

'I said, can you put it on a lead? My dog is a rescue; she's extremely nervous,' the woman called.

'I heard you. I'll try. But I can't do anything until he comes back.'

Bear, spotting that they'd been joined by the little Yorkshire terrier and her owner, bounded back at breakneck speed.

Eliza tried to call him to her. 'Bear ... here boy ... come to me.'

'Get him on a lead!' The woman was waving her arms around, which served to make Bear even more excited.

Ignoring the treat Eliza was desperately holding out for him, he vaulted over to the terrier and sniffed the other dog's rear.

'If you can't control him, he should not be off the lead! Get away from my dog.' The woman tapped Bear hard on the nose.

'Hey, there's no need to hurt him.'

'Get him on a lead – now!'

'I'm trying. If you could stop shouting it would help.' The more Eliza lunged for Bear's collar, the more he sidestepped away from her. 'Bear, come here, right now. I mean it!' She tried again to make a grab for the pup. Her face flushed.

'If he doesn't stop snapping, I'll have no choice but to kick him away.'

'Don't you dare! Anyway, he's not snapping. He's friendly.'

'You're not in control of your dog.'

'He's not mine. I was just trying to help my neighbour.' Eliza felt tears begin to trickle down her cheeks.

COUSIN ASH

The woman kicked out at Bear with her sturdy walking shoes. 'Get away from my baby. She's been attacked.'

'Please don't do that! Listen, I'm sorry. I'm trying to get him …'

By now, Bear was swatting at the little dog with his enormous paws; everything about him was just so large and clumsy. The terrier yapped loudly. Eliza couldn't help thinking that she took after her owner.

Finally, as Bear danced past her, bouncing as he went, Eliza managed to grab him by the collar and clip the lead on. Holding tightly onto him, she tried her best to calm him down, which wasn't easy, given that she was almost hysterical herself. She really shouldn't have listened to her neighbour when he said Bear would be okay off the lead.

'You're pathetic,' the snooty woman said.

Eliza tried again to apologise. 'I'm sorry. He's just a bit excited. He's much better when my neighbour's with him. I shouldn't have let him off. It just seemed so deserted, and he needs a good run and—'

The woman interrupted her, 'Do you have any idea what you sound like? Calling him in your silly voice – come here, come here. Babbling away like an idiot. You need to learn how to control him before you let him off the lead. My poor girl was terrified.'

'I'm sorry. You're right.' Eliza wondered how many more times she could say it.

'He's too lively for you. You need to join puppy classes or something.'

'I'm trying to explain to you – I just wanted to help.'

Clearly not prepared to listen to anything further, the woman walked off across the park, her little dog trotting along obediently beside her. As soon as she was a few feet from Eliza, she called out. 'Some people are not meant to have dogs, and you're one of them.'

Eliza knew she was in the wrong. There was no excuse for letting her neighbour's dog bound about like that. But the woman's remarks had hurt her. She suspected the spiteful words would stay with her for the remainder of the day, and she would question herself countless times. Why did she assume a dog would come back to her just because she called him? If God, or the cosmos, or whoever it was that made the bigger decisions in life, had decided she absolutely was not going to be lucky enough to become somebody's mother, why did she stupidly think she could just borrow a puppy and pretend to be a mummy for the day? How naive was she to think she could simply replace the babies she'd lost with a borrowed puppy?

Writing the day off as a bad lot, Eliza was ready to return home and pretty much spend the day crying. That awful woman would soon forget the quarrel. She would no doubt go on with her day, happy that she had protected her baby, but Eliza would be unable to forget. Perhaps if people knew the consequences of their words, they might think before they spoke. Anxiety could be crippling – and not always evident from the outside. Tucking her windswept hair behind her ears, Eliza bent down, trying to wrestle a piece of stick from between Bear's teeth.

'Don't let him chew that – it's bad for his gums.'

Eliza glanced up to see a figure approaching. At five foot eleven he wasn't exceptionally tall for a man, but compared to Eliza and Ash, who had both only made it to the dizzy heights of five foot four, he seemed like a giant. She knew him by his walk. Head down, shoulders rolling as he went. It was not a confident stride.

Ignoring his comment, she asked, 'Scott! What do you want?' As if she didn't know.

'Is that any way to greet me?'

'It's the perfect way to greet you. You never get up this early on a Saturday. So, why are you here?'

'I just wanted to see you. I knew this was the weekend you were walking the dog.' Reaching down to stroke Bear, Scott added, 'Hello there, mate. Christ, you are big, aren't you?'

'Yes, he is!'

'D'you fancy getting a coffee or something? We could get one of those cardboard bacon things you like.'

'Scott, it's great to see you. Don't get me wrong. But ... I know you didn't come here for the sole purpose of joining me for a veggie bacon roll for breakfast. You're going to start talking about the money, and I just can't take it right now. I'm already having a shitty day; I don't need this.'

Scott's manner instantly switched. Screwing up his nose, he sneered, 'You've got a fuckload of money, Elz. You don't even need to work. You never have to worry about bills or letting people down, and you've just moved into a massive house. I would love to know how you could have a shitty day.'

'It's not massive. And even people with money can have a bad time, Scott. Don't be so stupid.'

'Tell me then. Come on. Tell me about your *bad time*.'

'I just had a row with a horrible woman. She really upset me. She told me I was pathetic.'

'Poor old Eliza.'

'Oh, get lost. I don't have to tell you anything.'

'Listen, I've got people texting me for money, looking for me, knocking on my mum's door. Having to juggle all this is giving me flamin' chest pains. That's a shitty day, Elz. Not arguing with some nut job in the park.'

Eliza began dragging a reluctant Bear towards the gates. 'I'm sorry you're in debt. But Auntie Miriam was very specific; she didn't want you to have her money. How can I go against her wishes and just start giving it to you now she's dead?'

'But that's the point – she's dead! So, she won't know. You

could help me out. It wouldn't kill you to give me some. Just a lump sum to get me straight.'

'But *I'd* know, wouldn't I? I'd know I was giving money to the one person that Auntie Miriam stated was not to have any. It would feel wrong.'

'It's not fair!' With his head down, Scott scuffed his trainers on the grass, appearing for all the world like a schoolboy denied sweets.

'I'm sorry.' Eliza felt perhaps life would've been simpler if Auntie Miriam had left everything to the Donkey Sanctuary, as she and Scott had always presumed she would.

'If Ash was still around you wouldn't have got a penny of that money, or inherited Miriam's house.'

'I realise that. She would've left it all to her daughter. Of course she would. But Ash *isn't* around, so she chose me.'

'I could contest it, you know. I reckon I'd have a good case.'

Eliza began heading towards the car park. 'You wouldn't.'

'How do you know?' Scott followed her.

'Because she was of sound mind, and she left her money to her niece. It's all perfectly acceptable. It was her decision to make.'

'And what about her nephew? Why wasn't it acceptable for her to leave half to you and half to me? Just because I was a nephew on her husband's side. I wasn't her flesh and blood, but that doesn't mean I—'

Eliza interrupted him, 'Do you genuinely think it was because you were related to her by marriage?'

'Well...' He shrugged.

After a minute, filled only with the sound of their feet on the path, they reached Eliza's car. Opening the back door, she ushered Bear in and clipped him to his seatbelt. Turning to Scott, she said, 'For the record. It made no difference to her that you were Uncle Robert's nephew, and I was *her* niece. When we were kids, we were both Ash's cousins; she was the link between us. We were all the same. You must know that, surely?'

'Maybe.'

Eliza looked up into his pale grey eyes, which were as familiar to her as a childhood story.

They had been so close, the three of them, almost like siblings. He didn't seem well; he was washed out, and his hair, what was left of it, was unkept. She felt sorry for him and angered by him at the same time.

Walking round and opening the passenger door, Scott indicated he'd like a lift. Eliza nodded. She knew he'd sold his car months ago. The least she could do for him was give him a lift home.

'I was serious about buying you breakfast, you know?'

'Were you?'

'Yes, I like hanging out with you, Elz. I always have.'

She wanted to ask if they could take a rain check for now; that witch with the little dog had totally ruined her appetite. But she knew he'd take offence and she'd already upset him enough by refusing to help. 'Okay. The café by the clock tower?'

'Yeah.' Scott nodded.

'And I'm paying.'

'If you're sure.'

'I am. We just need to drop Bear home first. Can you imagine the carnage he could cause in a café?' She started up the car.

Returning to his favourite subject, Scott said, 'You've got it so easy, Elz. I'd bloody love having that house to myself.'

'It's not all you think it is, Scott.' Eliza bristled. 'Honestly, it's ...'

'What?'

'I don't know.' She shook her head. 'When I'm there on my own, it feels kind of ... strange. And ... the other night, I popped to Blakes, you know the shop on the corner.'

'Of course. Remember when Uncle Robert used to give us 50p each to buy sweets?'

'And you always took ages choosing what you wanted.'

'Yeah. And you always chose a Mars bar. So, anyway, Elz, what's your point?'

'I realised I was out of milk, and it was just before nine p.m., so I threw on my coat and ran over to the shop. On the way back, I felt like someone was following me. I turned around to look, and whoever was behind me shone a torch in my face.'

'Odd. Probably nothing to do with you though. Most likely just a dog walker, picking up shit or something.'

Eliza disagreed. 'It was *in* my face, Scott. I couldn't see a thing. I tripped up the kerb and went down on all fours. And d'you know what? They didn't even stop to help me up. Just turned and buggered off.'

'You never saw them?'

'No. The light was too bright. I was seeing green blobs for ages after.'

'Did you hurt yourself?'

'Yes. I bruised my knee where I landed on the edge of the kerb.'

'Well, that's a bit crap. But it's not the end of the world.'

'Yes, I know it's not the end of the world. But it hurt. It still does a bit.' She rubbed her knee to emphasise the point. 'And … often when I'm in the house, it's like someone's watching me, but I don't know where from.'

'Like who?'

'I don't know. I'm just telling you, living there isn't as great as you think it is.'

Like picking at a scab, Scott said, 'I still say Auntie Miriam chose you because you were her blood.'

He wasn't going to stop until she said it. 'Auntie Miriam cut you out for one reason and one reason only, Scott. She blamed you for what happened to Ash.'

'That's just cruel.'

'I know.'

'I ... I ... loved Ash; you know I did.'

'We both did.'

'So why punish me now? Why leave *all* the money to you? Miriam knew how hard up I was.'

'She blamed you. She never got over it.'

'Well, maybe if she knew I wasn't the only one lying about that night, she'd blame you too.'

Eliza felt the usual guilt course through her veins. The same shame she always experienced when they talked about Ash. Was there something she could've done differently? Scott was right – maybe if Auntie Miriam had known the whole truth, she would've held them both responsible, and the donkeys would now be very rich indeed.

How had it come to this? How had she and Scott ended up on opposing sides? As children they were so close. Scott had always been like the little brother she never had.

ELIZA – 2002

'Ash, Elz, get me down. I'm stuck!' Scott cried.

'You're not stuck,' Ash replied, her usually pretty face twisted in anger, as it always was when she spoke to Scott. 'You're just a baby.'

'I am not!' At seven, Scott was the youngest and smallest of the three.

'If you're not a baby, jump down from that tree. Go on, do it!' Ash called up.

'It's too high.' He continued to cry.

'Stop it. Don't make him jump.' Eliza was already making her way back up the tree to rescue her cousin.

Ash snorted. 'He's so lame.'

'Don't be mean,' Eliza said.

'He's a baby and he knows it,' Ash laughed.

'*I am not!*' Scott's frightened tears were clearly becoming those of frustration. His greatest wish was to be an equal to Ash and Eliza. They might both be nearly ten, but he never took it well when Ash treated him this way.

'Just wait there. I'm coming.' Eliza put her feet on the lower branches, picturing how she'd just got down. Due to the recent rain, the branches were slightly slippery. She needed to be careful. 'I'll get you. Just stop crying and wait for me.'

'He can't stop crying. Because he's a baby.' Ash seemed determined to make the situation worse.

'Get Auntie Miriam. She'll help me down.'

'We're not going to bother her. Anyway, we don't need a grown up. I've told you – I'm coming,' Eliza replied.

'My mum's too busy, making us lunch. Cutting the crusts off the sandwiches for the baby.' Ash laughed again. A cruel, sarcastic sound.

Scott placed his hands over his ears. 'Shut up, shut up, shut up.'

'Come down here and make me!'

'Fine. I will.' Without warning, Scott launched himself from the branch he'd been perched on for the last ten minutes.

Eliza watched him plummet to the ground. He hadn't been that high, maybe just the height of a tall man. Even so, she hadn't expected him to jump. 'Scott, no!'

His small body hit the ground with a thud. Landing awkwardly, his left arm trapped underneath him, he screamed, 'Ouch! Oh, God, it hurts.'

Climbing back down, Eliza ran to him. 'It's okay. I'm here.'

She cradled his head in her lap, wisps of his auburn hair splayed out on her jeans.

He looked up at her, his eyes wet. 'It really, really hurts, Elz.'

Checking his wrist, Eliza could immediately see it was at a grotesque angle. Turning to Ash, she called, 'Go and get your mum.'

Ash had the good grace to look a little guilty. 'I was just kidding.'

'You're always just kidding. You're horrible,' Scott sniffed.

'I didn't think you'd actually jump.'

'Just get your mum. He's going to need to go to hospital.' Eliza could hear the panic in her own voice.

At this information, Scott's wails increased.

Ash strolled back towards the house.

'At least run!' Rocking Scott gently, Eliza reassured him, 'Auntie Miriam will be here in a minute. It'll all be okay.'

'It's hurting more,' he moaned.

'Why did you jump?'

'I'm not a baby.'

'I know you're not. Ash knows it too.'

'I hate her.'

'No, you don't.'

Auntie Miriam appeared at the back door and tottered towards the children, her kitten heels sinking into the damp grass. 'Oh, Scottie, what have you done now?'

2
HANNAH – 2022

LOTTIE AND HANNAH were eating bacon butties in the café by the clock tower. It wasn't as flash as the new coffee places that seemed to spring up every other day in town, but it was clean, the food was amazing, and the staff were friendly. Both girls were comforted by its familiarity.

'I still don't get how you managed to say I love you to the man in the hardware store though,' Hannah laughed.

'Oh, yes, I never finished telling you the story. So, anyway, I got the paint stripper and the other bits and pieces, and as he handed me the stuff, I said thank you and turned to leave. And he said – lovely.'

'*Lovely?*'

'Like, kind of, lovely doing business with you, I guess. But I misheard him at first. I thought he said – love you, and before I knew it, I was saying it back.' Lottie threw up her hands. 'I have no idea why!'

Hannah smiled. 'Probably made his day.'

Lottie agreed. 'Maybe.' She grinned at her friend. 'It's so good to catch up, Han. Feels like I never see you these days.'

'I've just been so busy. Still, I mustn't complain.' Hannah savoured another bite of her sandwich.

'I'm pleased you're happy and that you have loads of people clambering for your attention.'

'Hardly, Lottie! Talk about exaggerate.'

'Can I help it if I'm proud of you?' Lottie tilted her head, causing her long chestnut hair to swing in front of her face.

'You sound like my gran. Mum says she's always talking about me to her friends at Bingo.'

'Aww, Granny Annie. She has every right to brag.' Lottie moved her silky hair away from her face. 'By the way, you have brown sauce on your chin.'

Hannah swiped at her face with a napkin. 'I bumped into Dave in Tesco's this morning; he was with Noah. He introduced me as his boss.'

'So he should! What was Noah like?'

'Cute. He must take after his mum.'

'Absolutely.'

'Dave's earning his keep, you know?'

'Good.'

'He rarely makes so much as a politically incorrect comment these days!'

'From Neanderthal to the soul of discretion,' Lottie laughed.

They ate in silence for a couple of minutes, before Hannah asked, tentatively, 'Heard anything from Chen?'

'Not for a month or so.'

'Where is he now?'

'Somewhere in Greece. He's been hopping about from island to island.'

'You haven't sent him any more money, have you?' Hannah waited for an answer, watching Lottie stare intently into her orange juice. 'Lottie …?'

'*What?*'

'Tell me.'

'Oh, all right, calm down. I sent him a few hundred quid. It wasn't much. Money goes a lot further in Greece.'

'You already bought him a fancy backpack.'

'I had to. D'you know what his mum was planning to send him travelling with?' Without waiting for an answer, Lottie continued, 'A nineteen eighties suitcase. Borrowed from his grandma. Honestly, he would've looked like he was heading off to bloody Hogwarts!'

'You don't have to buy him stuff or give him money. You don't owe him anything.'

'I know!' Lottie snapped.

'You say you know, but ...' Hannah shrugged. 'How many other times have you sent him a few hundred quid, I wonder?'

'Listen, I know it seems odd to you, like I'm paying him to keep quiet about what my dad did.'

'I'm not saying *that*.' Hannah rolled her eyes. 'Jesus, that really *would* be dark.'

'I just want him to have a good time. He had to wait ages before he could travel, and I want this to be an amazing trip of a lifetime type of thing.'

'It already is. I just think he shouldn't be depending on you for it.'

'Do you need reminding what an awful childhood that man had?'

'No.'

'And do you need reminding where all that awful shit took place?'

Hannah sighed; they'd had this conversation before. She hated that Lottie felt such guilt. Her dad had been an awful man, who had done awful things, and it had taken Lottie the best part of a year to even begin to come to terms with it. Hannah often found her awake in the middle of the night, dunking cookies into hot chocolate in an effort to get back to sleep. She knew her friend had struggled to adjust her memories from the father figure who had been a part of her childhood to the monster who had ruined Chen's. Loads of times, Hannah had joined her at the kitchen table, consuming far too many cookies and reassuring her it wasn't her fault, and no, it didn't mean she was a monster too. 'I don't need reminding about any of it, but, like I've said before, you need to get it into your head that *none* of it was your fault.'

'I know, I know. You're right. I can't change it. I need to let my mum rest in peace too and stop trying to fathom out her decisions.'

'Of course you do.'

'It's just … sometimes it's there in the background of my conversations with Chen. The elephant in the room. And … well, I feel like I'm the only one left from the family, so who else are all those boys going to blame?' Lottie shrugged.

'*Not you!* Chen adores you. He's never spoken badly of you. *Me*, yes. He spoke terribly of me when I was questioning him, but never you,' Hannah said.

'I just like to treat him. He's a nice guy.'

'You said when you first met him you couldn't be bothered to give him the time of day.' Hannah tilted her head. 'Bit different now!'

'That was when I couldn't hold a decent conversation with the idiot. Now … we talk about lots of things. Besides, don't forget – I've changed since then too.'

'I know you have. You definitely swear a lot less than you did when we first met.'

'I had a lot to swear about back then!'

'Absolutely,' Hannah agreed. 'But … I hate to think of you holding yourself responsible. However Chen felt in the past, he's put it behind him now. You must understand that. I mean, you've managed to forgive Vincent, haven't you?'

Lottie paused for a second. 'I don't know that I'd go as far as to say *forgiven*. But I refuse to allow what he did to keep affecting me.'

'Well, there you go. Who's to say that's not how Chen feels about your dad?'

'What a mess!'

Hannah placed her hand over Lottie's and squeezed gently.

Pushing her empty plate away with a sigh, Lottie asked, 'So, are we having cake, or what?'

Hannah smiled. Once they came to the part where Lottie began requesting cake, it usually meant things were okay. 'For breakfast?'

'Why not? We're adults, aren't we? We can do what we want.'

'Okay. If you like, although I could do without the calories.' Hannah patted her tummy.

'Oh shush. You know you'll burn it off. Anyway, we can make it carrot cake and kid ourselves it's healthy.'

As Hannah tried to catch the waitress's eye, Lottie leant forward and whispered, 'I can't think where I know that woman from.'

'What woman?'

'Just sat down behind you – don't look.'

Grabbing her phone, Hannah switched the camera to selfie mode and moved the phone from side to side, trying to spot the woman behind her.

'Great trick. I can tell you've done that before.'

'D'you mean the brunette? Early thirties. Quite attractive, but rather uptight?'

'Yes, I guess you could say that.'

'Can't help you, I'm afraid. I've never seen her before in my life.'

'Are you sure? I was hoping you'd be able to put me out of my misery. It's really bugging me!'

'Definitely. I never forget a brunette ... or a blonde, come to that. Actually, I never forget anything!'

COUSIN ASH

The waitress took their order for carrot cake and soon returned with two huge slices.

'Bloody hell, the size of that, we could've shared.' Hannah patted her belly again. 'Talk about the elephant in the room!'

Lottie laughed. A second later she let out a squeak. 'I've got it. I know who she is. Oh, the relief!'

'Who is she?'

'She went to St Bede's College for Girls. She was older, a good three or four years above me. I knew her a bit when she was in her last year. Eliza something.' Lottie tapped the table, obviously trying to remember a surname. 'Griffith, Grylls, Griffin, something like that.'

'Another one who liked to wear those silly kilts,' Hannah said.

'We didn't *like* them; they were just part of the school uniform.' Lottie pulled a face.

'How come you remember her if she was older than you?'

'Because …' Lottie leant in again and dropped her voice back to a whisper, 'her cousin went missing the year after they left school.' Her eyebrows shot up.

'Oh!'

'Eighteen and just disappeared. That makes a person stick in your mind. I can't believe it took me so long to remember.'

'So this cousin of hers, was he or she never found then?'

'She. Her name was Ash. No, never. I remember seeing posters all over town asking if anyone knew where she was. There were a few on my way home from school. Quite creepy – just her face, staring out at you. Eventually, they all got blown away or pulled down. And, like I say, she never came back.'

'Interesting.'

'Look at you – your Spidey senses are working.'

'Shut up! It's just intriguing, don't you think?'

'Sad, I think.'

'Yeah, that too.' Hannah tried her trick with the phone again. 'Who's the guy with her?'

'No idea. Could be a brother or something. They don't go together as a couple, do they?'

'No. If you ask *me*, he's ill. Looks like he could do with a bit of sun. Maybe you'd like to give him some money to go backpacking in Greece, Lottie.'

'Oh, ha bloody ha. No thank you. He's not my type. In fact, I can't see how he would be anybody's type. You're right, he seems like a bit of a pasty-faced loser to me. I'm surprised she's hanging out with him.'

'I just said he looked ill. Blimey, Lottie!'

'What?'

'Nothing.' Hannah shook her head. 'Sometimes I'm reminded you used to be a posh little princess, that's all.'

'Too judgy?' Lottie wrinkled her nose.

'Just a bit. Of course, now you've told me all about her cousin going missing, I'm going to have to ask you to introduce me to her.'

'Really?'

'You know I can't resist a mystery.'

'We'll pop over on our way out.'

'Okay.' Hannah placed a large forkful of carrot cake into her mouth. It was deliciously sweet and spicy.

Their bill was paid, and they were ready to leave. Pushing in their chairs, they casually stopped at the table behind Hannah. Lottie said, 'Hi, are you Eliza Griffith, by any chance?'

'Griffins. Yes.' Eliza looked a bit worried.

'I'm Charlotte Thorogood. Lottie.'

'Oh yes, from St Bede's?'

'That's right. I wasn't sure if you'd remember me.'

'Of course I do. You live in that lovely house, where they have the fetes.'

'Yes. Well …' Lottie didn't seem sure how to finish her sentence.

'It's good to see you.' Eliza smiled politely. She had perfectly straight teeth.

A rather awkward silence followed, during which it was clear from her face that Eliza expected that to be the end of it.

But Lottie had promised an introduction, and she was true to her word. 'This is my friend, Hannah.'

Hannah ran her fingers through her spiky blonde hair and nodded a hello.

After a slight delay, Eliza pointed towards her male companion. 'This is my cousin, Scott.'

The man mumbled something inaudible.

'Well, technically, he's not actually my cousin. He's my cousin's cousin.'

'Right.' Lottie's brow creased. 'Your *cousin's cousin?*'

'His mum is the sister of my mum's brother-in-law.' Eliza was clearly used to trying to explain it.

'R … ight.' The crease grew deeper in Lottie's forehead. 'The sister of your mum's brother-in-law.'

'I get it. You share a common cousin, although you're from different sides of that marriage. Yes?' Hannah asked.

'We did share a common cousin, yes. But she's … erm.'

'Our cousin Ash is dead.' Scott spoke over Eliza.

'Well, she's presumed dead. She's … well, you probably remember it all, Lottie,' Eliza said.

'Yes, I do. I'm so sorry for your loss.'

It must be about a decade since she'd disappeared. Hannah wondered if it was still correct to give one's condolences.

Eliza thanked Lottie.

Hannah couldn't help herself. 'So, what happened to her?

Who was the last person to see her? Who might have an idea where she is? Do you think she's actually dead?'

Lottie held up her hand to stop the barrage. 'Han, I think that's enough questions.' To Eliza and Scott, she said, 'Sorry. Hannah's a private investigator.'

'Well, we can answer all those questions for you,' Scott replied, dispassionately. 'We don't know, we don't know, we don't know, and we don't know.'

Clearly a little embarrassed, Lottie said, 'Sorry. It was nice to see you again, Eliza. You're looking good.'

Hannah whipped a business card out of her bag, 'If you need me, give me a call.' She handed the card to Eliza, who took it with a look of confusion.

'We won't need you. Ash's dead – I just told you that.' Scott gave her an angry look.

'Keep it, just in case.' This comment was directed towards Eliza. Hannah had already decided that Lottie's first analysis of Scott had been correct; he was a pasty-faced loser.

3
ELIZA – 2022

BACK AT THE park the next day, Eliza kept an eye out for the woman with the terrier. All she needed now was another confrontation with her. If only she'd spotted her and her tiny dog a second earlier and had time to grab Bear, she would've popped that lead on him quicker than he could've said, 'Can I sniff your bum?'

'Sorry, Bear, I know this is not as much fun as yesterday, but I just can't risk another encounter with that woman. You're staying on the lead today, like it or not.'

Seeing Scott yesterday had been good, but also tough. He thought she'd won the jackpot; he was convinced she was living the life of Riley. He knew nothing of what went on in her head.

There *was* a woman approaching, but she didn't have a dog, so Eliza paid her no more attention.

'So, this is the dog your neighbour asked you to walk?'

Recognising the annoyingly nasal voice, even before the woman came into focus, Eliza sighed. 'No, I just stole him off some lads over the other side of the park.'

'All right, no need to be sarky.'

'Well, what do you think?'

'I'm just surprised. You never seemed like a dog person.'

Eliza looked at Kristen. Taking in the immaculate blonde bobbed hair and the beautifully applied makeup, she wished she had done more than simply throw on a pair of joggers and a sweatshirt when she'd hopped out of bed this morning. What made Kristen think she had the right to make any assumptions about her? Keeping her voice as calm as possible, she replied, 'You don't know what sort of a person I am. And, anyway, how did you know I was walking him?'

'I think Ryan said something about it.'

At the mention of her ex-husband's name, Eliza bristled. 'Why are you here?'

'He's had me up most of the night,' Kristen gestured to the baby strapped to her front. 'I thought a bit of fresh air might get him off to sleep.'

'Right, and this was the only place you could think of?'

'It's nice here.'

'I wasn't born yesterday, Kristen.'

'What does that mean?'

'This park is right across town for you. You must think I'm an idiot. Leave me alone. Take your baby somewhere else.'

'His name is Otto. You know that.'

'I don't care what his unfortunate name is. Why did you have to bring him here to ruin my peace?'

'He's your family,' Kristen said. 'Can't you try to be kind?'

Eliza felt the anger swell inside her. 'He is *not* my family.'

'Close enough.'

'No. *Not* close enough. He's yours and he's Ryan's. He's got nothing whatsoever to do with me.'

'Are you sure you don't count as a step-mum?'

'Are you being obtuse?' Eliza asked incredulously. 'The fact that I was married to Ryan before you does not, by any stretch of the imagination, make me your baby's step-mum. And you, as a reasonably intelligent woman, know that!' Eliza could feel the blood rushing around inside her head. Kristen always did this to her. Of all the people in the world, all seven billion of them, this woman was the one she hated most.

'Okay, I'll go. Otto seems to have finally nodded off anyway.'

'Good for him.'

'But … can I just ask you one question, please?'

Eliza already knew exactly what the question was going to be. 'Come on then, ask away, if you must.' She might as well get it over with.

Kristen faltered slightly. 'Have … umm … have you thought any more about—?'

'Have I thought any more about sharing my inheritance with Ryan? No, I haven't. Because I don't need to. I made my decision the day I got that letter from my auntie's solicitor, and nothing has changed.'

'But … put yourself in Ryan's shoes. He knew Miriam for years. He loved her too. He visited her at that house, and had he known—'

'Had he known she was going to leave it to me, and all her money, he would've hung on and not divorced me when he did. Yes, I realise that. But he didn't hang on, did he? He left me for you, which, to be honest, was rather insulting. Auntie Miriam died after Ryan and I were divorced. What terribly bad luck for him.' Eliza copied Kristen's pseudo posh accent. 'What's more, as he's married again, I am under no obligation to share the money or the house with him, you, or baby Otto. So you can stop trying to guilt me into this. Watch my lips.' She pointed to her mouth. 'The inheritance is mine, and I will never share it with you two. Now, because of you, this poor dog's walk is going to have to be cut short again.'

'I don't know why you have to be like this, Elz.'

'Don't call me that. Only family call me Elz, and we've established that neither you nor him,' she indicated towards the now sleeping Otto, 'are my family.'

Once back in the car and on her way home, Eliza tried taking deep breaths. How dare that woman sneak up on her like that? She hadn't seen much of the baby, just the side of his face, but it had been enough. Otto looked like Ryan. Otto looked like her babies would've looked. How proud Ryan had been the first time she'd seen him with his son. Her heart had ached with jealousy. She always tried her hardest to avoid any situation where she might have to look at Kristen's smug face or catch sight of Ryan's son. It still stuck in her gut that he was a parent. He had achieved the thing she had longed for, strived for, and been prepared to give anything for. Ryan had it, and she didn't. Heartbreakingly, it had seemed about to happen five years ago, but that had been then. A world away from now. That had been when Ryan was hers, before the disappointment began.

ELIZA – 2017

'But you had your costume all worked out.' Ryan's voice on the phone sounded slightly petulant.

'Did you hear what I said?'

'Yes, I heard you. You've had a small amount of bleeding.'

'Right. So, I need to rest.'

'It's only a Halloween party at work. It's hardly going to be a raucous night. We'll probably be home by eleven. You could rest then. Besides, you're young, you'll be fine.'

'*Ryan*. There isn't supposed to be blood when you're pregnant. I need to rest. *Now!*'

'Okay. So don't come.'

'I won't.' Eliza hung up, squeezing her eyes shut to stop the tears.

The midwife was marvellous. She managed to get Eliza an urgent scan appointment, where the sonographer told her it was a bit early to say exactly what was happening. There was no sign of a heartbeat, but at six weeks it could simply be too soon. The sac was there, and there was nothing to suggest the bleeding was anything sinister. It could well just be the little one implanting. Eliza went home and googled 'implantation bleed' for a solid hour. She thought about calling her mum, but since her dad had taken early retirement from the civil service and her parents had relocated to America, she had learnt to rely on them less and less. Why worry them too? With nothing else to do but rest, she went to bed and remained there for the rest of the day. Creating a heart shape with her thumbs and index fingers, she placed it over her belly. Trying to think calm thoughts, she sent positive vibes to her baby.

———

She was awoken by Ryan, coming home just after midnight. 'You should've come, Elz, it was such a laugh.'

'I told you why I couldn't come.'

'I know. I know. But there were chairs. You could've just sat and drunk orange juice.'

'Sounds like a blast.'

He seemed not to notice the sarcasm in her voice. 'Everyone went to so much trouble with their costumes. Derek from accounts even put these weird contact lenses in. They made his eyes look all bloodshot. Who would've thought he would bother with all that?' Ryan chuckled to himself as he pulled off his Dracula costume. Dropping it on the floor, he fell into bed next to her.

Eliza wondered how long it would be before his thoughts turned to how she was. Was he even going to bother asking if there had been any more bleeding?

'You see a different side to people when they're all dressed up and full of booze, you know?' Ryan appeared to be waiting for an answer.

Eventually, she mumbled, 'Do you?'

'Oh yeah. Take Kristen for example. You'll never guess what she came as.'

'Won't I?'

'Nope. Go on – guess.'

Eliza didn't want to guess. She couldn't give a monkey's what Ryan's colleagues went to a Halloween party dressed as. All she cared about was the tiny foetus that was currently nestled in her womb. How was it possible he didn't get that? She decided not to reply. Perhaps if she remained silent, he would take the hint and realise she wasn't interested.

'Go on – guess.'

God, he was like a stuck record. 'I don't know. Umm … a witch?'

'No. Way better than that.'

'*Ryan*, I was going to go as a witch, and you said I looked great.'

'You did. But this was …' Ryan chuckled again, 'such a great costume.'

Eliza just knew that even if she managed to guess the astoundingly brilliant costume idea that Kristen had had, she was never going to be as impressed as Ryan, who was uncharacteristically behaving like a giggly child. It all seemed so trivial. She had much bigger fish to fry now. When they'd first talked about the works' party, she'd been as enthusiastic as him. Trying on different outfits, making up her face. Determined to come across as sexy and witchy at the same time. But then she'd got the positive result on the pregnancy test, and everything else had paled into insignificance. Dressing up, getting drunk – none of that had mattered once she'd known she was going to be a mum.

Clearly disappointed at her lack of guesses, Ryan blurted out the answer. 'She came as Daenerys.'

'Who?'

'Daenerys Targaryen.'

Eliza shook her head, nonplussed.

'From *Game of Thrones*.'

'Oh, *Game of Thrones*?'

'Yeah.'

'The programme I made you watch on your own, because I thought it was more boring than watching grass grow. How was I ever supposed to guess that?'

'She had the long blonde wig and everything. I've got some photos. Hold on.' Ryan reached for his phone, which he'd just plugged in to charge on the bedside table.

Eliza gritted her teeth. 'Honestly, don't bother.'

'I thought you liked her. You were friends way before she came to work at my place.'

'We weren't exactly friends, we just happened to go to the same school. Anyway, I didn't say I don't like her. I just said – don't bother showing me a photo of her dressed as a character from fucking *Game of Thrones*.'

'Why are you swearing at me?'

'Because, Ryan, earlier on, I went to the loo and there was more blood. And no matter how much I try to convince myself it's all okay and the baby is just getting settled, I think the truth is, I'm having a miscarriage. And you don't care. You haven't asked me how I am, or how the baby is. All you've done is bang on about bloody Kristen!'

4
HANNAH – 2022

'Thanks for letting me tag along,' Dave said.

'I'm not just letting you *tag along*; I value your input,' Hannah replied.

'It's great to hear that.'

'Seriously, this is a good contact. I want Sandlin PI to appear professional.'

'Ahh, so that's why you made me wear a friggin' suit.'

'Yes, and very smart you are in it too.'

'I feel like "the accused".'

'Admittedly, it's not your usual style. I've not seen you in anything with buttons for a while,' Hannah laughed. 'But I've told the client you're my IT expert, so it's necessary.'

'And that explains why *you're* not wearing one.' Dave tugged at his shirt collar. 'Anyway, tell me more about this Wilson guy.'

'He says he's hoping to get away without involving the police, but to be honest, if his employee is doing what it sounds like he's doing, I reckon they're going to need to be told.'

'Right, so …?' Dave sounded impatient.

Stopping at a red light, Hannah turned her head. 'All right,

Mr Eager Beaver, I'm getting to it. Mr Wilson imports art. Not paintings, more your objet d'art – you know, collectables?'

'I may be a total moron at times, but yes, I do know what you mean.'

'Well, he's been importing and selling all these beautiful things for years. He's a contact of Lottie's; she knew him from the auction house.' The traffic light changed to green, and Hannah pulled away. 'Anyway, a friend of his, a woman he knew back in his high school days, asked him if there were any jobs going. Her son needed work and she thought he'd be great at Mr Wilson's place. He's travelled a fair amount; in fact, he's been living overseas for a while. So, Mr Wilson, said – yes, why not, I'll take him on on a trial basis. I need a pair of young eyes and strong arms. The trial went well. So he took him on permanently. That was a few months ago. Things were going well, until … Mr Wilson got a bit suspicious.'

'That the youngster was stealing from him?'

'No. Well, yes, but he was cleverer than that. When he contacted me, Mr Wilson said that he recently took a look at the bank statements for the first time in ages and noticed that large sums of money were coming out of the current account and then being repaid before month end. Since the new guy started, he's allowed himself to be, let's say, distracted by the parts of the job he prefers. Meaning he hasn't checked anything money related for a good while, just leaves it all to the lad.'

'Wow, that's an easy way to get ripped off. Imagine what someone could do if you leave them unchecked.'

'Well, yes, and he now realises he was a bit too trusting.' Hannah turned left into a multi-story car park and headed for the nearest space.

'So … the young bloke is embezzling?'

'Sure seems that way.'

'What's he doing with the cash when he gets his hands on it?'

'That, my little IT expert, is where *we* come in.' Hannah

parked perfectly between the lines and pressed the button to turn her wing mirrors inwards. She never trusted other people to open their doors carefully.

———

Ten minutes later Hannah was pressing the buzzer for Wilson & Cavendish.

After a loud click, a female voice politely asked, 'Hello. How can I help you?'

'We're here to see Mr Wilson,' Hannah responded.

'Can I take your names?'

'I'm Ms Sandlin. I'm with my colleague, Mr Chipperton. Mr Wilson has asked us to call in today.'

'Hold on, please.'

The microphone clicked loudly, and they could do nothing but wait.

A couple more minutes passed and the microphone clicked again. 'He says you can come up. It's the second floor.' After a long buzzing sound, the door juddered and Hannah was able to push it open. Keen to meet with the client, she wanted to sprint up the two flights of stairs to Wilson & Cavendish, but she knew she would need her voice when she reached the top. So, instead, she compromised and simply took the stairs briskly. Dave followed along behind. Now a little out of shape, he chose to take a more leisurely approach. Arriving at the top, they were greeted by Mr Wilson himself, a man who appeared to be in his sixties, of larger than average size. Mr Wilson dressed to impress. He was wearing a Hugo Boss shirt and tie and some well-cut trousers, but had chosen to forgo the suit jacket. Hannah suspected that he might well perspire more than a smaller man, and it was immediately apparent that the old building was not air conditioned.

He held out a hand to them as they approached, before

retracting it, saying, 'Oh no, no, it's not the done thing anymore, is it?'

Hannah smiled. 'It's fine. We're fully vaccinated, as I'm sure are you.'

'Oh, indeed. But some people still prefer to keep their distance.'

Hannah suspected this was more down to his large sweaty palms than anything COVID related. But Mr Wilson seemed like a nice man. He was nothing like the sweaty supervisor she and Lottie had had when they first met. 'I'm happy to forgo the handshake,' she confirmed. 'To be honest I'm just pleased to be here.'

'I'm pleased too. I can't tell you how much this has been playing on my mind,' Mr Wilson said.

Settled into the chairs opposite Mr Wilson, Hannah asked him to tell them everything he knew.

Mr Wilson immediately handed them a Polaroid photo of a very tall, handsome young man. 'This is Charlie Bradbury. My ... I think we settled on the job description of Customer Services Assistant.'

'A polaroid,' Dave said. 'Very retro.'

Mr Wilson smiled. 'I found the camera in with some bits and pieces I bought at a flea market. Reminded me of different times. We thought these things were amazing back then, you know. An instant photograph – you couldn't make it up. I took that of Charlie when he first worked here. I was so proud, you see.'

'Proud?' Hannah asked.

'Yes. I wanted to give him a chance. I was once extremely fond of his mother.' Mr Wilson sucked in his sizeable stomach. 'I was more of a catch in my youth. We could have been something, you know; it was all down to bad timing. When I was free, she was not, and vice versa.'

Hannah nodded, acknowledging the regret of missed chances.

'So, when she asked me if there were any jobs for her son, I honestly wanted to help. I thought that had things gone another way, the boy could've been mine.'

'Absolutely.' Hannah felt it was probably wrong to explain that had Mr Wilson truly got together with his lost love, the son they would've had would clearly have cut quite a different shape. Anyway, she got the idea.

'When he came for the interview, he looked every inch the businessman. As you can see – Armani suit, shiny shoes. He mentioned studying business management at sixth form. He was the young blood this company needed.'

'I take it Cavendish is not young?' Dave asked.

'Cavendish was my father-in-law. He's no longer with us. I keep the name for balance. You'd be surprised how many people ask for him when they call up. Some even claim to have made a deal with him on price.' Mr Wilson smiled.

'I'll bet they do,' Dave laughed.

Hannah leant forward in her chair, eager to get to the meat of the matter. 'May I ask you, Mr Wilson, exactly what the problem is?'

'Yes, sorry, sorry – you're busy people,' Mr Wilson flustered. 'I'm wasting your precious time.'

'No, not at all. I'm just keen to get started and solve your problem,' Hannah replied.

'Well, Charlie proved to be a Godsend to begin with. No job was beneath him, and he quickly showed his worth. Within weeks he was explaining easier ways to invoice and recommending fancy computerised bookkeeping. I'm afraid he found my handwritten ledgers annoyingly antiquated. So I agreed to go digital and I let him get on with it. I was glad of the rest, to be honest. At the end of every month he told me how much money we had in the account, and it always sounded correct.'

Hannah and Dave exchanged a sideways glance.

Mr Wilson seemed not to notice and continued, 'But, just the other week, there was a query. A customer called stating that they'd paid an invoice, but it was still showing as owed on his statement. Charlie was out, picking up some picture frames, and I didn't have a clue how to ... erm, log on to the system and try to work it out. So I dug out the last few bank statements, which Charlie had kindly filed away.'

'And?' Hannah asked with anticipation.

'I sorted out the query with the customer. Yes, he had paid, but I remembered he'd had two separate deliveries for items that cost the exact same amount. A coincidence, but a fact, nevertheless. Then, after I hung up from the call, I just happened to notice something on the bank statements. I may be mistaken, but as I mentioned to you on the phone, Ms Sandlin, it seems that a large sum of money comes out of the account in the first week of every month and is replaced in the last. I thought maybe that was how these youngsters did it. Maybe Charlie was investing it elsewhere, but surely he'd check with me first.'

'You'd like to think so, wouldn't you?' Dave said, adding, 'Have you questioned him about it?'

Mr Wilson shook his head. 'What if I'm wrong?'

'I really don't see how you can be.' Hannah tried to soften the blow, but she couldn't help feeling angry with this young man for taking advantage of such a nice chap. 'Can I ask what exactly you mean by a large sum of money?'

'Oh well, it varies, but we're talking roughly ten thousand pounds a month.'

Hannah gave a small whistle. 'Well, if that kind of money is being removed every month and then replaced, and you're not the one doing it, I'm afraid Charlie is obviously using it for his own means. Unless someone else ...' She nodded towards the closed office door, wordlessly querying whether Mr Wilson's secretary could be the culprit.

'Oh, no, no. Absolutely not. She's been with me for years.' Mr Wilson shook his head. 'It has to be Charlie.' His eyes dropped to his lap. 'I just didn't want to believe it. All the time I thought he was trying to help with the business, and it would seem he's abusing my good nature. But what the devil can he be doing with the money?'

Giving a sympathetic smile, Hannah said, 'We plan to answer that question for you as soon as possible. But the first thing we're going to need to do is to take a look at these bank statements. Let's get the full picture, shall we? We could also do with logging into your accounts system. Do you have a login name and password?'

Mr Wilson rose from his chair. 'Yes, indeed. One thing I made sure to do when Charlie set up this new system was to insist that my secretary be given a copy of the details. Charlie wasn't happy; he said passwords and the like ought never to be written down, but I didn't trust myself to remember. I'll just nip to my secretary's office.' He left the room.

As soon as the door closed, Dave whispered, 'I know that lad.'

'You do?'

'Yep. I've had dealings with him in the past. He's not what Wilson thinks he is.'

'What did you nick him for?'

'He was usually drunk and causing trouble outside the Two Bishops, as it was called then. Often to be found with a few grams of weed in his pocket.'

'Not such a perfect young man after all.'

'No. And I'll bet you he's not been living abroad either. I reckon he's been in the nick somewhere.'

Hannah picked up the polaroid of Charlie. Waving it at Dave, she said, 'It just shows you what an Armani suit and a pair of shiny shoes can do.' She tossed the photo back onto the desk, scornfully.

The door opened and Mr Wilson reappeared with a yellow post it note. 'I'm assured these are the details you require. Now, how about I ask my secretary to make you both a drink whilst you're looking?'

'That would be great,' Dave said, taking the note and seating himself at the computer.

'We'll both take a white coffee, no sugar, please.' Hannah joined Dave at the computer, keen to get to work.

5

ELIZA – 2022

FINDING RYAN at her front door was most unexpected. She was used to standing on the doorstep with him waiting for Auntie Miriam to open up, but here they were, on different sides. Just like her and Scott. Seeing Otto the other day had unnerved her and set off a chain of thoughts in her head that she could've quite happily done without. Now this – her ex on the doorstep. His face always made her feel jittery somehow. It would've been so much easier if he'd not been so handsome. If his features weren't so even. Anything, just one thing wrong with his face would've made it easier to look at him.

'Ryan?' She raised her eyebrows quizzically as she opened the door.

'Hi … is this a good time?'

'It depends – what do you want?'

'Can I come in?' Ryan glanced around, as if he was somewhere he shouldn't be.

Eliza stepped back, allowing him entry into the hall. 'I suppose so.' She led him into the lounge, wishing she'd cleared up.

'It's different.'

'Yes. A bit.'

'Although, you've kept a lot of your auntie's stuff. Like the little nest of tables.'

'They're handy.'

'Yes, we always thought that when we came for tea.'

Wondering how long he was going to keep this perfectly pleasant conversation going, Eliza asked, 'Ryan?'

'Yes.'

'What d'you want?'

'Well, I haven't visited you since you moved here, and …' He tailed off. Obviously even *he* knew it was a ridiculous thing to say.

'I don't think you were under any obligation to visit me. I'm fairly sure it wasn't part of the divorce settlement. And you certainly didn't bother when I moved out of our marital home and into a pokey rented apartment!'

'Can I have a coffee, Elz? Would that be okay?' Ryan ran his fingers through his hair.

'Yes, of course.' She made her way into the kitchen. Politeness costs nothing, her auntie used to say.

Ryan followed her.

'Fresh or instant?' she asked.

'Fresh, please.'

Why had she bothered to ask? She knew. She knew all there was to know about this man who now stood in her kitchen watching her. She knew the good and she knew the bad. She had seen this man in the throes of ecstasy, and she had seen him when he was so angry his jaw clenched and his nostrils flared. He looked different now, of course. Kristen had seen to that. His hair was shorter. Eliza preferred it when it had flopped onto his forehead. His stubble, which had been slightly random when they had been married, was now perfect. So even, she assumed he had a new fancy gadget to keep it this way. But his beautiful blue eyes were the same, sparkling and clear. They were what had first attracted her to him. To Eliza, meeting Ryan had been like the scene in the Wizard of Oz where everything changes. The instant he'd looked at her, her life had gone from black and white to technicolour.

Young, free, and single, and out for the night with her friends, she fell for him the first time those eyes turned their attention towards her in a busy pub. Slightly older and with an air of maturity she had yet to develop, he had swept her off her feet and into marriage at a young age. It had been a while now since he'd looked at her through loving eyes, but there was still a lot of fondness in his gaze. It was the fondness that nearly killed her, so close and yet so far. Either way, she still found it hard to stare directly at him. Not for the first time, she felt herself seethe inside. *He's with Kristen. He's hers now, not mine. He traded me in for that high maintenance bitch!* That fact still angered her. Not only that – it hurt her. But, as awful as it had been to lose her husband, he was not the worst thing Eliza had lost. Nothing could compare to losing three pregnancies in close succession.

Ryan remained silent throughout the coffee making process.

She handed him his drink, trying not to breathe in his aftershave – too many memories.

He smiled. 'Perfect, thanks. Are you not having one?'

'No.'

'So, what's been happening for you, Elz?'

She almost told him all about running into a girl she'd known at school and receiving a business card from a private investigator, before remembering he was not her husband, and he didn't need to know. 'Not much. I fell over and hurt my knee the other day, but it's okay.'

'You should be more careful.'

Eliza felt a bolt of irritation; she hadn't mentioned the bright torchlight in her face. Would that have made him more sympathetic? She continued to keep it vague. 'I had breakfast with

Scott recently.' No need for specifics. Nothing was his business anymore.

'How is he?'

Eliza nodded. 'The same.' Again, she stopped herself from adding details. Ryan had no right to know about Scott's problems. Besides, he was only asking for something to say. The real reason for his visit was obviously far more selfish. 'I've made you a coffee, as requested. Can you tell me now why you're here?'

Clearing his throat, Ryan paused annoyingly before launching into a speech that seemed well rehearsed. 'I'm not here for me, or for Kristen, I'm here for Otto.' He paused again.

Eliza said nothing, avoiding his gaze.

After a second, he continued, 'I know you don't owe me anything, and it was all settled financially. But ...'

'But you're going to ask anyway.'

'It's not for me or Kristen.'

'It's for Otto. You *literally* just said that.'

'Elz, I had to take out a hefty mortgage to buy you out of the house. It pushed me to a difficult place – financially speaking. What with Kristen not wanting to return to work, and with all the new stuff she bought for the house, it doesn't seem fair that—'

'*Not fair.* Bloody hell, Ryan,' Eliza interrupted. 'Do you hear yourself? You bought the house off me. The one we lived in together. You bought me out because I couldn't afford to buy it from you. How in God's name can you say things aren't fair?'

'It's just the mortgage. I can't keep—'

'You broke my heart. You left me, and then you, you ...' Eliza began to cry. Brushing the tears away, determined not to let him see how much she still cared, she carried on, 'You moved her in to our home and you had a baby. *A baby*, Ryan. The fucking holy grail.'

'I know, and I realise how hard it was for you.'

'You have no clue, not one!'

'You're right, I probably don't. But listen, if Otto was yours, you'd want the best for him, wouldn't you?'

'That's a stupid question. Of course I would.'

'Right, well, that's all I'm doing. Trying to do the best for my son, Elz. We've not even been there a year and we're already behind with the mortgage.

'Just tell your wife to go back to work!'

'It's not that simple. I need an injection of cash, now, today.'

'Why does everyone think I'm a bank? Or worse – a charity!'

'I know you're not a charity. I know I don't really have any right to the money. But, think about it – it was buying you out that did this.'

'Why did the building society give you the mortgage if it was just going to bankrupt you?'

'Kristen was still working then; we played down our outgoings, gave them the impression we could afford it. But you know what she's like.' He shrugged.

'Did you know Kristen has already asked me for money?'

'No, I didn't.'

'She's mentioned it before, when our paths have unfortunately crossed. But she sought me out and asked me again, just the other day, as it happens.'

Ryan seemed surprised, but continued, 'To be honest with you, she knows nothing. She wants money to put by for Otto's education, or to take him on his first skiing trip. It's nuts! She's planning a load of stuff for him, and all the time, I'm trying to keep a roof over his head.'

'So, sell the house. Downsize!'

'Kristen takes care of our home. She looks after it well.' He glanced around the room, critically.

'None taken!'

'I didn't mean ... I just meant; you know ...'

'Hooray for Kristen. She looks after the home!'

'She's made it nice.'
'It already *was* nice.'
'Smarter.'
'At what cost? You can't afford to live there!'

Ryan squeezed the bridge of his nose, a gesture he always used to do to indicate how unreasonable he was finding her. 'You have this place. It's big. Too large for just you. We bought the old house from you in good faith. It's where our son was born.'

And where our babies died, Eliza thought.

'Can you not just imagine in your head that your auntie died a little earlier, before we divorced, and give me a lump sum to get me straight?'

'Everyone wants a lump sum.'

'What does that mean?' Ryan snapped.

'Nothing. Listen, you got yourself into this mess. You chose her over me and I can't ignore that. Get a loan, tell your wife to get a job, sell your house – the choices are endless. But I'll tell you the same as I told Kristen – I can't help you.'

'Can't or won't?'

'Both.'

'I never had you down as such a selfish bitch, Eliza.'

'And I never had you down as a cheating bastard. Perhaps we both got it wrong.'

He drained the last of his coffee. 'I hope you don't regret this.'

'Is that a threat?'

'Not at all. I just think you're pushing everyone away. When did you last see your mates from work?'

'That's *my* business.' She walked to the front door and held it open. 'Goodbye.'

After she'd shut the door behind him, she thought about what Ryan had said – he made out he was concerned about her, and that he wanted to help her, but clearly the sole purpose of his visit had been to help himself. How was it possible that as recently as last year, she had still entertained the idea of getting back with him?

ELIZA – 2021

Eliza was almost asleep on the sofa. She'd called in sick from work. Her record of attendance must be so crap, she absolutely dreaded to think what her next return to work interview was going to throw up. But she'd just not been well enough to go in. Her anxiety was through the roof. The mere thought of showering and getting dressed had been enough to send her scuttling towards the sofa, never mind the prospect of speaking to clients on the phone.

With *Good Morning* playing in the background, Eliza was almost asleep. The sun was streaming in through the patio doors, its heat warming her bare toes.

The doorbell was a rude awakening. 'What the …?' Her first thought was to ignore it. No one knew she was here. It could only be someone trying to read a meter or sell her something. Worse, it could be someone trying to convert her to their religion. No chance, not after the hand their so-called God had dealt her.

But whoever it was, was not prepared to be ignored. The bell rang again. And then again.

Pulling herself into a sitting position, Eliza swung her feet onto the floor and placed them into her fluffy slippers. She shuffled towards the front door, realising even before she opened it that the visitor was Ryan. His silhouette through the glass was so familiar. His wonderful broad shoulders and strong arms that she had thought would always be hers alone to touch. Her breath caught in her throat. What could he possibly want?

She took a second to fluff up her shoulder-length, slightly greasy hair, and check in the hall mirror that she didn't have sleep in her eyes or bits in her teeth; there was no time to do anything more. She opened the door. 'Ryan?'

'Hi.'

'Why are you here?'

'I called your work. Stella said you were off sick. What's up?'

'The usual.' She shrugged.

His face took on an awkward expression. 'Elz, you need to try to put it all behind you.'

Eliza's jaw dropped. 'Do I? Oh, how silly of me not to have realised.'

'I just mean … shit, I don't like to think of you still suffering from the losses.'

'I'm sorry my anxiety is affecting you.'

'You know I don't mean that.' He took a step towards her. 'Can I come in for a minute?'

She opened the door further. 'If you like. It's still half yours until the sale goes through. But I'm warning you, if you mention the state of the place …'

'Of course I won't.'

———

They sat on opposite sofas. Eliza flicked the television off. 'So …?'

Ryan was staring at the now blank TV screen. He appeared to be composing a speech.

'Why did you phone my work?' She couldn't stand the silence, and she hated the way he always paused before he spoke.

'I needed to talk to you. It's important. When Stella mentioned you were at home, I figured I'd come straight away.'

'What do you want to talk to me about?'

'I … I umm …' A small smile appeared on Ryan's face.

Eliza took this as a good sign. *He's changed his mind. He's left her!*

Ryan paused again, clearly considering his words carefully.

Her stomach felt as if she was at the top of a rollercoaster, about to nosedive. 'Don't do that. Just tell me.' Should she get up and join him on the other sofa? Was he regretting the divorce? It was so close to being final. Was it too late to call it off? If he wanted to come back and share their home, she was going to have to make it clear that he was to have nothing more to do with Kristen, not even a single text message. His eyes sparkled when he smiled; he looked more like the old Ryan, *her* Ryan. Eliza returned his smile. She'd known, deep down, that this wouldn't be the end. Would he want to try for another baby? Could she bear it?

'Kristen's pregnant.'

The smile wouldn't leave her face. It was stuck.

'Did you hear me?'

'Uh huh.'

'Are you okay about it?'

Eliza said nothing.

'I wanted to tell you myself, before you heard it from a friend, or saw the scan picture on Facebook or something.'

'The scan?'

'Yes, the twelve-week scan,' Ryan confirmed.

Eliza heard her voice ask, 'She's past twelve weeks?' None of Eliza's tiny foetuses had made it as far as eight.

'Yes.'

Finally, the smile left her face. Good riddance to it. It had not belonged there for at least the last twenty seconds. 'I'm not Kristen's friend on Facebook.' What a pointless thing to say!

'I'm sorry, Elz.'

At least he understood. He wasn't so thoughtless that he couldn't see that the news he'd just delivered had caused her pain. In fact, he could not have caused her any more pain if he had taken off her skin with a razor blade. She wanted to howl and scream. But that would have to wait until he was gone. 'I appreciate you telling me yourself.'

'Of course. We plan to get married as soon as possible. It seems the right thing for the baby.'

'Yes, I see what you mean.'

'Elz, I never wanted to—'

'Would you mind leaving now?' She didn't need to hear what came next. She was quite capable of filling in the blanks for herself.

'Are you going to be okay?'

'I'll be fine,' she lied.

'Do you think you should call your parents?'

'No, it's five a.m. in Florida!'

'OK. But call them later, promise me.'

Eliza agreed, despite having no intention of complying.

Ryan rose from the sofa. Passing the large yucca plant that sat in a pot next to the TV, he brushed the leaves. 'This is dusty.'

6
HANNAH – 2022

'It's good to be back, isn't it?' Hannah blew on her latte and slumped down in the car seat.

'Yep,' Dave agreed.

'I'm glad you're here.'

'You totally need me. If you were doing these obs without me, who would feed your caffeine habit?' Dave nodded towards the collection of disposable cups that littered the floor of Hannah's car.

'True, true,' Hannah agreed. 'Actually, you make a good point.'

'Do I?'

'Yes. I ought to invest in a reusable cup.'

'You should. Our Noah would go mad if he saw this lot. He's been learning about sustainability at school.'

'At his age?'

'Oh yeah, it's all the rage.' Dave bit into a doughnut.

'And that's another thing,' Hannah said. 'Doughnuts? How stereotypical are you?'

'Huh?'

'Cops and doughnuts. They go together.'

'Ahh, yes.' Dave raised his eyebrows. 'But I don't think I need to remind you that we,' he wiggled his index finger between them, 'are not coppers.'

Hannah stared down into her latte, watching the creamy liquid move majestically around the cup as she gently rotated it. She knew it; it was a fact she woke up to every single day. She was not a copper, and neither was Dave. It was a sad truth that they would never again don the uniform and pledge to protect the public. But she knew they were something just as important. They were PIs. Every day they helped someone, someone who had a question and needed an answer. It was good enough for her. 'Remember when we first went out on the beat together?' she asked.

'I do, yes. And I know what you're going to say.'

'What am I going to say?'

'You're going to say that I was a rude, obnoxious git who never once got you a coffee, never mind a friggin' doughnut.'

'As if I would say that!' Hannah laughed. 'Dave, you were a bugger, a very selfish bugger, but you make up for it when you get me stuff now.'

He gave a resigned sigh. 'I hope that's true.'

Hannah took a sip of the cooling coffee. 'It is. I don't lie to you. You don't lie to me. That's the deal.'

'Yep,' Dave agreed.

'Anyway, as I was saying, it's good to be back on obs.'

'Yes, and you of all people know that too much time on my hands is never a good thing. So I'm grateful for this job.'

Hannah held up her hand. 'Okay. Enough fawning over me. Chuck me one of those doughnuts.'

Handing her the bag of calorific sweetness, Dave said, 'I hope my hunch is right, otherwise we're piling on the pounds for nothing.'

'Well, it sounds like a good hunch to me. You said you always suspected him of dealing, and if he is, then this is the place he'd hang out on a Saturday afternoon.'

'He was a crafty little shit. Well ... *big* shit. You know what I mean. Any time we searched him he made sure he was carrying just under the limit. "It's for personal use, mate," he'd say. The most we could do was take it off him. He never separated it. One bag – one person!'

'If we can catch him selling it or buying a large amount, we can prove to Mr Wilson that Charlie is using his money to fund his drug dealing.'

'But I need to be right about the place. He could be operating from anywhere.'

Hannah bit into her doughnut, skilfully catching a blob of jam with her tongue before it made its way to her white t-shirt. 'Only time will tell.'

Two hours later they were rewarded for their patience. Sauntering round the corner came a vastly different Charlie. The weekday Armani suit was nowhere to be seen; instead, Charlie wore pale ripped jeans and a grey Nike hoodie. He blended in well with the hordes of youth who dedicated their days to hanging around the shops, or to be more precise, the benches outside the shops. But it was clearly him. Charlie was tall and thin – Hannah estimated six foot four minimum. He also had a good strong jaw line; it was definitely him. She thought he could've made his fortune modelling. His height and his manly jaw would surely sell aftershave or the like.

'That's him,' she whispered. Despite being way across the street, it was always a habit to whisper on stakeouts. 'Now we wait for a customer.'

The customer was not far behind. A woman pushing a buggy approached from the other direction. Barely glancing to check the traffic, she crossed the road in a hurry and made her way over to Charlie. A couple of words were exchanged, and a package handed over. Immediately, the woman turned on her heels and rushed off in the other direction. Her desire not to be seen with Charlie was evident.

'Not your usual pot-head,' Dave remarked.

'No. Unless the whole *baby in a buggy* thing is a front.'

'D'you want to take her, or shall I?'

'I'll go,' Hannah offered. 'You keep an eye on him.'

'Boss.' Dave nodded.

Getting out of the car, Hannah walked behind the woman with the buggy, stopping now and again to peek in shop windows to allow the gap between them to widen. Within a couple of minutes the woman headed into the Co-op. Hannah followed suit. Grabbing a basket, she idly picked up a couple of items and examined the packaging, all the time watching the woman with the buggy. It didn't take her long to complete her shopping. Throwing nappies, baby milk, a loaf of bread and a jar of coffee into a basket, the woman joined the queue for the kiosk.

Hannah joined behind her.

'Give us thirty grams of Cutter's Choice and some papers, please.'

The man behind the counter handed over the tobacco and ran it all through the till. Hannah watched as her mark checked the total on the till. Then, reaching into her pocket, the woman took out a small plastic bag containing a roll of notes, all held together with an elastic band. There were quite a few tenners in the roll. Placing the change back in the plastic bag, she took her shopping and left.

Hannah bought the odd collection of items she'd placed in her basket and asked for a carrier bag.

Swinging her shopping as she walked, she made her way back to Dave.

Charlie was still there when she got back to the car, so she slipped in quietly. Handing Dave a pack of four Crunchies, she said, 'For Noah. If he likes them.'

'Oh, he does. Thanks.'

Hannah peeled one of the bananas she'd also purchased. Taking a bite, she asked, 'Any more customers?'

'Yes. Two more.'

'Let me guess – they didn't seem like druggies either?'

'Exactly,' Dave agreed, taking the banana he was offered and almost demolishing it in four large bites.

'A bit healthier than doughnuts.'

'Yeah,' Dave agreed, through a mouthful of banana. Swallowing, he added, 'How did you know the customers weren't druggies?'

'Its money he's selling, not drugs. That woman just went to the shop and bought stuff for her and her baby. She pulled out a wedge of readies. All neatly wrapped up in a plastic bag. Just like the ones businesses use to take change to the bank.'

'I thought that. It didn't look like weed he was handing over. But it was difficult to see – he does it so quick. Like a friggin' conjurer.'

As they spoke, a young man with a mop of blond hair tentatively approached Charlie. It was clear from his body language that he was afraid. They watched as an altercation took place. It was subtle, but the threat was there, nonetheless. Charlie leant down, his face right up in the other man's. The blond man backed away, his eyes wide, but a bench halted his escape. Stopping abruptly, he almost fell. Looking up into Charlie's sneering face, he appeared to be pleading for something. No doubt he just needed more time. It was sad to see. His posture was one of a begging man, who was genuinely scared. They couldn't hear what was said, but fear is a universal language.

Hannah and Dave leant forward, staring through the windscreen, determined to catch what they could of the conversation. Both had studied rudimentary lip reading, and a few words jumped out at them – can't pay ... extra ... next week. Charlie towered over the customer, who by now was frantically gesticulating and repeatedly saying sorry. It made Hannah feel sick to see how scared he was. Perhaps he had a young family; maybe he'd simply lost his job. There could be people depending on him for food. He was clearly in way over his head, in more ways than one. She grabbed her phone and took some photos. 'I think we can safely say Charlie's taking money out of Mr Wilson's business account to lend to needy people.'

'I think we can,' Dave agreed, his jaw clenched.

'But this is no Robin Hood scenario. He's bound to be charging them extortionate interest.'

'The other customers who came whilst you were off buying bananas didn't look like the kind of people who could get a legitimate loan either. That scrote, Charlie, is loaning to the poorest of the poor, the people who have no other way of getting money in a hurry.'

'What a total bastard.' Hannah was disgusted. 'How the hell are they supposed to pay him back?'

'Makes me wanna ...' Dave made a fist and banged the dashboard hard.

'Easy, tiger. Mind the airbag!'

'Sorry. It just makes me so ...'

'He's clearly using force or threats to get the money back, then he just pops it back into the account and keeps the interest.'

'The scumbag is making a mug out of Wilson and causing untold misery to the people he lends to.'

'Not for much longer.' Hannah scrolled through the photos she'd taken. 'Did you get any of him handing over the money to the others?'

'Of course. Loads.'

'Right. Let's start putting our case together. Then we can get it all back to Mr Wilson. After which, I reckon a tip off to the cops might be in order. We've got him, Dave!'

'Absolutely, boss.'

'Fancy another banana?' Hannah asked, with a satisfied grin.

7
ELIZA – 2022

'I'M TELLING YOU, Elz, I don't even wanna go back home.'

'Scottie, it can't be as bad as you're making out.'

'It is! You think I'm overreacting, don't you?'

'No. I don't think you're overreacting; I *know* you are. No one's going to kill you – this isn't a movie.'

'You don't know this guy. He's huge. Like, six foot eight or something. Who even knew you could pile shit that high! Anyway, I owe him, he's nasty, and he's not going to let this go.' Scott was sweating unpleasantly.

'I thought you were just behind with a credit card or something. The way you're talking, you owe some hoodlum.'

'It was a loan. It was meant to tide me over. I didn't think about the interest.'

'For God's sake.' Eliza rose from her chair and crossed over to the fridge. Taking out a bottle of wine, she asked, 'D'you want some?'

'Why not? I'll probably be dead by Tuesday anyway.'

'Don't joke like that.'

Scott took the glass she offered. 'I'm not joking. He wants his money. It's not like the council tax; you can't juggle with them.

You can't buy yourself time and they don't send polite letters. These kinds of people communicate with their fists.' He gulped at the wine, noisily.

'All right, all right.' Eliza couldn't help feeling that Scott was somewhat overstating his case. 'Tell me, who exactly do you owe?'

'Just *someone*, that's all you need to know. A guy I used to hang about with put me onto him.' Scott held out his glass, indicating he wanted a refill.

'Go easy!'

'What for? Elz, you're just not getting this. You're sitting here in your bloody detached house with money in the bank; you think I'm exaggerating.'

'I just think maybe you've watched too much TV.'

'Except it isn't *your* house, is it? It's Miriam's.'

Eliza ignored the dig. 'What does your mum say? Can't she help?'

'You know what my mum's like. She's not got the time of day for me. She never did have.'

'Is your dad back?'

'No. He's doing a long stretch.'

'Maybe he'll get out early for good behaviour.'

Scott raised his eyebrows.

'Right. Of course. Fergus O'Connor wouldn't know good behaviour if it bit him on the arse.'

'She doesn't learn. She's always taken in by him and his blarney. Well, fuck her, she can waste her life waiting for him and not giving a toss about me. Next time she needs my help, I'll tell her to get lost.'

'I wish she'd been different, Scottie. I wish you'd had a mum like mine or Auntie Miriam.'

'You and me both.'

'It just seems so unfair. She put all her energy into Fergus and couldn't see the dear little boy in front of her.'

'Dear little boy?' he scoffed.

'Yes. You were cute.'

'Crap. Ash knew what I was. She never tired of telling me I was a useless twat, and she was probably right.'

'You're just feeling down. Things will get better. You just need to get some work and sort yourself out.'

'Sort myself out? Elz, it's not that simple. It was all right for you; you went to a fancy girls' school. What did I get? I got to finish school a year after my cousin went missing. With everyone talking about me. How was I supposed to pass any exams? My head was mashed.'

'Listen, I can't give you money, and you know why. But I would like to help. Maybe I can speak to the people you owe money to.'

'Shove it where the wet don't get, Eliza. This isn't a legit loan company. We're not talking about phoning up and making an appointment. Christ, you're way too naive and trusting. You wouldn't have a clue. What makes you think you can talk to anyone for me? If you were a hostage negotiator, you'd be all like, can we have some of the dead ones back, please?'

Eliza ignored his taunts. 'I just hate to see you like this.' She felt the usual pity. Scott had never been able to catch a break. His life had been a mess since the day his mother had grudgingly pushed him into the world, all ten pounds two ounces of him. 'Well, what about my idea that you try to get a job? I know you're not qualified for anything, but you could still try.'

'Or I could just sit at home and wait for the inevitable moment when that bastard sends someone round to beat the shite out of me.'

'D'you want to stay here for the night? You can. I don't think Miriam would mind.'

'Of course she wouldn't mind. She's fucking dead!'

'You know what I mean. She didn't want you to have her

money, but she wouldn't mind me putting you up. You could sleep in Ash's room.'

'That crypt. No thanks. It's like a shrine.'

'It's not anymore.'

'What?'

'It's not a shrine to Ash. I took everything out and white-washed the walls.'

'It must've taken a fair few coats to cover the black.'

'It did – about six, I think.'

'What did you do with all her stuff?'

'Took some to the charity shop and binned the rest.'

'Did you keep anything?'

'No.'

'Wow. That's pretty cold-hearted, Elz.'

'Not really. Ash is dead. Auntie Miriam is dead. I didn't like seeing all her stuff from years ago. It took me back each time I went in there.'

'Took you back?'

'Reminded me of Ash, and ... you know!' Eliza shuddered.

'Auntie Miriam never gave up hope, did she?' Scott said. 'I mean, she agreed to the declaration of death thing, but I don't think she ever imagined she'd die without seeing Ash again.'

'I know. What about you, Scott?'

'Me?'

'Have you given up hope?'

'Of course. Haven't you?' He poured himself a third glass of wine.

'Mostly, yes. But, just occasionally, I do wonder, you know ...'

'If she's going to come back and say – this is *my* house now!'

'No. Not that. For goodness' sake, you're obsessed. I just mean, I do wonder if she's out there somewhere. Living her life. Without us.'

'Why though? What would be the point? Why stay away so

long?'

'The relationship between her and her mum was never good. A fresh start, maybe.'

'Well, you obviously don't think she's ever coming back, or you wouldn't have cleared out her room.'

Eliza gave herself a shake. 'Enough about all this. Do you want to stay or not?'

'I don't think I have a whole lot of choice, seeing as you won't give me the money to clear my debts.'

'Auntie Miriam said—'

'Fuck off.' Scott downed the wine in one go. 'Don't keep parroting the same thing. Auntie Miriam didn't want me to have any of her money. I know that. But she thought I was solely to blame. *We know the truth.*'

Placing her glass on the worktop, Eliza left the kitchen, shouting over her shoulder, 'Take a shower if you want. I'll go and freshen up the room for you.'

As she left, she heard Scott mutter under his breath, 'You do that small thing.'

―――

Eliza woke with a start. She'd been dreaming about a hospital. It hadn't been a nice dream. There was talk of babies and sad losses. She was glad to have left the dream behind. But what had woken her? There had been a bang somewhere off in the distance and she had assumed it had been part of the hospital dream, but now she was awake, she wasn't so sure.

A second later she heard the noise again. It was definitely here in the real world.

Jumping out of bed, she shoved her feet into her slippers and grabbed her dressing gown from the end of the bed. This took no time at all, and in less than a minute she was at the top of the stairs, listening for further sounds.

When no additional bangs occurred, she wasn't sure what to do. Should she go downstairs and investigate? She hated living alone. This was always Ryan's thing. As old fashioned as it might be, to her, exploring strange noises in the night was man's work.

In the middle of her deliberation, the front door opened. She stood stock still, her breathing shallow.

'*Who's out there?*'

Eliza allowed the air she had been holding in to leave her body. Thank God. Scott's voice. She'd forgotten he was here. 'What's happened?' She made her way tentatively down the stairs.

'Bastards!'

'What? Tell me!'

'Someone's kicked the fence in.' Scott appeared in the hallway, wearing nothing but his boxers and the faded black tee shirt he'd had on the day before.

'Scottie, you'll freeze to death.'

'I wasn't going to mess about getting dressed, Elz. I wanted to know what was going on.'

'Okay. But shut the door now. You haven't even got anything on your feet.'

'Someone's kicked your fence in – doesn't that bother you?'

'Yes. Of course it does.'

'Probably drunk or stoned.'

'Who is?'

'The person who just purposely defaced your property. Why else would someone make a point of kicking your fence in?'

Eliza paused before asking, 'Do you think it could be someone who's after you?'

'The loan?'

'Yes. Is it a warning?'

'Doubt it,' Scott replied. 'He doesn't know I'm here. Actually, he doesn't even know we're related.'

'Well, then yes, you're right. It was probably a drunk. Did you not see anyone?'

'No. Just a couple of holes in the side fence.' Scott made his way back up the stairs.

'Are you going back to bed?'

'What else is there to do? Whoever it was has gone.'

'D'you think it's got anything to do with the person who shone that torch in my face?'

Pausing at the door to Ash's old room, Scott said, 'I don't know.' With a shrug, he added, 'I'll try to fix the fence for you tomorrow.'

'Thanks. I'm glad you were here.'

'Yeah, me too. Wouldn't want you to have to face some drunk prick alone.' He stepped into the room and closed the door behind him.

It took Eliza a long time to get back to sleep. All she could think of was how scared she'd been when she'd first heard the dull thuds of what she now knew to be someone kicking her fence. Somewhere in that place between wakefulness and sleep, a jumble of thoughts cascaded around her mind. Happier times in this house when Uncle Robert was still alive. A hundred games of hide and seek with Ash and Scott. The three of them sitting on the stairs, listening to the adults talking and joking in the lounge. This house was as much Scott's as it was hers. Was it right to keep it all for herself? Then she heard a voice she hadn't heard for an awfully long time. As clear as day – *this house does not belong to either of you; it's mine!* Eliza jerked awake. Once again, her heart was pounding. It had sounded so much like Ash. So clear. Had she dreamt it, or heard it for real? Of course, it had to have been a dream. But it had sounded so familiar. As always, it had been harsh and disapproving. Typical Ash.

ELIZA – 2002

Two weeks after he fell out of the tree, Scott sat with his arm in plaster – well and truly on the subs bench. 'It's crazy that Ash is having a football party. They're meant for boys.' He spoke to Eliza, throwing his good arm up in disgust. 'And she doesn't care one bit that I can't join in!'

Eliza felt sorry for him but couldn't think how to make him feel any better.

Scott called out to Ash, 'Who ever heard of a girl having a football party? It's stupid.' He wrinkled up his nose.

Joining him on the bench to tie her laces, Ash gave him a shove. 'Move over. You're the one who's stupid. You don't know anything about anything.'

'I know that all the other girls in your class had a princess party or whatever they called it.'

'That's rubbish. What rule says girls have to do that shit on their birthdays?'

'Shush.' Eliza tried to place her hand over her cousin's mouth. 'Someone will hear you swearing.'

Ash shook her hand away. 'You two are so lame.'

Holding up his plastered wrist, adorned with swear words by Ash, Scott asked, 'And why go ahead with a football party when you know I can't join in?'

'Are you still here?' Ash asked, sarcastically.

'I mean it. Why not change it?'

'Because my world doesn't revolve around you, that's why!' Giving him another shove, Ash stood up. Jumping up and down, she seemed satisfied her boots were comfortable.

'What did your mum say about your wrist?' Eliza asked.

Scott pulled a face. 'Nothing much.'

'You shouldn't take it out on Ash, though.' Eliza tried to calm the water. 'It's not her fault you broke it.'

'Actually, it *is*!' He left the bench and walked off towards a wobbly table that held cups of weak orange squash and a few packs of biscuits. He called back, 'Looks like I'm stuck watching you guys play.'

'You're crap anyway,' Ash sneered, tying her long dark hair back.

'It is a shame he can't join in, though. He won't be able to play any sport for ages. His cast won't be off for another four weeks, and even then, he has to be careful. They said it was a nasty break.'

Ash gave a cynical shrug. 'I didn't want him to play anyway. He's so young, it's embarrassing. Besides, he's a ginger minger!' She sneered.

'Ash!'

'Oh, shush. Anyway, Elz, are we playing football or standing here talking about the baby?'

Eliza gave up. 'We're playing football, I guess.'

———

Ash's dad was the referee and he'd gone all out to look the part, dressing in black shorts and top and even the correct socks. Blowing the whistle, he called out when there was a foul or when the ball went over the line. He threw himself into the role, but by half-time he was panting and had to admit defeat.

Hunched over on the subs bench, he tried to explain to his daughter. 'I'm sorry, Ashley, I just need ...' His cheeks puffed out as he let out a long slow breath, 'a rest. I think I'll head inside for a while.' Pointing down the field he added, 'My mate, Mick, is going to take over for me.'

'But Dad ... you promised. You even bought the socks!'

'I know. I'm just not feeling too good.' Uncle Robert's head dropped between his knees.

Eliza didn't like to say anything, but she'd been quite shocked by how pale her Uncle Robert had looked when they'd arrived. He seemed different. Somehow there was less of him than usual.

'Darling, are you okay? I told you this would be too much for you.' Auntie Miriam hobbled over as fast as her unsuitable shoes allowed on the turf.

'I'm all right; don't fuss.'

'You're not all right. Look at you. You're not breathing well.'

'I said don't fuss. Not in front of Ashley.'

'Can I get you anything? A glass of water from inside?'

'In those shoes? I'll be dead by the time you bring it back.' Uncle Robert gave a dry laugh.

'I'll get you a squash.' Auntie Miriam made her way unsteadily to the refreshment table.

'What's wrong with you, Daddy? Why is this too much?' Ash asked.

'Nothing. I just overdid it on the whisky last night. You know how greedy I am. I'll be fine.' Uncle Robert winked at his daughter.

'I don't want to play if you're not watching.' Standing in front of her dad, Ash made a grab for him, holding him tight around the middle.

'You must, sweetheart. You must squeeze all you can out of this wonderful day. It'll never be your tenth birthday again. I won't be inside for long.'

'But Daddy—'

'There's lots more to look forward to. Mum's organised a fabulous after-match tea. There's a beautiful cake.'

'It's bloody pink, Dad!'

'I know. But, least said soonest mended.' Uncle Robert nodded, adding, gently, 'Don't swear, please.'

'Mummy doesn't get me.' Ash hung her head.

'She tries, and she loves you. Never forget that.' Heaving himself up off the bench, Uncle Robert waved away any attempts to help from those standing around him. 'I'm just going to pop inside the changing rooms a minute.' Gesturing to his mate, he called, 'Start the game up, Mick. It's seven-nil, so all to play for.'

Auntie Miriam was on her way back, a plastic cup of squash in her hand. She was about as unsuitably dressed as it was possible to be on a football pitch. A tight-fitting skirt and a cashmere jumper clung to her dainty frame. Eliza thought she must be embarrassed to have dressed so inappropriately.

Uncle Robert seemed happy with her appearance, though. His eyes glistened as he said, 'Here she comes now. Thank you, my sweet.' Taking the paper cup, he sipped the squash and began walking slowly towards the changing rooms, Auntie Miriam fretting by his side.

Sucking on a piece of orange, Eliza watched from the pitch. She knew the game was ruined for her cousin. As much as Ash loved football, she loved her dad more, and now he was going to be indoors. 'He'll probably watch out of the window,' she called across, trying to make Ash feel better.

'He won't. He's gone in to be sick. He's always sick these days.'

'Is he?' Eliza walked over to the bench.

'Yeah. I need to have a serious conversation with him about not drinking so much bloody whisky!'

Mick blew the whistle. 'Play on!'

'Hopefully he'll feel better when we have the food,' Eliza said, although she doubted it.

From the refreshment table, where he'd spent most of the first half scoffing custard creams, Scott shouted, 'They've blown the whistle; I think you're meant to go and play.'

'Oh, shut up, stupid.' Ash flipped him the finger. 'When will you realise that no one cares what you think?'

8
HANNAH – 2022

'NICE OF YOU TO buy me dinner.' Paul sawed off a large piece of steak and shoved it unceremoniously into his waiting mouth.

'Nice of you to pick something cheap!' Hannah replied, sarcastically.

'What can I say? I don't get treated often.'

'So when you do, you like to really stiff the person who's treating you!' Hannah laughed.

'You said – order whatever you fancy.'

Hannah waved away his comment. 'Oh, fine, fine.' She was used to her ex-colleague by now. He was still in the police force and always ready to help her with information that she no longer had access to, but he made sure he got paid for his trouble. What he didn't know was that she planned to put the meal on Mr Wilson's expenses anyway.

Hannah picked at her Caesar salad. The place she'd chosen was nice; the décor was a little tired, but the staff seemed pleasant. Most important of all, it was well away from Kingshurst. The last thing either of them needed was someone they knew to walk through the door and spot them.

'Anyway, getting down to business.' Hannah leant across the

table towards her ex-colleague. 'Spill the beans. What can you tell me about Charlie Bradbury?'

Spearing another piece of bloody meat with his fork, Paul said, 'Nasty piece of work.'

'I'm going to need a bit more than that in return for a fucking rib-eye.'

'Of course. I'm getting there.' Paul took a swig of Rioja, taking his time to answer and not even attempting to hide how much he was enjoying the attention. 'Chippy was right.'

'Dave.'

'Sorry, I forgot you don't like to ...' Paul paused, clearly not sure how much of the past to mention. '*Dave* was right. That Charlie fella was into drugs before. Nothing too big. Small-time supplying. He was also a regular face down the nick on a Friday night. He may be a drainpipe, but he can't handle his drink. There were a few charges of causing an affray, that kind of thing. I'll be honest with you; I don't understand how your fella Wilson could be fooled by him. One google of Bradbury's name, and he'd have got the gist.'

'Mr Wilson doesn't google. He's not from our world. I don't think it would occur to him that you can actually look people up on that there interweb thingy.' Hannah smiled. 'Besides, he was blinded by the young love he felt for Charlie's mum.'

'Well, it's a shame he didn't think a bit before he took him on.'

'Absolutely. I hate the idea that such a nice man can be ripped off.'

'Should've employed someone through a reputable agency. Something like that.'

'Paul, I know that, and you know that. But Mr Wilson is from the era when getting a job was more about *who* you knew than *what*. It's not his fault he's so trusting.'

'But I see so many naive old people getting done over by

bloody chancers. I just want to put my head on their shoulders, you know?'

'To comfort them?'

'No ... It's an expression. I wish I could put my head on ...' He stopped. 'You knew what I meant, didn't you?'

Hannah laughed. 'Of course, you twat. Anyway, give me the whole story. We're talking about drug dealing and affrays, yes?'

'Yeah. But a few years ago he hit the big time. If you get my drift.'

'Uh huh.' Hannah sipped on her sparkling water. Paul was expecting a chauffeur as well.

'GBH.'

'Right. When?'

Paul waved his empty glass at a passing waiter, indicating he needed a refill.

'Perhaps I should've just got you a bottle?' Hannah said.

'Well, it would've worked out cheaper for you in the long run.'

'Fine, order a bottle. Just tell me about the GBH.'

Paul called the waiter back and changed his order from a single glass to a bottle. Tuning back into their conversation, he said, 'So, yeah ... GBH!'

'When was it?'

'About four years ago. It was just after you and Chip ... Dave, you know ... left the force.'

'I see. How long did he get?'

'He served two years. Should've been more in my opinion. I looked at the case. He kicked a young bloke outside a nightclub. Some argument about a girl.'

'More details please?' Hannah opened notes on her phone and began typing.

'Picture the scene. They're all in some arsehole of a nightclub in town. Charlie tries it on with this girl. The guy next to her turns out to be her boyfriend, and he warns Charlie off. Charlie's being watched by the meatheads on security, so he just sneers, and does nothing. But he doesn't forget it. Later, as they're all getting kicked out of the place at four in the morning, and everyone is a little worse for wear, especially lanky Charlie, he finds himself leaving at the exact same moment as the girl and her boyfriend.'

'Shame.' Hannah shook her head.

'Yeah. Bad timing. Charlie, full of his own piss and importance, makes a grab for the girl. You know – grab 'em by the pussy.' Paul did an excellent Trump impression.

Hannah shuddered. 'Please don't ever do that voice again.'

'Anyway, the girl …' Paul stopped as the waiter approached with his wine.

Hannah also sat in silence, watching the young man wrestle the cork from the bottle.

Taking the taster he was offered, Paul swirled the glass dramatically before downing its contents in one. He nodded, handed the glass back to the waiter and said, 'Thanks, that'll do nicely.'

The waiter poured Paul a modest glass of wine, placed the bottle on the table and politely backed away.

Once he was out of earshot, Paul topped up his glass considerably and resumed his story. 'The girl, quite rightly, makes a fuss. She shouts at Charlie to get the hell off her, how dare he touch her, he's a creep, etc. etc. I don't blame her; women shouldn't have to take that shit from men. But the problem is, there's always some schmuck stood next to her who gets roped into a fight. The boyfriend feels he's got to protect her, every time. Tough situation for him. I doubt he wanted to take on a six foot five giant.'

'Wow. I knew he was tall, but …'

'Six-five, that's what it says on his record.'

'So the poor guy felt he had to say something as well.'

'Yeah. Gotta back up the Mrs, haven't you? According to

witnesses, he just politely told Charlie to keep his hands to himself.'

'Charlie didn't like that?' Hannah guessed.

'Charlie did not! Went ballistic, apparently. Shoved the guy up against a wall. Fists flying.'

Hannah was reminded of Charlie forcing the blond man backwards into a bench. She remembered the fear on the poor man's face.

Finishing everything on his plate, Paul placed his knife and fork together. 'Long story short – the other guy ended up on the ground, in the fucking foetal position, with Charlie kicking seven shades of shite out of him. Luckily, the bouncers pulled him away. But not before he'd done some damage.'

'Poor guy,' Hannah said. 'What were his injuries? Had to be something substantial for the CPS to go with GBH.'

'Broke his right leg in two places. The guy was off work for weeks, and Christ knows how it affected him psychologically. Witnesses said it was bloody lucky Charlie didn't go for the head. The way he was kicking, it could've been a whole other story.'

'He definitely should've got longer than two years.'

'Definitely,' Paul agreed. 'But Charlie boy was an exemplary prisoner. So he got out early.'

'I guess anyone can be exemplary, if it's going to help their cause.'

'Personally, I'm delighted to hear you've got all this stuff on him. Although I can't believe he would take such a risk. Stealing from his boss every month.'

'Great way to bankroll your business though. No outgoings for him whatsoever.'

'Well, with a bit of luck he'll be back inside soon.' Paul took a large slurp from his glass. 'Hopefully, they won't fall for the old model prisoner act twice. Maybe he'll do a decent stretch this time.'

'You know we've got to tell the client first, though,' Hannah said.

'Course, I get it. But he'll come straight to us, surely?'

'I really hope so. The sooner that lanky drink of water is locked up again the better.'

Paul shouted across to the waiter. 'Can I order a dessert, mate?'

Hannah laughed. 'You greedy fucker!'

Dropping his voice, Paul said, 'You do know I'm not supposed to go digging about in files for you, don't you? Plus I got you all that stuff you asked for on the missing teenager.'

'I know. But I do pay you!'

'Not a lot.' Paul laughed.

'Fine.' Hannah gave in. 'Fill your boots. I guess I couldn't do it without you.'

Paul grinned. 'Cheers.' To the approaching waiter, he said, 'Two sponge puddings, please. Plenty of custard.'

'*Two?*' Hannah asked.

'One of 'em's for you. You can't survive on friggin' water and salad, Han.'

9
ELIZA – 2022

'THAT'S US DONE, love. You've got yourself a smart new fence there.'

'Thank you so much.' Eliza reached for her purse. Handing the two men the money they had previously agreed, plus a generous tip, she couldn't stop herself from saying, 'It's not true, you know? What it said on the fence.'

Both men smiled. The man who had just spoken, the younger of the two, a tall man with a baritone voice, said, 'Don't you worry about it. We're not judging.'

'I know you're not. But I wanted you both to know. I'm not a bitch.'

His partner, a mature chap with a round belly and a balding head, was quick to reassure her, 'We don't think you are, honestly.'

'Someone did it, as a … joke. No one thinks that about me. They wouldn't. I mean – why would they?'

Putting the money in his toolbox, the taller man nodded. 'Righty ho. We'll let you get on. We'll take the old fence away, as agreed.'

Embarrassed, Eliza changed the subject. 'Thank you for

coming at such short notice. My neighbour recommended you. In fact, he contacted you for me. Do you have a business card I could take? Just in case …' She didn't want to say it, but she was fearful the fence might receive further damage.

The taller man ferreted around in his overall pockets and came up with a slightly bent, greasy card, which had clearly been hanging around in there since he'd worked on the ark. She wondered how often his overalls saw the inside of a washing machine.

'There you go, love. Give us a call if you need anything else doing.'

Eliza read the card, *Small and Waddle. Carpentry and Joinery.* 'Which one of you is …?'

'I'm Small,' the taller man said. 'And he's Waddle.' With a slight flick of his head, he indicated his rotund mate.

'I see.' Eliza smiled.

'We don't just put up fences; we can do all kinds of work. Inside and out. We've had nearly fifty years' experience between us,' Waddle said.

'Really?' She asked the question merely to make conversation, not because she doubted his word.

'Oh yes. I've been at this job a long time. I'm no whipper snapper, you know? You don't get a hairstyle like this in a hurry.' Waddle rubbed his bald head.

Eliza giggled. 'No, I don't suppose you do.' He'd clearly made that joke countless times before. Showing them to the door, she said, 'Well, thanks again for coming so soon. I'll keep hold of your card. Hopefully I won't need any more rude words removed from my property, though.'

The men left and Eliza wished she could just keep her mouth shut. What did it matter if Small and Waddle did think she was a bitch who'd stolen the house? Chances were they were never going to see her again.

A few minutes after they left, Scott arrived on the doorstep. He was sweating heavily.

'What's up, Scottie?'

'You're not going to believe it. I think I've just seen Ash.'

'*What?*'

'Down by the Co-op, of all places. Just walking along the road, like it was all perfectly normal.'

'You must be mistaken. Remember before? How many times did we think we'd seen her?'

'I know. But that hasn't happened for years, Elz.'

'It's funny …'

'What is?'

'Well, not funny,' Eliza said. 'But odd. I thought I heard her voice the other night.'

'What did she say?'

'You'd love it. She said this house wasn't mine.'

Scott raised his eyebrows.

'It really did sound like her. I was thinking … I haven't heard her voice for twelve years, but I still recognised it.'

'Well, that's how I feel about this person I just saw. It was definitely her.'

Eliza was lost in thought. *The last thing I heard Ash say was - run for it!*

'Are you listening, Elz?'

'Huh?'

'I said, this was definitely her. She was wearing one of those horrible long coats she used to wear, the ones that trailed along the ground, long black hair, the boots …'

'Scott, if she was alive today, I doubt she'd still be a goth. She'd be thirty years old, the same as me. She wouldn't have that stupid hair hanging in her face or the ridiculous clothes. You're just remembering her how she was when we last saw her –

when she ... ran off.'

'This person walked like her. It's freaked me out – I'm not gonna lie.'

'Lots of people walk the same way.'

'No, they don't. Ash use to walk like she had the weight of the world on her.'

'That is true. But, like I say, she wouldn't be a goth now. She only did that because of the funeral, then it became a habit. She just wore that stuff whenever she wasn't at school.'

'Uh huh. She never chose to wear anything other than black from the day he died to the day she—'

'There's something *I* need to tell *you* too.' Eliza couldn't wait for him to finish his sentence.

Scott pulled up a chair. 'Go on.' He braced himself.

'Did you notice I've got a new fence? I got it put up today.'

'I wasn't really looking, sorry. But – bloody hell, Elz, I thought it was going to be something life changing! I'm sorry. I know I said I'd fix it.'

'I'm not telling you because you didn't fix it, you idiot. I'm telling you because ...'

'What?'

'They didn't just kick it. They wrote on it in red paint. I'm surprised you didn't see it when you left the morning after.'

'I turn right at the gate to get home, don't I? What did it say?'

'It said *the bitch that lives here stole my house.*'

'Shit!'

'I know. I was going to just get the broken panels replaced, but after I saw those words, I decided to get the whole thing done straight away. I couldn't have people reading that.'

'No, I guess not. Now you mention it, it did seem different. Nice.'

'I don't think Auntie Miriam would approve of the colour. It's called Sunset, but she'd say it was orange.'

'Well, she's not here, is she?'

'No. Besides, once I knew I had to get it all changed I thought I'd go for something brighter.'

'Do you think it was Ash? The writing, I mean,' Scott asked.

Eliza shook her head. 'I don't know what to think any more. It can't be, can it?'

'I'm telling you, the woman by the Co-op was her. I'm sure of it.'

'But it doesn't make any sense. If she's alive and she wants her mum's house, why doesn't she just come and knock on the door?'

'Because we all declared her dead. I reckon she's probably a bit pissed off about that,' Scott said.

'Well, she shouldn't have stayed away so long.'

'We should have done more ... the next day.'

'Stop it, Scott, please. It's too late to say that now.'

'Fine. I'll stop. But I'm telling you, it was her.'

Checking the time on her phone, Eliza groaned. 'I have to walk Bear again. I promised to do it about four-ish, so he doesn't get too hot.'

'Want me to come with you?'

'Yes, please. I think I'd feel so much better about letting him off the lead if I was with someone. I can't bear the responsibility alone.'

'Ha! I see what you did there.'

'Wha ...? Oh, yes, very droll. Come on.' She grabbed her trainers. 'Let's go before I chicken out and keep him on the lead.'

'I'll be with you, Elz. You can let him off. I promise I won't let anyone call you pathetic.' Scott grinned.

'You're all heart.'

As Eliza unlocked the door to her neighbour's house to collect Bear, she saw Scott stop to check his phone. Heading towards him at full pelt, being dragged by the massive puppy, she noticed he was furiously texting. 'Are you okay? What's that all about?'

'Nothing.' He shook his head.

'Tell me. You look worried.'

Scott's phone pinged and he checked an incoming message. Exhaling loudly, he said, 'It's all right. He's letting me have more time.'

'Who is? Oh, I see, the guy you owe?'

'Yeah.' Scott sounded relieved. 'I was meant to meet him later. I texted to say I can't get the money together today. I thought he'd send the heavies after me. But he said he won't be there. He wants me to leave it for now. He's got to go away for a while. That gives me a bit of breathing space.'

'Why?'

'Why what? Why won't he be there? Jesus, Elz, you sound like you don't want me to get a break.'

'I do. Of course I do. It's just ... before ... it was urgent.'

'Like I said, I told him I can't get the money. *Which I can't!* And he's being okay about it. End of.'

'I'm sorry I can't help you.'

'Yeah, yeah.' Scott waved away her apology. 'Give me the lead; that dog is gonna pull your arm out of its socket in a second.' Taking charge of Bear, he marched on ahead.

'Mind your wrist. Don't let him pull it.'

'My bad one is on the left. I thought you knew that.'

Eliza brought up the rear. Not for the first time, she felt like the world's worst cousin.

―――

After an hour in the park, Bear was far less boisterous. In fact, he was walking quite nicely to heel, back to the car.

'He behaves so much better for you,' Eliza said.

'Just gotta show him who's boss.'

'He'd never come back for me like that. You just called him and there he was.'

'Probably a bit of luck, Elz. Maybe my voice sounds like his owner or something.'

'Thank God, we didn't see that woman again. She made me feel totally inadequate.'

'Not a good way to feel.'

'I guess you're familiar with it, huh?'

'Erm…' Scott cocked his head, 'let me think. Yeah, every time I did anything in front of Ash.'

'She wasn't that bad.'

'You don't know the half of it.'

They parked outside Eliza's and deposited a now far more placid Bear back into his house. Making sure he had plenty of clean water in his bowl, Eliza slammed the front door behind her.

'Let me know when you're next walking him,' Scott said. 'I'll try and join you. It was good.'

'It was, wasn't it?'

They opened the gate and made their way down Eliza's front path.

'What's that?' Scott pointed to a bag on the front doorstep.

'I don't know.'

'Did you order something?'

'Not that I can think of. Besides, that's just a carrier bag, it's not a parcel.'

They took the last few steps and reached the bag. Eliza picked it up and plunged her hand inside.'

'Careful; it could be dog shit!'

'Scott, why would you even think …?' Eliza withdrew her hand. 'It's a CD.' Almost throwing it at her cousin, she exclaimed, 'Oh, God!'

'*Automatic for the People*, REM. So what?' Confused, Scott examined the CD, turning it over in his hand. On the back, in red permanent marker and large letters, were the words *Everybody hurts*.

ELIZA – 2004

The vicar announced that they would lead out to Uncle Robert's favourite REM song, and there it was – the tune he had played for them on so many occasions, at home and in the car. A classic, Uncle Robert called it. The haunting instrumental opening, so familiar, and then those heart-breaking lyrics. Ash, who had thus far managed to hold her emotions in, became distraught. Unable to stand whilst she waited to leave the church last, as was the plan, she crumbled back onto the smooth wooden pew. Her sobbing became loud, too loud, devastatingly loud! The sound forced its way into Eliza's brain, where it remained, for ever more. That song and Ash's sobs entwined themselves in her memory.

10

HANNAH – 2022

No matter where they both were or what they were up to, Hannah and Dave always made time to get together at least twice a week. Today they were at Dave's place. Hannah couldn't help wanting to know exactly what he was doing. She never lost sight of the fact that the company was hers, or the fact that Lottie had invested heavily.

'So, have you managed to put all the evidence together ready for Mr Wilson?' Hannah asked, taking a swig of cheap instant coffee from the slightly dubious black AC/DC mug Dave had provided. His selection of mugs would most definitely not have passed the test back when she and Lottie were office cleaners.

'Yep. We've got enough proof,' Dave replied. 'There's a clear financial trail and more than enough incriminating photographs.'

'That's great news.' Hannah automatically took another swig of coffee, before remembering how bad the first one had been. 'I asked Mr Wilson if he wanted us to hand over everything we had to Paul at the station and let him take it from there, but he's hesitant.'

'Can't be easy shopping someone you thought of as a surrogate son,' Dave said. 'Especially when things seemed so good at the start.'

'I know.' Hannah placed her mug on the small table next to an iPad. 'This yours?'

Dave shook his head. 'Noah's.'

'Already?'

'He's got one at his mum's too. Kids pretty much get given them as they leave the womb these days.'

'What a time to be alive!' Hannah rolled her eyes. 'Anyway, where were we? Oh yes. You're right, it can't be easy shopping him, but … I'm not a hundred percent happy about simply giving Mr Wilson the evidence. Especially since I met Paul. That stuff he told me about the GBH charge proves that Charlie has a temper.'

'He's worse than we originally thought. I get what you're saying, but I think Wilson just wants to digest it all first. Once he hears what we've got on dear, sweet, helpful Charlie, he'll see sense and take it to the police himself, I reckon.'

'But what if he confronts Charlie?' Hannah asked. 'I like Mr Wilson. He's a decent bloke. But, like I said to Paul, he's not from our world. He might not realise what he's dealing with. He probably thinks a stern word from a fatherly figure will do the trick. Charlie's a nasty piece of work, who's been unashamedly stealing from his boss. Who knows what he'll do if Mr Wilson just asks him outright about it?'

'I get you, but I think you have to do what the client wants.' Dave jumped up. 'I've just remembered, I've got some biscuits somewhere.' Offering the opened packet, he continued, 'He wants to see the evidence first. So, we have to take it to him.'

'Keep them for Noah.' Hannah waved away the biscuits, adding, 'You're probably right.'

'D'you want me to go in with it or should I leave it to you?' Dave asked.

It was written all over his face what he wanted. Hannah

considered for a second. 'You know what, Dave? I'm going to let you deal with this. You researched all the financial stuff; you knew where to find Charlie; you deserve the credit. Take him what we've got and wrap it up. Tell him I'll send an invoice.'

'Will do, boss.' Dave was clearly pleased.

'And don't forget to wear your suit.' Hannah laughed. Checking her list on notes, she continued, 'Next, where are we at with the debugging of the investment company?'

'All done. Nothing there. I was in and out in no time.'

'And you're sure?' Hannah checked. 'It was clean?'

'As a whistle! That gear Lottie bought us is the dog's bollocks. You can debug a couple of offices without breaking a sweat. I trust the equipment completely.'

'Great. I'll invoice for that as well.'

'You keep the money rolling in. I'm pleased to have the work.'

Hannah forced herself to take one more gulp of her drink; she needed the caffeine. Pulling a face, she said, 'Try and get something better to drink before we meet here again, can you, mate? I don't insist on a latte, but I do like it to taste vaguely like actual coffee.'

Dave nodded. 'For you ... anything!'

'Good luck with Mr Wilson. Text me, okay?'

'Sure.'

There was something about his expression, his over-exuberance. It was just a little too much. It worried her. So, before she left, she asked, 'You're all right, aren't you?'

Dave took a second too long to reply, eventually stuttering, 'Ye ... yeah, I guess so.'

Her hunch had been right. 'You can't change it.'

'I know.'

'You have to think of Noah.'

'I do.'

'But it's still there, isn't it?'

Immediately Dave's eyes became swimmy. 'It's just when I'm

alone. I'm all right if I'm working or with Noah. But when I'm here, alone, there's too much time to think. You know?'

'I know.'

'The things I said. The stuff I did. I was—'

'Dave!' Hannah grabbed him by the arm and gave him a shake. 'What we did was wrong. We shouldn't have put Dawn in that position. You know it and I know it.'

'She died on the street like a dog.' Dave swallowed hard, clearly trying for the millionth time to rid his mind of the image of their colleague bleeding out in the gutter.

'You didn't stab her.'

'I wasn't there to stop it, though.'

'No. Neither was I. We messed up badly. But we have to move on.' It had taken Hannah a long time to admit to her own guilt, and stop trying to make it solely Dave's responsibility that they hadn't turned back when they'd first seen the fight in the street. Now, she waited to see if he would pull himself together or if he would lose it. She knew it could go either way.

After a minute he took a deep breath and said, 'I don't know what I'd do without you giving me work.'

'I give you work because you're good and I need you. I never employed you out of pity. Just remember that. I'm happy to give you as much work as I can. But I need to know you're on track, Dave. I have to be sure. This is my reputation on the line.'

'I get it.' Dave gave himself a shake. 'I'm good. Honestly, I'm okay.'

Hannah reached out for him again, only this time she was gentler and gave his arm a rub. 'We're both allowed to lose our shit now and then. We have every right to feel bad about not turning back sooner and going to help her, but when push comes to shove, we have to keep our eyes on the ball and have each other's backs, okay?'

'Absolutely. It was just a wobble. I promise.'

Checking out his cluttered lounge, Hannah said, 'When's Noah coming next?'

'Not for a few days.'

'Okay. I think you're right – maybe you've been on your own for too long. Sort this place out. Make it comfortable for Noah and get him back here as soon as possible. Too much thinking time is not your friend.'

Dave looked at the lounge. As if seeing it for the first time, he said, 'You're right. Fuck! What a mess.'

'Tidy it for him. Maybe run a vacuum around the place. Then make an appointment to go and see Mr Wilson. I'll wait for your text to tell me how it went.'

'I'm on it.'

'Like a car bonnet.'

They both laughed. It relaxed the tension. Hannah knew it was okay to leave him.

11
SCOTT – 2022

'Thank you for walking Bear with me again, Scottie.' Eliza gave him a broad smile.

'You're welcome. How's your knee doing?'

'Better, thanks. It doesn't hurt anymore.'

'I meant what I said before.' Scott grabbed the puppy by his scruff and gave him a friendly shake. 'I like this big wally.'

'We ought to try taking him somewhere else for a change next time. I'll bet he's sick of the park.'

'Like where?'

'We could drive to the beach.'

'A bit of a trek for a flamin' dog walk.'

'Not really,' Eliza disagreed. 'We could be in Lynton in forty minutes.'

'Yeah. Maybe.' Scott shrugged, noncommittally.

'Or … we could … do you think we could …?'

'Spit it out!'

'I was thinking … maybe the woods. I reckon Bear would absolutely love it.'

'*No!*'

Eliza stopped walking. 'Really?'

'Yes, *really*.' Scott stopped too, wrestling Bear to a standstill.

'I don't mean *those* woods. I just mean ... you know ... woods.'

'Not *any* woods. Thank you.'

'Okay.' Eliza resumed walking.

Scott and Bear joined her.

'Would you still be scared?' she asked.

'I just don't like the woods. Okay? Can we talk about something else now, please?'

'Of course.' Eliza agreed, but seemed unable to think of a new subject, so they settled for silence.

Scott felt the tension start to build in his chest. Try as he might, he couldn't help but imagine himself in a deep dark wood, and the old fear and adrenalin started coursing around his body. He began to feel lightheaded. Breathing deeply, he focused on Bear and Eliza and the wide, open spaces of the park. He tried not to think about the past.

SCOTT – 2002

'Do those look like witchy woods?' Uncle Robert asked.

'Yes. Stop the car, stop the car!' the three children shouted in unison.

Uncle Robert sing-songed, 'Are you sure?'

'Yes, yes, yes.' The children couldn't contain their excitement.

'Okay. But you've got to be brave.' Uncle Robert parked in a layby. 'Coming, Miriam?'

Auntie Miriam shook her head. 'You lot go. I'll be all right here. I have the wrong shoes on. But ... be careful, please, Robert.'

'Come with us?' Eliza asked.

'I'll read; you go.' Auntie Miriam had already taken a magazine out of the glove box and began thumbing through it. 'Just be careful of that plaster cast, Scottie.'

'You should come – it's so much fun,' Scott replied, amazed as always that Auntie Miriam didn't mind missing it.

'Leave her. It'll be better without her.'

'Ashley, there's no need to be rude.' Uncle Robert undid his seat belt.

'Sorry, Daddy, I just meant – if she doesn't want to come, let's not make her.'

Auntie Miriam looked a little sad for a second. 'You meant exactly what you said, child.'

———

'Stick to the path; we don't want to traipse mud into the car when we get back,' Uncle Robert advised.

'*If* we get back – you mean,' Eliza said.

'Yes, you're right. *If* we get back.'

They walked further into the woods. Already Uncle Robert's car was out of sight. They'd played this game before. Many times. If they spotted some woods that were spooky, Uncle Robert would always ask if the children thought they were witchy. If there was time, they'd stop. Uncle Robert was everything Scott wished his father would be.

It wasn't long before they were in the thick of things and the bright sunshine was gone. Overhead the trees blotted out the sky and the children felt they were now in a dark, mysterious place.

Scott's nostrils filled with an earthy aroma. He could hear his own heartbeat. If he was in these woods alone, he would probably die of fright, but it was always okay when he had Uncle Robert, Ash, and Eliza. He could never be sure if he was excited or scared; all he knew was that he loved this game.

Even though he loved it, as usual, after a few minutes, he began to panic and suggested that maybe they ought to turn back.

Ash had no time for him. 'Stop it. You always spoil it.'

'Hold my hand, Scottie,' Eliza offered.

'He does this every time. Why don't you just admit you're a cry baby and stay with my stupid mother in the car?' Ash asked.

Uncle Robert tutted, 'Don't say that, Ashley. Your mum just prefers her magazines, that's all. Besides,' he put on a fake scary voice, 'not everyone enjoys the witchy woods!'

Taking Eliza's hand, the hairs on the back of Scott's neck stood on end. Once Uncle Robert put on the voice it usually meant he was going to do it soon. Scott's stomach fluttered. He could almost taste the fear. 'Don't do it, Uncle Robert,' he begged.

'*Stop spoiling it!*' Ash clenched her fists.

Eliza squeezed Scott's hand. 'You always like it when he does it, you're just erm ... apprehenceful.'

'Apprehensive!' Uncle Robert laughed. 'Anyway, Scottie, there's nothing to be apprehensive about. We're just out for a walk in the witchy woods. What could go wrong?' He began to hang back, making sure he was to the rear of the group.

He was going to do it. Any minute now. Scott caught him, just outside his peripheral vision, bending and pretending to do up his shoelaces.

A second later, Uncle Robert shouted, '*What's that?*'

'*What?*' the children all shouted together.

'Over there, in the witchiest part of the woods. What is it?'

Scott's heart was almost beating out of his chest. He longed for this part, but he dreaded it too.

As always, Uncle Robert managed to surreptitiously throw whatever stone or rock he'd picked up, sending it flying into the bushes. As it collided with a tree it made a thud off in the distance. The children turned their heads towards the sound.

'What is it, Dad?' Ash asked, her expression one of pure elation.

'It's ... *a witch!*' Uncle Robert shouted. 'Run for it!'

All four turned and ran, back along the path they'd just walked down.

Scott could feel the cool air rushing in and out of his lungs as he breathed. All three children screamed at the top of their voices. Eliza's hand slipped from his and just for a second, he fell back.

Reaching out, she grabbed him. 'Don't get left behind!'

Once again, his sweaty little hand made contact with hers.

Within seconds they'd reached the road. Even though it felt like a long way, Uncle Robert never actually took them far into the woods.

They were at the car in an instant. Uncle Robert always parked on the same side of the road as the woods; they all knew he couldn't risk an over-excited child running out of the woods and into the road.

Opening the car doors, the children threw themselves onto the back seat, gasping for air.

Uncle Robert arrived at the car last.

'Did you see any witches?' Auntie Miriam asked calmly, closing her magazine.

'No, but we heard one, didn't we, Uncle Robert?' Eliza replied.

'Yes ... we ... did.' He seemed even more breathless than the children.

'I'm so scared. I'm so scared,' Scott muttered, but he was laughing at the same time. The adrenalin was doing what it always did to his body.

'Can we go home now?' Auntie Miriam smiled lovingly at her husband.

'Of course.' Uncle Robert started up the engine with a slightly shaky hand.

'Do you need me to drive?' She asked.

'I'm fine.' He placed his hand over hers. 'Seatbelts on, kids. Wave goodbye to the witches.' He pressed play on the CD player.

No more than ten minutes had passed since they'd parked up.

12

HANNAH – 2022

IT WAS a couple of days since their meeting, and Hannah hadn't received the text she'd been expecting from Dave. Surely, he wanted to show off and tell her how pleased Mr Wilson had been with their efforts? Perhaps he'd spent too long tidying up and had had to put off visiting Mr Wilson. Or maybe Mr Wilson himself had been busy. Either way, she needed to get in touch with Dave. Trying to call him, she felt slightly uneasy when his phone just rang and rang. Texting him, she asked, 'All okay? How did it go at Wilson & Cavendish?' *Keep it light, give him the chance to reply before you panic.*

She didn't want to let on that she was worried, but if she was honest, he hadn't been brilliant the last time they'd met. Should she have gone in with the evidence herself? No, she was right to send him. He'd done the work putting the case together. He was a whizz on the computer system Charlie had insisted Mr Wilson buy. He'd found the anomalies immediately. Besides, it was the PI work that kept him sane, kept him on the wagon. Still, it was worrying that he wasn't picking up his phone.

Vowing to keep trying to get hold of him, Hannah rustled up a couple of lattes and took them through to the garden. 'I'm glad to see you're doing that on the patio. That stuff stinks.' She handed Lottie one of the mugs.

'Woah! You made me jump.' Lottie took the mug and placed it on the patio where she was kneeling. 'Thanks.'

'Too engrossed in your stripping.'

'Ha ha. Actually, underneath these layers of paint lies a beautiful piece.'

'I'll take your word for it. It looks like a hideous monstrosity to me.'

'Han, you have to look beyond the obvious. You know that! This is going to be a quick seller for my website once it's back to its natural wood, I promise you.'

'Like I say, I'll take your word for it. You know your furniture, no doubt about it. Are you still loving this whole restoration thing?'

Lottie leant back on her heels. 'Yes, but ...'

'What?'

'I know it sounds daft, but I miss all the stuff from before. You know, the things we did together. Searching for Vincent.'

'You hated the stakeout!'

'Admittedly, I don't have the patience to do your job, but it was fun, looking for him together, you know?'

'I loved it too.'

'How's the latest case going? Dear old Mr Wilson and that guy who's misappropriating company funds. As you put it.'

'It's all done. I feel sorry for Mr Wilson. Charlie took advantage. He knew Mr Wilson wasn't familiar with the accounting package he'd persuaded the poor man to buy. He could've carried on until year end. Did I tell you what he was doing with the money?'

'No. I've not seen you for days.'

'Bloody loan shark, by the looks of it. You know the kind of thing, probably ridiculously high interest.'

'Wanker!' Lottie shook her head.

'But we got him. We found the evidence we needed to nail him. Hopefully, Dave's taken it all to Mr Wilson.'

'*Hopefully?*'

'I can't get hold of him to check.'

'Oh right. Charlie sounds like a proper chancer. Money can be an extremely strong motivator though,' Lottie said. 'Take fucking Vincent for example.'

'Classic case,' Hannah agreed.

'Is it exciting? Knowing you've nabbed him.'

'Well, Dave did most of the groundwork, to be fair. He's good at digging around in accounts, and he knew exactly where we'd find Charlie doing his dodgy dealing on the street. To be honest, it was a lot of waiting around and taking photos. You would've hated it!'

'Maybe.'

'What d'you mean?'

'Don't get me wrong – I love restoring furniture, and I adore it when a piece I've poured my heart into, like this one, gets a new forever home, but nothing makes my pulse race like the day we went after Vincent at the hospital.'

'If I remember correctly – it also made you want to pee!'

'Yes, it did.'

Hannah laughed. 'Happy memories.'

'Let's hope Mr Wilson is impressed and that he's going to write a review for the website.'

'I won't know until Dave picks up his flippin' phone. But I'm sure he will be impressed.'

'He'd bloody better be!' Placing the lid on the paint stripper, Lottie stood up, rubbing her knees. 'That needs to be left to work its magic for a while.' She carried her mug over to the garden chairs and joined her friend.

Reaching down to pat Lottie's slightly deaf, but rather sweet Spaniel, Dixie, who was sunning herself on the grass, Hannah said, 'I do have a new case that I'm keen to run by you.'

'Go on then. Who's the client?'

'After all, you are an investor in the company, and I think you'll be interested.'

'I am!'

'It's definitely one you'd like to hear about.' Hannah grinned.

'Stop messing about and just tell me!'

'All right.' Hannah stopped teasing. 'Remember the woman in the café? You went to school with her.'

'Eliza Griffith?'

'Griffins, yes.'

'She called you?'

'Yes. This morning.'

'What the …? Why have we been wasting time talking about paint stripper?'

'I was waiting for the right moment,' Hannah smiled.

'So, she wants you to find her cousin?'

'No. Sadly, that's not the job.'

'What then?'

'It's still interesting. I'm looking forward to getting started straight away. I just came home to grab a change of clothes, in case I need to do some surveillance in the car.'

'What's the case?'

'Let me tell you from the start.' Hannah drew in a breath, dramatically. 'When I got the call from Eliza, I could tell she was worried, so we arranged to meet as soon as possible. That's where I disappeared to earlier. We met in the same café we first saw her in. She seemed happiest meeting there, and, you know me, I don't mind where I go, as long as there's something decent to drink.' Hannah thought briefly of the stuff Dave had tried to pass off as coffee.

'So, Ms Griffins, what can I do for you?'

'Please, call me Eliza. I've only recently gone back to my maiden name, and it still sounds weird, and like I'm a bit of a failure.'

'Oh, I'm sure that's not true.' Hannah used her most professional voice to try to reassure.

'Well, we don't need to be that formal, do we?'

'Of course not. It's your call entirely. Carry on, Eliza.' Hannah waved her hand to indicate all formalities were forgotten.

'I almost don't know where to start. Do I start with Ash? Do you need to know all that?' Eliza shook her head.

Hannah assessed her new client for a second time, and concluded again that she was indeed an attractive woman, but she was just so tense. 'Why not tell me what you need from me right now and I'll soon let you know if I have any questions?'

'Okay. Well, when I was growing up, I was very close to my two cousins. None of us had brothers or sisters, and we just ended up like siblings. Like I told you the other day, Scott is Ash's cousin on the other side; he's not related to me by blood at all. But I've known him all his life and he's like blood, you know?'

Hannah nodded. 'It's about how the person makes you feel in here.' She tapped her breastbone.

'Exactly. Scott's three years younger than Ash and me. We kidded around with him a fair bit. Well, Ash did. But once he caught up in size, that eased off. You know what testosterone does when it hits. He was way taller than both of us by the time he was thirteen or so.'

Hannah discreetly made notes on her phone, all the time saying 'Uh huh' to encourage her client.

'Anyway, Ash disappeared not long after she and I turned eighteen. It was a terrible time. The not knowing nearly killed us all. Her mum, my Auntie Miriam, was distraught, as you'd imagine. I kept thinking she'd come back. I couldn't believe she would just …' Eliza's eyes filled with tears. 'I'm sorry. This isn't helping, is it?'

'It must have been hell for all of you.' Hannah grabbed a paper napkin and handed it to Eliza, indicating she should continue. 'Go on, when you're ready.'

'My Auntie Miriam died last year. I think she had always assumed she would see Ash again, but the more time that went by, the less likely it became. Anyway, she did this thing about four years ago where you can declare someone as missing, presumed dead. I don't think she wanted to do it, but my mum and dad and Scott's mum, well, everyone really, they all encouraged her. They thought it would help her to put it all behind her. Like you can do that. Like you can put something that horrific behind you. I've lost more than one pregnancy. But my babies were tiny. They had all just started on their journey through life. When I'm feeling philosophical, I say to myself that for some reason that I cannot figure out, they weren't meant to be. But Auntie Miriam lost so much more. She lost a child who had been with her for eighteen years. They didn't always see eye to eye, and anyone who knew them would tell you Ash got on better with her dad, but Auntie Miriam loved her daughter. I cannot imagine her pain.'

Hannah gave her condolences for Eliza's own losses, still silently hoping the job was going to be to find Ash.

'A few weeks after my auntie died, I got a letter from a solicitor telling me I was her only beneficiary.'

'Right.'

'Not me and Scott. Just me.'

'I see, and he had expected to be included?'

'Yes. I understood why she didn't leave everything to someone else, my parents for example. They're living overseas, they're sorted financially. I get why she wanted to help the younger generation, and I know if Ash had not been presumed dead, she would've left it all to her. But it was a shock just how one sided it was.'

'Why do you suppose she didn't include Scott?'

'Oh, I don't need to suppose at all. She stated it, in her will. *Nothing* was to go to him. Not property, not money, not a stick of furniture. Everything for me.'

'Do you know why?'

'Auntie Miriam blamed Scott for Ash's disappearance. She said it all along. I knew she was angry with him, but I didn't realise how deep the anger went.'

'And *was* Scott responsible for Ash's disappearance?'

'I ... he ... no, he wasn't.'

'You don't seem too sure.'

'I am sure. He wasn't.'

'So why do you think your auntie was adamant that he was?'

'Scott and I were asleep in Ash's room the night she went missing. We don't know anything about it. I didn't ask you here to talk about that night.'

'Fair enough.' Hannah tried to hide her disappointment. She would've loved to have been given the mission to find Ash. She'd found Vincent bloody Rocchino, hadn't she? 'What do you want me to help with? If it's a legal issue regarding allowing Scott to have some of the money I would suggest a solicitor.'

'It's not that. Scott's asked me for money, a few times. But I've always said no. I decided early on I was going to stick to Auntie Miriam's rules. If she didn't want him to have anything, then I won't give it to him.'

'Right. So ...?'

'Scott's not the only person who's been asking me for money.'

'Who else?'

'My ex-husband is pissed off because he divorced me and immediately remarried. His timing was so bad.' Eliza gave a cynical laugh. 'I got the letter from the solicitor on the same day as I heard about his second marriage. I've researched it. I don't have to pay him anything. It's entirely my inheritance.'

'You've told him this?'

'Yes.'

'So, what's the issue?'

'He's not happy about it.'

'Tough!'

'Then there's his wife.'

'Ah ha, the notorious second wife!'

'Yes, Kristen. She's a total bitch. We went to school together; Lottie might remember her. She has a face like a horse.'

Hannah thought it was unlikely the new wife was as unattractive as Eliza portrayed, but chose to remain quiet on the subject.

'A few years ago, she started working at WB Electrics, where my ex works, and she ... well, she stole him off me.'

'I'm sorry.'

'She found a chink in our armour, and she took advantage of it.' Eliza sniffed. 'I was distracted, well, heartbroken actually. I'd just lost three pregnancies in close succession, and she leapt in.'

Hannah shook her head disapprovingly to demonstrate solidarity with her new client.

Eliza continued speaking, 'She's mentioned the money before, but only tentatively. Then, just recently, she came to the park where she knew I'd be, and she badgered me, directly asking for money. Saying, I'm family.'

'What does she mean by that?' Hannah queried.

'I'm still struggling with the fact they have a baby. To be honest with you, it gnaws at my insides. She turned up, with the baby in tow, asking me to consider giving them money for his sake.' Eliza gave an incredulous look. 'She's so thoughtless?'

'I'm sorry. It must be difficult. But you know, legally you owe them nothing. I still don't see—'

'I don't need your help explaining to these people that I'm

not going to give them any of my inheritance. That's not why I called you.'

'Okay,' Hannah said, 'you've told me two reasons why you *didn't* call me. How about you tell me why you *did*?'

'Someone is threatening me.'

'I see. Go on?'

'The other night, someone came to the house and kicked in the fence. Scott was staying – he heard it all.'

'How do you know they were threatening you? It could've been an accident, a drunk, something like that?'

'I did think it could be that. Also, Scott's in debt and we thought maybe it was someone after him. But he's gone now. He went back home the next day. He said just in case it was someone after him, it wasn't fair to bring that to my door and he'd rather sort it out from his mum's.'

'He lives with her?' Hannah asked.

'He's never really got himself together enough to move out.'

'Doesn't he worry about bringing violence to *her* door?'

'Apparently not!'

'I assume something else has happened since he left?'

'Yes. When I checked out the fence in the daylight, I realised that not only had someone kicked it, but they'd written on it too. In red paint.'

Hannah raised her eyebrows enquiringly.

'Just some stuff about how I was a bitch and I'd stolen the house.'

'Right.'

'Then Scott and I found a CD on my doorstep.'

'A CD?'

'Yes,' Eliza said, 'it was my uncle's favourite group. It included the song that was played at his funeral. They wrote *Everybody Hurts* in red marker pen.'

'Ah ha, a theme.'

'Sorry?'

'Red for anger. To show you just how mad this person is. That they're serious.'

'I guess so. After that I got a text from a number I didn't recognise.'

'Can you show me?'

'I deleted it.'

Just about managing to stop herself from swearing, Hannah said, 'For fu ... you shouldn't have done that, Eliza.'

'I know. But it scared me, so I blocked the number and deleted it.'

'What did the text say?'

'That's not your house and that's not your money. That kind of thing.'

'In red?'

'No.'

'Shame. I do like continuity. So, you think it was from your cousin Ash?'

'I don't know. I mean, that's the suggestion, isn't it?'

'Very much so. Almost too much so, in my opinion,' Hannah said.

'Meaning?'

'There could be lots of reasons for a text like that. Anyone can pretend to be Ash.'

'True. Let's be honest, there are a few people who don't like me much at the moment.'

'Well, you've blocked the number now.'

'But,' Eliza looked really concerned, 'what if it *is* her?'

'Is that what you honestly believe?' Hannah asked.

'I think it's possible that she isn't dead after all. And if she is still alive ... I think she hates me!'

13
ELIZA – 2022

The only way to get through this nightmare was to keep busy and wait for Hannah to solve everything. The next room that needed decluttering in the house was the walk-in pantry. If you could call it a room.

She had lots of memories that revolved around the little closed off corner of the kitchen. When Eliza, Ash and Scott were children, Auntie Miriam kept all manner of tasty delights in there. Sometimes, Eliza would choose the pantry as her hiding place when they played hide and seek, just so she could search for treats.

People didn't really have walk-in pantries anymore. They were very much a thing of the past. Instead, one opted for a fully fitted kitchen. The random assortment of items that used to sit on the shelves in Auntie Miriam's time would now be found in cupboards or integrated fridges. It was a shame. Auntie Miriam had been so proud of her walk-in pantry back in the day, always stating that if there was ever another World War, she would be ready.

Now, all that remained was for Eliza to filter out all the

products that had reached, or in some cases, outlived, their sell-by date.

Eliza placed her phone on one of the shelves, making sure the volume was up. If Hannah managed to work anything out, she needed to be ready to take the call.

Picking up a tin of spam, she turned it over and noted the date printed on the base – Best by Oct 2009. Before Ash went missing. *How odd. This tin was actually on this shelf on the night that Ash ...* Eliza stopped herself from thinking about it. Instead, she chucked the tin into one of the large black plastic sacks that were destined for the tip. Auntie Miriam was usually quite thorough about tidying and sorting, but she'd definitely missed that one.

Eliza continued to sort through the items on the shelves; each one was closely examined and either placed in the keep pile or discarded. Once she had sorted everything, she planned to wipe down all the shelves with a weak bleach solution and itemise anything she needed to buy to restock, although clearly spam would not be on the list. She was very much a vegetarian now. Eventually, she thought she might get someone like Small and Waddle back in and have them rip it all out and maybe make her some nice bespoke cupboards. But she couldn't think about all that right now. Plus, there was always the possibility that they would make a comment about the writing on the fence. Better to leave it a bit longer. Give them the chance to forget those embarrassing words. There would be time enough for all that upheaval when Hannah had solved her current conundrum and life was a bit more normal.

With just two shelves left to clear, Eliza seriously questioned if she was going to be able to lift the heavy black bags into the boot of her car. Deciding that perhaps she ought to wait for Scott's help, she left the bags in the middle of the pantry. She'd done enough reminiscing for one day.

ELIZA – 2002

Eliza knew it wouldn't be long before she was found. But hiding in the pantry gave her a chance to quickly search for something sugary. In the weeks leading up to Christmas, the shelves always began to contain interesting jars and packets. She could hear Ash stomping about overhead, annoyed as usual by how good Scott was at hiding. Ash hated Scott to be good at anything. Eliza ran her hand along the shelves, trying not to disturb anything. What could she eat? Maybe something that was already open, so Auntie Miriam wouldn't know exactly how much had been in there. She came across a jar of maraschino cherries. Their purpose was to provide a colourful addition to Auntie Miriam and Eliza's mum's festive snowballs. Eliza had seen the little cherries bobbing around in the cloudy yellow liquid on previous occasions. The jar had already been opened, and thanks to her small, dexterous fingers, Eliza was able to scoop out the cherries with ease. First one, then another, then more.

By the time she heard Ash's feet on the squeaky bottom step of the stairs, Eliza had almost munched her way through the contents of the jar. Sadly, she was starting to feel a bit sick, but, oh, the excitement of secretly gobbling up all that delicious sweetness in the dimly lit pantry! She hoped Auntie Miriam wouldn't work out it was her. What if she'd ruined Christmas? Sadly, Eliza knew that the chances were Scott would be the one to get the blame for her crime.

With sticky fingers, she hastily replaced the lid and shoved the jar to the back of the shelf. Then she waited for the inevitable.

Ash yanked the pantry door open. 'Found you. What a totally lame place to hide, Elz.'

'Have you found Scott yet?'

'No. The little idiot must be in a good place.'

'Shall we look together?'

'If you like.' Ash shrugged.

'Well, we have to find him.'

'Do we?'

Eliza secretly licked her fingers. 'Of course.'

'I vote we leave him. Let's go and climb some trees. He'll come out and join us when he gets bored.'

'He can't. Your mum said he's not allowed to climb trees anymore. Not since his wrist.'

'Oh God, he's such a baby.

14
HANNAH – 2022

'This was a lovely idea. Thank you so much.' Lottie gestured to the cooked breakfast Hannah had made her.

'You're welcome. I fancied something more than just coffee and toast. Not sure when I'll next get to eat.'

'Stakeout?'

'Mmmm ... sort of.' Hannah spoke with a mouthful of scrambled egg. 'Sorry!'

'My mother would never forgive you, but *I* will.'

'Bless you.'

'Is it Eliza's case you're working on today?'

'Yeah. I'm going to do a bit of nosing about. Eliza's already called this morning to see if I've found anything out. She said she was waiting all day yesterday for news.'

'She can't expect you to solve it in a day!' Lottie squeaked.

'I did go over there and wait outside her place for a while, but there was nothing to see. I think she just really wants to get answers quick.'

'She's not coping well, is she?' Lottie stood up, indicating she was going to make more coffee.

'Oh, yes please.' Hannah passed her mug to Lottie.

'You'll need to pee!'

'I'll deal with it,' Hannah laughed, adding, 'No, she's not coping. She's freaking out. I know she's trying to keep busy, sorting out her new house. But she's got herself convinced Ash is out for revenge. That useless cousin of hers isn't helping matters. He's like a wet weekend in Morecombe.'

'Have you actually been there?'

'Morecombe? No.' Hannah shook her head. 'But I can imagine.'

'Do *you* think it's Ash, out for revenge?'

'I doubt it. I think someone wants to get their hands on her inheritance; it's as simple as that. I won't be surprised if the messages begin demanding money.'

'Really?' Lottie paused. 'Blackmail, you mean?'

'Extortion. A threat of some kind. Trust me, they'll ask for money soon. And when they do, they'll start making mistakes or giving too much information away, and that's when I'll nab the bastard!'

'But ...' Lottie placed a coffee pod into the machine, 'how can you be sure it's not Ash? How can you know she's definitely not just angry at Eliza for inheriting what's rightfully hers?'

'Because it's all so unnecessary. Let's be honest here – if she is still alive, she could just go to a solicitor and ask them what her rights are. Why paint on fences and leave CDs on the doorstep?'

'True. Do you think she is, though? Do you think she's been alive all this time and just not bothered to come home?'

'I haven't told Eliza this yet, but I know I can trust you. I did find out a bit about the case, actually.'

'Ohhh, what?' Lottie sat back at the table, abandoning the coffee.

'After we first saw her in the café, I spoke to Paul, my mate in the service. You know he gets me info sometimes.'

'What did he say?' Lottie asked.

'He read the file and gave me the essence.'

'Which is?'

'The family didn't treat her as a missing person to begin with. She was considered to be just a runaway teenager who would return of her own free will.'

'Why?'

'Evidently, by the time this Ash character was eighteen, she'd run away from home for the odd night or two quite a few times. She didn't get on with her mother.'

'I see. So, they just thought ...'

'Uh huh,' Hannah nodded, 'just another attempt to get away from home. There was a fairly large sum of money in the sideboard around the time she was last seen, and it was missing too. It must've seemed like she'd taken the money and scarpered.'

'Eliza must know about the money,' Lottie said.

'I guess so. Anyway, the mum didn't involve the police for the first week. She was hopeful that the girl would return. When she didn't come home, it became clear it more than likely wasn't just a case of a young woman running off to stay at a friend's house. The family had contacted everyone they could think of, and no one knew where she was. Once the police were involved, Ash was labelled as a missing person, but it was only deemed a medium risk case. An eighteen-year-old – medium risk, for Christ's sake! Honestly, I don't think it was ever thoroughly investigated.'

Lottie said, 'That's quite sad.'

'It is, yes. After she'd been gone for two weeks, the family told the police they were going to make posters and put them around the neighbourhood. Remember you told me about them?'

'They had a black and white picture of Ash right in the middle. Staring out at you with those angry eyes.'

'You'd think they'd go for a colour picture.'

'It wouldn't have made much difference, to be honest. Ash was a goth. Everything about her was black; hair, clothes …'

'Well, anyway, the posters didn't yield much of a response.'

'Imagine being gone for twelve years.'

'I would never leave my mum and dad wondering for a minute. But then, by the sounds of it, Ash wasn't all that considerate to her mum. It seems like a total clash of personalities. It happens.'

Lottie was silent for a second.

'Are you okay?' Hannah asked.

'Just thinking, you know, I wasn't much older than Ash the first time my mum brought fucking Vincent into our home. We think we're so grown up at that age. Ash can't have given any thought to how much she was making her mum suffer. Just as I never gave much thought as to why my mum needed the attention of that useless little git.'

'You'd think she would've worked out that leaving her family in limbo was cruel. She could at least have written or called,' Hannah said.

'That's the bit I struggle with. That's why I think she must be dead.'

Hannah continued with her report. 'Paul said that about a month after Ash went missing, a witness came forward. It was a woman who had been on her way to an early morning cleaning job.'

'Been there, done that!' Lottie grimaced. 'I wonder if she worked for Fat Face Bale?'

'God, don't make me think about him now. I've just eaten breakfast.' Hannah pretended to gag. 'Anyway, this woman said she remembered seeing a girl who matched Ash's description around the date in question. This girl was hitching a lift by the side of the road, near Lullaby Woods, and the witness thought she might have got into a lorry. But she couldn't remember what was written on the lorry and the driver was never traced.

Unfortunately, just like now, there was no CCTV on that strip of road. So, there's no way of knowing if it was Ash or just some other young woman who matched the description.'

'Which was?'

'A young female, approximately seventeen to twenty years of age, about five foot four, with long dark hair and dark clothing.'

'Could be lots of people, I suppose. It's a shame it took the witness a month to come forward.'

'Sometimes people just need a trigger. Maybe she'd only just noticed the posters. It was probably dark at that time of the morning – maybe the witness couldn't be sure what she'd actually seen.' Hannah picked up her mug and shook it at Lottie, indicating she'd like a drink.

Lottie rose from the table and continued making the coffee. 'I guess so. There was nothing else Paul could say to help you?'

'Nothing. She didn't have a phone with her. I think we were all still using pay as you go Nokias back then. She had a bank account, but it had hardly any money in it and there was never any activity around it. Over time, it became a cold case, and once the family had her declared dead the file was archived.'

'And now she's back.'

'Well ...'

'Maybe.' Lottie handed Hannah a fresh coffee.

'Thanks. Goodness me, this bloody woman. Is she alive? Is she dead? I'm going to do my best to find out. But I'm not taking my eye off the ball. This little charade with Eliza could have less to do with Ash and a whole lot more to do with one of the people who feels put out about the inheritance.'

'So, what kind of research are you doing today?' Lottie asked.

'A bit of a chat with the neighbours, that sort of thing.'

'What ... undercover?'

'You bet your sweet arse.' Hannah winked.

'You're so lucky.' Lottie looked crestfallen.

Hannah didn't hesitate. 'Want to come with me?'

'Really?'

'I'm sure I can think of a way to weave you into my narrative. Or did you have plans?'

'I was going to paint a chair.'

'Watch paint dry or come with me: which would you prefer?'

'Do you need to ask?' Lottie smiled.

'Okay. We can grab Dixie too.'

Lottie immediately scooped up her dog. 'Got her!'

'You're keen. Let's finish these drinks first. Oh yeah, I also need to swing past Dave's place on the way.'

'Still no reply?'

'No.' Hannah had texted a few times. Each time she'd tried to keep it light, but her concern was growing. They never went this long without speaking, and no matter how much she tried to justify the total radio silence, it was starting to worry her. He was a grown man, and he wouldn't like her checking up on him, but in truth, what choice was he leaving her?

———

Dave's old banger was outside his flat when they pulled up. 'You and Dixie wait here, okay?' Hannah said. 'Hopefully, this is just going to be a quick debrief and then we can be on our way.'

'No worries. Dixie's nodded off anyway.' Lottie grabbed her phone and clicked on Facebook.

Two flights of stairs later, Hannah rang Dave's doorbell confidently, sure that he was going to open up. She waited. Not a sound came from inside the flat. A few seconds later she rang again. Still nothing. Flipping the letterbox up, she tried to see inside. It was impossible to tell whether he was in or not. The front door led to a tiny hallway. If he was inside, he would most likely be in either the lounge or the bedroom, neither of which was visible from her rather limited vantage point. Placing her mouth as close to the grubby letterbox as she dared, she shouted, 'Dave!'

No response.

'Are you in there?'

The entire place was silent, not even the usual hum of the TV he always had on for company.

Taking out her phone, Hannah rang his number. As before, it simply rang and rang. She couldn't hear a ringtone inside the flat, but that meant nothing – they tended to keep their phones on silent because they were usually trying to be inconspicuous.

Making her way back to the car, she weighed up whether it was time to talk to Paul at the station. Should she be thinking about reporting Dave as missing? It was a tough call. He was a man who could take care of himself; he might not thank her for telling the whole station his business. But, on the other hand, the last thing he'd been about to do was take some evidence to a client, and that evidence would almost certainly have upset the employee. Charlie might be a beanpole, but they both knew how he behaved when he was angry.

She joined Lottie in the car.

'Guess who texted me?' Lottie waved her phone in the air, triumphantly.

'Erm … Chen?' Hannah guessed.

'He's just arrived in Santorini. He sent me a photo of him at the beach. It looks amazing, doesn't it?'

'Nice.' Hannah nodded, slightly distracted.

Still staring at the smiling, sun-kissed Chen in the photo, Lottie asked, 'That was a *very* quick debrief. Everything okay?'

'Not really,' Hannah sighed. 'He's not in.'

'Did you ring the bell more than once?

Hannah chose not to dignify such a question with an answer.

When she didn't reply, Lottie added, 'And call through the letterbox?'

Hannah threw up her hands, 'No, I just hoped the smoke

signals I sent from the ground floor would do the trick! Yes, I rang the bell more than once, *and* I called through the letterbox. What do you take me for?'

After a short silence Lottie burst out laughing. 'Sorry.'

'Seriously, though,' Hannah replied, 'I'm worried about him. I'm halfway convinced I ought to let someone at the station know.'

'He might not want them all to know he's missing, though. What if he's on a bender?'

'I know. I know. I could tell Paul, but he's not exactly discreet. To be honest, I'm not so worried that he's on a bender, I'm more worried about what Mr Wilson's shit-for-brains employee might've done to him. We should've gone in together.' Hannah rubbed her forehead.

'So?'

'I'll think about it whilst we're doing our covert research. I can always call Paul on the way home if I'm really worried.'

'Good idea,' Lottie agreed. 'Oh, by the way, what sort of car does a nun drive?'

'Is this a joke?' Hannah asked. 'Am I supposed to say – I don't know, what sort of car *does* a nun drive?'

'No. A pastel pink, smart car drove past just now, and I could've sworn it was being driven by a nun.'

Hannah laughed. 'I'm sure nuns can drive whatever car they like. Now, let's get on with it. Stop gawping at that bloody phone.' She started up the engine and headed in the direction of Eliza's neighbourhood.

Halfway there, Lottie let out a squeal.

'What's up?' Hannah kept her eyes on the road.

'Facebook.'

'What about it?'

Lottie tried to wave the phone in front of Hannah's face.

Swatting it away, Hannah instructed, 'I thought I told you to leave the phone alone. We need to get in the right frame of mind for work.'

'But look!'

'I'm driving, Lottie. Just tell me, please.'

'They're restarting the fetes at Mulberry House.'

'Oh! D'you want to go?'

Lottie shrugged. 'I don't know. I'll think about it.'

Still keeping her eyes on the road, Hannah patted Lottie's knee. 'We can go if you want to. It's entirely your call. Now put that phone down. Let's talk tactics.'

'Bringing Dixie was such a good idea; it makes us seem like we're just out for a dog walk.' Lottie grinned.

'Exactly. We're just two normal people out for a stroll.'

'Brilliant.' Lottie's grin widened.

'Just one normal person and an inane grinning fool, out for a walk,' Hannah corrected herself.

'Sorry. Am I making it too obvious?'

'Just a bit. Try to act a little less … umm … a little less *Lottie on a stakeout*.'

'I'll try. Come on Dixie,' Lottie added, about three octaves higher than her usual voice.

'What we're looking for are neighbours who are out the front, doing a bit of gardening, or people coming and going. It's a nice day.' Hannah looked up at a clear blue sky. 'There should be plenty of people about.'

'Right. What do we do when we find them?'

'We ask them questions. You'll see. Just follow my lead.'

The first person they encountered was a woman who appeared to be in her forties. She was wearing a fluffy leopard print dressing gown; her hair was tied in a messy ponytail and her face was devoid of colour. She was sorting out the recycling in her front garden.

Hannah gave her a wave and called out, 'Morning!'

In return, the woman gave a small tight smile, which didn't reach her eyes. Instead, they remained focused on the wine bottles she was trying to quietly drop into the large green bin.

'No good?' Lottie asked.

'She doesn't want to talk; she's got enough on her plate trying to dispose of those bottles quietly. Keep walking'

The next person to cross their path was a young woman who was pushing a toddler in a buggy. She was gorgeous.

Hannah smiled.

The young woman returned her smile.

'Sorry to bother you,' Hannah said. 'Can I ask you a question?'

'Sure. What's up?'

'Do you live in this street?'

'No.'

'Oh, okay. No problem.'

'Soz about that,' the young woman said. 'I live a couple of streets that way.' She pointed off to the right, causing her large breasts to swing mesmerisingly.

'Thanks, anyway.' Hannah tried not to stare.

'Why d'you ask?'

'Just trying to get some local info. Before we move around here.'

The toddler, aware that his buggy had stopped moving, instantly became fractious.

Giving the buggy a shake, the young woman said, 'Shush, I'm tryin' a help these girls. Just wait a second.' Grabbing a small bar of chocolate from her bag, she unwrapped it and passed it to her son. 'Have a bit of this.'

The toddler took the bar in his dainty hands gleefully.

'He's such a little bugger, this one is. He wants everyfing. Like his father.'

Lottie leant into the buggy and surveyed the lad, who had a shock of dark hair and the face of a cherub. 'Have I met him before?' she asked.

'Doubt it.' The young woman laughed, awkwardly.

'Yes, of course. Daft question.' Lottie backed away from the buggy, obviously realising she was coming across as slightly weird. 'He's a lovely boy.'

'Yeah, he is.' The young woman reached in and ruffled her son's hair. 'But he don't half know it. Like I say, always gets what he wants does our Dwayne.'

'We'd best get going,' Hannah said. 'We really need to do some research on the area.'

'Well, I fink it's a good street. I don't live far, and I'd recommend it. It's nice round here. Cute dog, by the way.' The woman bent and stroked Dixie on the head.

'Thanks for your help.' Lottie smiled, taking one last glance at the boy, who had already all but demolished the chocolate bar.

'Yes, thank you,' Hannah added.

They watched as the young woman made her way down the road, her bum wiggling as she walked.

Hannah asked, 'What the hell was all that about?'

'What?'

'Wondering if you'd met the boy before. Were you trying to get into character or something?'

'No. Of course not. I genuinely thought ...' Lottie shook her head. 'Did that kid look like Vincent to you?'

'*Vincent!*'

'It was strange. He just reminded me ...'

'Well, I didn't know your wicked stepdad as well as you did, but I can't say that kid looked much like him. I mean ... he was short!'

Lottie laughed. 'You wally.'

'Come on, let's get on. If it takes us this long to get to work, is it any wonder I don't often bring you with me?' Hannah gave Lottie a shove.

'All right, all right. I'm moving.' Lottie set off at such a pace Dixie struggled to keep up.

They continued around the block, and as they came back to the street that contained Eliza's house, they spotted an elderly man parking his Honda Civic on the driveway a few houses down. 'We're on! Try to act normal this time. No more strange questions.' Hannah walked purposefully towards the neighbour, calling, 'Excuse me?'

Clearly a gent; the man removed his cap. 'Yes?'

'Have you got a minute?'

'Well ...'

'It's just that my wife and I have seen a house for sale at the end of the road,' Hannah grabbed Lottie's hand affectionately, 'but we're not familiar with the area. Before we go as far as calling the agent and booking a viewing, we thought we'd suss out the street, you know, see if it's for us.'

'Oh, right.' The neighbour seemed relieved they were not canvasing for votes or trying to sell him something.

'Have you lived here long?' Hannah asked, casually.

'Oh yes, donkey's years.' The neighbour stroked his bristly chin. 'Must be getting on for thirty now. I came here with my wife; God rest her soul.'

'Wow. Thirty years in the same house. That speaks volumes about the neighbourhood, I'd say.' Hannah smiled, adding, 'Sorry for your loss.'

'Thank you.' The neighbour nodded. 'It's a very nice street. Never any trouble. Quiet, you know.'

'Perfect!' Lottie squeaked, determined to join in, but clearly now unsure how to sound normal.

'We were round this way last week as well and we noticed some graffiti on a fence; it was a bit disconcerting. I don't suppose you know anything about that, do you?' Hannah asked.

'Well,' the neighbour gave a slight cough, 'that was a shame, yes. But it was swiftly removed. I called the carpenters myself, sorted it all out for the new lady there. She seems lovely. I can only assume it was a case of mistaken identity. We never normally have anything like that.'

'New lady?' Hannah asked.

'Yes, in Miriam's old house. I believe she's a niece or something.'

'So, we don't need to worry about vandals kicking in our fence if we decide to move here?'

'Absolutely not. We've had no trouble for years. Not since ...'

'Since?'

'Well, we once had a girl go missing. Miriam's daughter, actually. She disappeared. Terribly sad. But that was over a decade ago now.'

'Goodness, yes, it must've been awful. How dreadful for the mother.'

'They didn't get on well, Miriam and her daughter. What was her name now?'

Spotting that Lottie was about to provide the man with the answer, Hannah gave her a nudge in the ribs.

'Well, anyway, I'm sure it was terrible for Miriam. You're right,' the neighbour agreed, then added, 'Ashley, that was the name.'

'I guess you knew her quite well.'

'A bit of a funny one. Halloween every day for that little madam. You get my drift.'

'Right.'

'Miriam couldn't cope with her. She was a wild child.'

'Really?'

'Well, not when Robert was around. But afterwards, once it was just the two of them, Miriam was lost.'

'What do you think happened to the girl?' Hannah asked.

'I think she was killed. No one drops off the radar like that. She was there one day and gone the next.'

'That's fascinating, isn't it, darling?' Hannah turned to Lottie.

'Yes, fascinating.' Lottie's voice remained ridiculously high.

'But who would've killed her?'

'The boyfriend, of course.'

'Boyfriend?' Hannah hid her surprise.

'Yes, I think he did her in.'

'But surely the police would've questioned him?'

'I don't think they knew about him. I saw him sneaking about near the house after dark. It wouldn't surprise me if poor old Miriam didn't even know he existed.'

'Right. And you didn't think *you* ought to mention him to the police?'

'They never asked me.'

15
ELIZA – 2022

ELIZA WOKE with such a start she couldn't be sure what time it was, or even what day. Was it a workday or a weekend? Was it early in the morning or late at night? Why was it so cold? She waited, shaking her head in an effort to return to reality. Hating that feeling of bewilderment that sometimes comes with waking in the middle of a deep sleep.

It didn't take her long to get a handle on things. She quickly came to the realisation that there was no such thing as a workday for her, not at the moment. She was in Auntie Miriam's house, except it was hers now. As for the time, a quick glance at her phone on the bedside table told her it was two a.m. The only question that remained was why it was so cold.

She lay still, trying to figure out what had woken her. Was Scott staying? No, she remembered him saying he had stuff to do. No doubt he was playing cards, frantically trying to win back the money he owed.

A noise downstairs in the kitchen made her blood run cold. Maybe that was what had woken her. But, if Scott wasn't staying, who the hell was in the kitchen? Immediately each breath she took came quicker. In and out. In and out. Barely a second between them. So fast it made her dizzy. What was she supposed to do? Go downstairs? Confront the person in the kitchen? What if they hurt her?

Eliza got out of bed and threw on her dressing gown and slippers. Making her way down the stairs, she carefully stepped over the noisy bottom step, moving her head to the left as she did so. Once in the hallway she thought to herself, *I'm going to need a weapon.* This thought was instantly followed by another: *nothing ever ended well that began with I'm going to need a weapon.* Shit! There was nothing. Unless you counted a lone umbrella that stood in the umbrella bucket. She picked it up. Turning it over to feel its weight, she concluded it wouldn't do much damage to anyone. However, it was at least a long thin one, and given that there was nothing else, it would have to do. She figured she could hold it out in front, and it would provide an illusion of distance between herself and the intruder.

Taking the last few steps towards the kitchen, she strained to hear if the noises had stopped. With a strange sense of déjà-vu she gently pushed the kitchen door open, allowing the hall light to lead the way.

The kitchen was empty. The fridge door hung open, providing an eerie light. Switching the overhead fluorescent strip light on, she waited for the flickering to stop. When it did and the room became bathed in light, she realised all the jars of preserves and jams had been removed from the fridge and placed on the kitchen table. They stood in neat rows, evenly spaced apart, resembling a queue of people. Most noticeable of all though was the fact that the back door was swinging on its hinges. No wonder the house was so cold. She ran to the back door, throwing her weight at it and slamming it shut. It was a big, old door and it made a fair racket as it closed. Reaching up onto her tiptoes, she slid the top bolt across and vowed to be more conscientious about locking up at night. With the back door bolted, she allowed herself to breathe again. Switching from shallow inhalations she took a couple of good lungfuls of air.

Turning back to the kitchen table she pondered why anyone would want to mess with the contents of her fridge. About to begin reloading it, her eye was caught by something – the door to the pantry was slightly ajar. Had she closed it after she'd finished sorting? A hideous thought struck her – when sliding the bolt across the back door, had she actually locked the person *in*, not out? Had the place of wonder from her childhood become the hiding place of something dreadful? What now?

Eliza stood in the middle of the kitchen, waiting for the faintest of sounds. Nothing. Placing the umbrella out in front of her, she took a step towards the pantry door. She needed to pee, she needed to poo, she needed to vomit. Her insides were fluid.

Taking a deep breath, she wrenched the door open and stabbed at the inside of the pantry with the umbrella. 'Arghh, arghh, arghh.' Several stabs into the darkness.

Pulling the light cord, she scanned the small room in the dim light provided. No one. It was just as she'd left it after tidying up. Three large black bags remained on the floor awaiting Scott's assistance to remove them. She backed out, pulled the light cord again and firmly closed the door. Dropping the umbrella, she went back to her task of replacing the jars in the fridge. She was contemplating whether to call Scott or Hannah when the garden security light came on. It was annoyingly over-sensitive and was often set off by foxes or badgers. But when it did come on, it flooded the garden with a glaring light. Glancing up from the kitchen table, at first, she could see nothing to warrant the trigger of the light. No wildlife at all. But then, as she squinted further down the garden, she saw something that made her heart want to crawl out of her mouth.

At the end of the garden, by the gate that led into the fields behind, she could just make out a figure. Dressed all in black, it was walking away. Its long, dark hair blew in the wind, and it moved slowly, slightly hunched over with its head down. For the last six years that Eliza had known Ash she had dressed entirely in black except for her much begrudged school uniform. Whenever in black, Ash had carried her grief on her back. It was her, it had to be.

'Ash?' Eliza whispered.

Passing by the tree that Scott had jumped from when they were kids, the figure disappeared into the fields.

Eliza rushed to the kitchen sink and threw up. All the fear, all the adrenaline, and the contents of her stomach came rushing out.

As soon as she was able, she ran back up the stairs and grabbed her phone from the bedside table. Fumbling, she almost dropped it, but managing to click on her contacts, she pressed Hannah's name.

Hannah answered on the third ring.

Sobbing into the phone, Eliza cried, 'Can you come now, please?'

'What's happened?'

'It's definitely her. She's back. Ash is back. I've just seen her!'

'You're sure it was her?'

'Yes. She was dressed in those awful mourning clothes. She wore them every chance she got after the funeral. She's been inside the house!'

'It's okay. Sit tight. I'm coming now,' Hannah assured her.

ELIZA – 2004

Ash and her mum were classed as the chief mourners. That sounded strange to Eliza's young ears. Had she known the term at the age of twelve, she would've considered chief mourner to be an oxymoron. Chief was good, it meant they were the best, the top of the range, but mourners meant people who had lost someone they loved. How could Ash and her mum be the best losers? It made no sense.

Being the chief mourners also meant everyone else got to sit and wait for the coffin to be carried in, and the chiefs had to walk along behind it. Eliza wondered if her cousin felt on show. All eyes were on her and Auntie Miriam. Did she wish they would stop looking? Ash had never liked to be stared at. Did the gazes dig into her head? Twice she watched Ash flick at her long dark hair; perhaps she could feel the touch of those stares, like small, burrowing animals making their home.

Eliza studied the men in front of Ash, the men from the funeral home. They wore jackets that hung down at the back, like two tails; she had seen men wear the same thing at a wedding once. They walked slowly and surely as they held the coffin. Not once did it wobble. How were they so good at carrying it? Didn't it freak them out that her dead uncle was inside it?

Afterwards, outside the church, Ash took Eliza to one side. Dressed from head to toe in black, she presented a sombre image. Almost a caricature of a Victorian widow, just like the pictures in their school textbooks, she was a world away from the Ash who would previously have rocked up to every occasion in jeans and trainers, no matter how much Auntie Miriam had insisted that she dress up.

'Are you okay?' Eliza asked.

Ash shrugged.

'That song, by REM. It was …' Eliza didn't know how to finish the sentence.

'She shouldn't have picked it. I told her not to.' Ash gritted her teeth. 'But she wouldn't listen to me.'

'Try not to think about it now. We'll make a pact never to listen to it again, okay?' Eliza gave a weak smile.

'I don't plan to.'

'How do you feel?' Eliza tried to imagine losing her mum or dad.

'Like I'm going to die too.'

'Oh, Ash.' Eliza blew her nose. 'It doesn't seem real, does it?'

'I don't know how I'm going to live another day without him, never mind the rest of my life.'

'It all happened so quickly. Just last year he was okay. Kind of.'

'He wasn't really. He was sicker than he let on. Anyway, the doctor said you never know with cancer; it can be quick or slow.'

'Oh.' Eliza didn't know what to say. She had never had to comfort someone who was grief stricken before.

'I shall never get over this. I know I shan't.' Ash's mood matched the dark clouds that gathered overhead.

Eliza gave her cousin a hug. 'I'm sorry. He was lovely. It's so unfair.'

'It's totally shit, that's what it is.'

Eliza glanced around to check that her parents or Auntie Miriam weren't listening. Supporting her cousin, she replied, 'Yes, it is. It's totally shit!'

'What's totally shit?' Scott began wandering towards them.

'What d'you think, stupid?' Ash left the group before he had the chance to join it.

16

HANNAH – 2022

No sooner had Hannah rung the doorbell than Eliza was on the doorstep, throwing herself into her arms. 'Thank you so much for coming so quickly. I've been so scared.'

'Well, that was all down to Lottie,' Hannah said. 'She doesn't always sleep well, and we were just sitting at the kitchen table talking, when you called. Actually, I brought her with me.' She shuffled aside to reveal a sheepish Lottie a few paces behind her on the path. 'I didn't want to leave her. I hope you don't mind?'

'No, of course not. The way I'm feeling right now, the more the merrier. I just don't want to be alone in this house.'

'Let's get inside and you can tell me what's been going on.' Hannah peeled Eliza's arms from around her neck.

'She was here. She disappeared into the fields at the back. It was awful. I don't even know if she was real or a ghost or … what she was.'

'Right, calm down. Tell me exactly what happened.'

Eliza explained about hearing noises in the kitchen and finding the jars on the table. She described how the pantry door was slightly ajar, including a re-enactment of her stabbing the umbrella into the darkness, and finally she told them about finding the back door wide open.

'I'm surprised to hear you didn't lock it last night, to be honest.' Hannah had her law-enforcement face on.

'I thought I did; I'm usually so careful.'

'And you use this key, correct?' Hannah unhooked a large, nickel-plated key that was hanging next to the back door.

'Yes, that key is as old as the hills. There used to be two of them when we were kids.'

'What happened to the other one?'

'God knows. I'm talking way before Ash went missing.'

'Right. So, you usually lock the back door with this key and then you hang it up here?'

'Yes.'

'Meaning,' Hannah pondered, 'if someone could make a copy of the key, they could unlock the back door from the outside?'

'Well ... yes ... I suppose so. If I hadn't slid the lock across, which I must admit, I don't always do, because it's right up the top. It's such a tall door and I'm usually in my slippers when I lock up.'

Hannah frowned. 'No excuse!'

'Are you suggesting Ash kept a key all these years?'

'Forget about Ash for a minute. Was there an opportunity for anyone else to have somehow taken the key and put it back later?'

'Like whom?'

'Like anyone who wants to put the frighteners up you and start demanding money.'

'Demanding money! Why would you say that?'

'I'm pretty convinced it's the whole purpose of this exercise. It makes more sense to me than Ash reappearing after twelve years.'

'I don't know. Maybe there were opportunities, but ...' Eliza turned to Lottie. 'Has Hannah told you what's been going on?'

'I ... umm.' Lottie clearly wasn't sure if she was supposed to be in the know. She appeared to be trying to avoid getting Hannah into trouble concerning client confidentiality.

'It's okay if she has. I don't mind. I just wanted to get your take on it. Do you think it's Ash, or do you agree with Hannah that it's someone trying to scare me?'

'I don't know for definite. But Hannah is one smart cookie, and if she thinks it's not Ash, I guess I'll go with that.'

'It's strange you should mention demanding money. I got this text a couple of minutes before you arrived.' Eliza unlocked her phone and handed it to Hannah. 'I did as you said – I didn't delete it.'

'Good. Now you're learning.' Hannah took the phone and read the message aloud. 'Your a selfish bitch! The money isn't even yours. You should share it.' She asked Eliza, 'How did Ash do at school?'

'At school?'

'Yes, was she good at English like you?' Hannah had noted Eliza's correct use of the word "whom" earlier.

'I don't know. Maybe. Why?'

'The person who sent this text used the wrong "your", that's all. It's a fairly common mistake.' Hannah shook her head. 'It could mean nothing. Anyway, this tells me someone wants you to start sharing the readies around. Nice timing; get you when you're still freaking out from their visit. I'm sorry, Eliza, but I'd say we're talking about one of the people who's been asking you for handouts.'

'But – that would include Scott.'

'Most likely, yes.'

'No way. He's like a brother to me. He wouldn't—'

'Scott is the most obviously in need of cash. We'd be mad not to consider him.'

'But I saw her. I told you, she walked through the gate and into the fields. She had the exact same hair and clothes.'

'What you described was a person with their head down and long black hair. It could've been friggin' Cher for all you knew.'

'It really seemed like it was her.'

'Did you get a photo?' Hannah asked.

Eliza shook her head. 'I left my phone upstairs.'

'You don't have an iPad or anything lying about that you could've used?'

'An iPad? Why would I?'

'I don't know. My employee's kid has got one. Can you believe it? He's not even into double figures yet.'

'Madness! When I was his age, I was still playing hide and seek with Scott, and climbing trees.' Eliza gazed out of the kitchen window. Returning to the subject of the eerie figure, she said, 'Honestly, it was horrible when I saw Ash. Like a ghost was walking over my grave or something.'

'Firstly, you don't have a grave yet, and secondly, what you felt were cold shivers, right?'

'Exactly.'

'Because the fridge was open, and you'd only just shut the back door!' Hannah threw her arms up in the air. 'Don't let it get to you. Don't allow this charade to trick you. Someone wants to get their hands on your money, and you must keep a level head to stop them. If you start believing this is Ash, returned from the dead, or even returned from the living, you'll allow yourself to be manipulated into all kinds of things.'

Lottie nodded. 'She's right, Eliza. She's definitely right.'

'I don't know what to think anymore. Why put all the jars on the table and leave the door open? It doesn't make any sense.'

'I take it this text was from an unknown number?' Hannah asked.

'Yes.'

'Is it the same as the number that sent you the other message?'

'No, I think it's different.'

'Probably just a burner phone. I'll check the number out with my contact at the station, but I doubt we'll get anywhere. Oh, by the way, just a quick question about your cousin – did she have a boyfriend at the time she went missing?'

'Ash? A boyfriend? No!'

'You're sure?'

'Absolutely. She never liked men much.'

'Just like you, Hannah.' Lottie butted in.

'I'm gay, not anti-men. There is a difference. Was Ash gay? Is that what you mean?'

'I don't know,' Eliza shrugged. 'It's hard to say what she was – I wouldn't like to label her. She just didn't like men. The only man she ever liked was her dad. But … boyfriends? No, I can't imagine that. Why d'you ask?'

'Just curious.' Hannah shook her head. 'Right, I suggest you try to get some sleep, Eliza. I'll be on watch.'

'Outside in your car like before?'

'No, right here in the kitchen. Whoever is tormenting you clearly knows their way around the fields at the back. I think I'm far more likely to see something from this vantage point. Have you got a sofa where Lottie can get her head down for the night?'

'I'll be okay. I'll stay up with you,' Lottie volunteered.

'Oh no you won't. You'll either distract me with all your chatter about matey in Greece, or you'll get bored after a couple of minutes.'

'We could play twenty questions.'

'No way. I said I need to stay awake!'

'Bloody cheek!' Lottie gave Hannah a shove.

'There's plenty of room. You can have a bedroom if you like. There's Ash's room or the spare bedroom,' Eliza offered.

'I'll take the spare room,' Lottie replied, rather too quickly.

S.E. SHEPHERD

Hannah figured the thought of Ash's room probably creeped her out, especially after Eliza's story about the dark figure disappearing into the fields.

'What about you, Hannah? You can't sit on a hard chair all night.' Eliza looked concerned.

'I've sat up all night on worse. I need to be awake. A comfy bed isn't going to do me any favours right now.' Hannah yawned.

'You must let me know how much this is going to cost. I'll pay straight away. I just feel so much safer now you're here.'

'Don't worry, I'll let you know the full cost implications tomorrow.'

'Honestly, money is no object. I almost wish I hadn't inherited it all.'

'And that is exactly how someone wants you to feel. Go and get some sleep, okay?'

'I'll try. But all I'll be thinking about is tomorrow night, when you've left, and if I can't get Scott to stay, I'll be on my own again.'

'How about I stay a few nights? Just until we get to the bottom of this. Would that make you feel better?' Hannah offered.

'Oh yes, definitely. I'd be so relieved. Lottie too, if she wants to. I don't want to separate you two.'

Lottie laughed. 'We're not together.'

'Oh right, I wasn't sure.'

'Although, I am definitely her type.'

Hannah rolled her eyes. 'Lottie, behave. You are so not my type! You'd need a few more piercings!'

'Sorry, I didn't mean to offend anyone.' Eliza blushed. 'It was just that you said you were up in the night at the kitchen table, and I thought, maybe if you lived together, you might be a couple.'

'You didn't offend us at all,' Hannah reassured her. 'Lottie owns the house. I'm a kind of lodger. I'm gay, she's straight. I usually like my women a bit quirky, and she goes for the most obvious blokes you can think of: tall, dark and handsome.'

Lottie smiled. 'Yes, definitely tall. I have an aversion to short-arses!'

'Umm!' Eliza clearly wasn't sure how to react.

'It's all right,' Hannah said. 'She doesn't mean it; it's a reference to someone evil, who has now shuffled off this mortal coil.'

'I see.' Eliza spoke to Lottie. 'Would you like to stay too?'

'I can't, I have a dog. It's okay to leave her for a while, like we've done tonight. But I wouldn't want to stay here without her for more than one night. I had to live away from her for a while a couple of years ago, and I hated it.'

'You could bring her too if you like. I might feel safer with her listening out for burglars or mad people who like to rearrange preserves.'

'She doesn't make a particularly good guard dog – she's a bit deaf. But she is very loyal.'

'Bring her along anyway. It would be good to have you all here. I'll sort you both out with a front door key.'

'Thanks,' Lottie said. Turning to Hannah, she smiled. 'You're better than a guard dog, aren't you, Han?'

'Oh shush,' Hannah returned her smile, 'we'll be fine. I promise. In the morning we'll pop home, grab our stuff, and collect Dixie, and then it's pyjama parties, Prosecco, and face packs every night!' She pulled one of her funny faces.

Standing up, Lottie giggled. 'You've always struck me as a sleep-over kind of gal!' She kissed Hannah on the top of her head. 'Good night.'

'Good night, beautiful.'

'Stay alert,' Lottie instructed.

'I will. Our country needs lerts.'

'And if you can't be a lert …'

'Be a loof,' Hannah replied.

They both laughed. It was one of Hannah's dad's favourite jokes.

17

ELIZA – 2022

'What did you forget?' Eliza opened the door with a smile. 'Oh, it's you. I thought—'

'Who were those women I just saw leaving?'

'What the hell has it got to do with you, Ryan?'

'Just curious. No need to bite my head off.'

'They're friends of mine. They've just gone to collect their stuff and they're coming to stay.'

'Here?'

'Yes, here! Where else would I be referring to?'

'Well, quite, this is *your* house.'

'Ryan,' Eliza exhaled noisily, 'what d'you want?'

'I was hoping you were going to be in a good mood.'

'I *was* in a good mood.'

'I noticed your new friends had put a smile on your face.'

'Yes, they *had*. If you must know, they've made me feel safe.'

'I didn't know you were *unsafe*.'

Exhaling again, Eliza asked, 'D'you want to come in?' Whatever he might be now, he was once the most important person in her life, and it might possibly be helpful to share her worries with him.

'Yes, please.' He gave her that smile that used to light up her day.

'Coffee?' She led him into the kitchen, already so sure of his answer that she got the coffee ready.

He nodded and took a seat at the table.

Eliza stared at the empty old oak table, remembering last night when it had bizarrely displayed the contents of her fridge. She made him a coffee, just how he liked it; she had learnt over the years to add the correct amount of milk and sugar.

Almost reading her mind, Ryan muttered, 'Perfect. I wish Kristen could get this right.'

It was on the tip of her tongue to say something along the lines of – your new wife can't make your coffee how you like it, oh my heart bleeds for you! But she decided against it. After years of anxiety and mental health issues, one of the ways she had learnt to cope was to try to turn a negative into a positive. So, in her head, she simply said to herself: *it's a compliment – he thinks I make decent coffee. I'll leave it at that.*

Joining her ex-husband at the table, Eliza wrapped her hands around her own mug of green tea and attempted a smile. God, this being positive thing wasn't easy.

'So, tell me all about it. Why have you felt unsafe? And how have those women helped?'

Eliza hesitated, hating the thought of showing her vulnerability to Ryan. She knew the reason he had so actively gone after Kristen during their marriage was because she had been wrapped up in their losses. She had been so focused on getting and staying pregnant, their sex life had become an all or nothing situation. She was either dragging him off to bed the minute the ovulation predictor smiled at her, or physically pushing him away when she found out she was pregnant, for fear of another loss. He had begun to feel unwanted, and on more than one occasion he accused Eliza of seeing him as nothing more than a sperm donor. But she was unable to change her actions. As her desperation grew, their love paid the price. In truth, she had never stopped loving him; she had always wanted to put him first, but the urge to conceive was all consuming. Ultimately, she became a nightmare to live with. It wasn't her fault, but then again, it wasn't *his* either. When she'd found out about his affair with Kristen, it had cut her like a knife. All the time she had thought they were striving for a future together and he was off, finding comfort in the arms of a woman who wasn't on the edge, and who didn't cry at the drop of a hat.

He had said something to her once, during one of their fights, when she had first found out about his infidelity; he had said – it's just much easier to spend time with her, Elz. I don't have to constantly think about whether I'll upset her by accident. You're so vulnerable and I hate doing this to you, but I don't know how to be me around you anymore.

Sitting at the table now, with Ryan so close, she didn't know whether it was a good idea to reveal her vulnerability. She had made a point of presenting a stony face to him ever since the day he had come to their old house to tell her Kristen was pregnant. She'd not allowed the mask to slip, choosing instead to cry in private. If she told him about Hannah and Lottie and the truth behind them staying at her house, would he look at her with pity again? She wasn't sure she could bear it. But, apart from Scott, there wasn't anyone else she knew well enough to talk to about Ash, and she needed to tell someone just how creepy it had been seeing her cousin in the garden last night. Maybe Ryan calling around today was fate?

'Hannah is a private investigator. Lottie is her friend; I was at school with Lottie.'

'What? I mean … why? Why do you need a private investigator?' Ryan seemed genuinely shocked. 'Are you okay? Has someone hurt you?'

She found his concerned expression a comfort. 'I'm not hurt, as such. But … I'm not okay.'

'What does that mean?' He grabbed hold of her hand as it rested on the table.

Unsure whether to pull away or let him touch her, Eliza hesitated. 'I've … I'm getting … I've had a couple of messages that appear, on the face of it, to be from my cousin Ash.'

'But she's dead.'

'We don't know that.'

'She must be.'

'Well, these messages suggest otherwise.'

'Are we talking text messages or voicemail?'

'Text messages.'

'Right. Well, we'll speak to the police; they'll trace the number. You don't need a private investigator, Elz, you need the police.'

Snatching her hand away, Eliza said, 'Please don't tell me what I need, Ryan. Hannah knows what she's doing. She's got a contact at the police station. She used to be one.'

'She used to be a police officer?'

'Yes. And she's good. She's going to work it all out for me and she's going to stay here to keep me safe.'

'But I don't see how a text message can make you feel scared. Just ignore it or block the caller.'

Eliza left her seat and paced the kitchen floor, already embarrassed at how much she had enjoyed Ryan holding her hand. 'There were other messages. Far more physical ones!'

'Like what? Why didn't you tell me this before?'

'It's only just happened. And anyway, why should I tell you? You have a wife and child to think about; they're your priority.'

Ryan stood up. Stopping her in her tracks, he held her by the arms. 'Elz, if someone is physically threatening you, you need to tell me, okay? Let me worry about my priorities.'

She allowed him to lead her back to the table.

He said, 'Tell me everything. I want to help.'

———

Over the course of the next fifteen minutes Eliza talked non-stop. She told him about the writing on the fence and the night Scott had heard someone kicking it. She also told him about the CD on the doorstep, and, just like Scott, he didn't get the significance of the song until she mentioned her Uncle Robert's funeral. Then she described the events of the night before, finishing with the ghostly figure of Ash in the garden and the latest text demanding that she share the money.

'Well, I'm all for sharing, but to be honest the whole thing sounds incredible.'

'I know. But I saw it with my own eyes.'

'Yeah, I guess you did.'

Eliza hesitated, then asked softly, 'Do you ever think about them?'

Instinctively, he knew who she meant. 'Yes. Often.'

'Even though you have Otto?'

'Of course.'

'I think of them all the time. I worked out all the due dates, and I think of those as their birthdays.' Eliza folded her arms onto the table and dropped her head into them. She couldn't hold back the tears any longer.

Ryan rubbed her back, like he used to. When her crying became louder, he searched the room for tissues. Unable to find any, he tore off a few pieces of kitchen roll and handed them to her. She lifted her head just enough to take the kitchen roll before dropping it back down. She cried for so long, he had time to refill the kettle and make her a fresh tea. He then returned to rub her back again.

Lifting her head from the table, Eliza spotted the full mug. 'Thank you.'

'No worries.'

'You know what really pisses me off?'

'Not specifically. Tell me?'

'We'd still be together if any one of my pregnancies had stuck. You wouldn't have left me if we had a baby. Look how you ran to marry Kristen because of Otto.'

'You shouldn't blame her,' Ryan said. 'She just saw something she wanted and went for it.'

'I'll always blame her.'

'There were cracks before she came along, Elz.'

'Yes, there were. But a baby would've filled those cracks. Instead, she just drove a wedge into them. The irony is, the doctors were finally going to investigate. You have to have three losses before it's a "problem",' Eliza scoffed. 'They were all a problem to me.'

'And me!'

'Yes, and you. Sorry.'

'I *did* care.'

'It's ridiculous – they won't start tests until you've lost three in a row. I was young and I was otherwise healthy. They actually said it could be a coincidence.'

'I remember.'

'No point testing now.'

'You'll meet someone else, Elz.'

'So he can shit on me too? Maybe Hannah has the right idea. Women are far more loyal.'

'Hannah?'

'I told you, the private investigator.'

'Right.'

With sudden realisation, Eliza said, 'I never asked why you're here.'

'It doesn't matter.'

'Tell me?'

Ryan sighed. 'I'm being made redundant; I was going to ask for money again.'

'You're persistent, I'll give you that. Surely you'll get a pay-out – you've been there a few years.'

'Yes, but nothing like as much as *you* got.'

'Well, that makes a mockery of everything we've been talking about, doesn't it?'

'No, it doesn't. You can always talk to me about the babies, Elz. Forget the money.'

Eliza paused before saying, 'Actually, Ash said I should share. What do you need?'

'I don't know ... I was just going to ask for help ...'

'Would ten thousand *help*?'

'Yes.'

'Okay. Text me your bank details. I'll send it.'

'You're sure?'

'Yes. I don't know why, but it seems like it's the right thing to do. Maybe somehow Ash will know, and she might stop haunting me.'

'Do you honestly think it's her?'

'Maybe. I don't know.' Eliza shook her head.

'But why now? Why all these years later?'

'I just told you – I don't know. I don't know if it's her, I don't know if she's alive or dead, I don't know *anything*!'

Ryan gave a small cough and paused, before saying, 'Whenever you used to talk about the last time you were with Ash, it always seemed like, well, like maybe you were keeping something back.'

'Why would you say that?'

'Because it's true. You always maintained you and Scott were asleep in her bed when she went missing.'

'We were.' Eliza's voice rose an octave.

'But I swear you once said that she was wearing her long black coat the last time you saw her. Why would she wear that in the house?'

'For God's sake, Ryan,' Eliza shook her head, 'who are you? Bloody Columbo! Leave it.'

'Your private investigator is going to want to know the truth. You won't be able to lie to her.'

'I *won't* lie to her.'

'By the way, which one was Hannah?'

'Blonde, cropped hair.'

'Are you sure she's a reputable investigator?'

'I'm not your wife anymore. You don't need to double-check everything I do. Google her, Hannah Sandlin – she's good.'

'All right, all right. She was just a bit trendy, that's all. I don't want you to get ripped off by someone who charges a load of money but doesn't know what they're doing.'

Eliza placed her hands on her hips. 'Well, as you, and Kristen, and Scott, and Uncle Tom Cobley and all like to point out, I can afford it.'

'I meant what I said: whatever happens, you can always talk to me about the babies.'

'What does that mean?'

'That they were my babies too.'

'No, not that bit. I know they were your babies. I mean the *whatever happens* part.'

'It's just an expression.'

'An odd one.'

'If you say so. Anyway, call me any time you're upset about them, okay?'

'Thanks.'

He texted her his bank details and thanked her for the ten

thousand pounds. 'It will help us enormously. It's just until I can get another job. You know how specialised my role is?'

'Yes. It's fine. Anyway, Hannah and Lottie will be back soon. They're bringing their dog.'

'Oh, that'll be a great help. A guard dog.'

'Not really. Apparently, she's a bit deaf. But it'll be nice to have her here and I'll bet she's better trained than Bear.'

'From what you've told me about him, she would have to be.'

'I'll see you out.'

He followed her down the hall. At the front door, he said, 'If there's anything else you want to talk about, I'm always here for you.'

Eliza nodded.

'If you want to get it all off your chest, about Ash. If you want to tell me the truth about the night she went missing, I'm happy to listen.'

Her face fell. 'Oh, get lost, Ryan.' She was disappointed that once again they were parting on bad terms. 'I've already told you the truth. Scott and I were asleep in Ash's bed. There's nothing else to tell!'

ELIZA – 2017

Eliza poured herself another drink. Waving the bottle of red wine at Ryan, she suggested he might like a top up too.

Moving his glass away, Ryan said, 'I've had enough. And so have you, Elz.' He squeezed the bridge of his nose.

'Me?' Eliza swung the bottle back towards her own glass.

'Yes.' He moved closer, attempting to take ownership of the wine bottle. 'Go easy, sweetheart. You're not used to it.'

She yanked the bottle away from his reach. 'No. I'm not. And why is that?'

His gaze dropped to his lap.

'Look at me!' Eliza shouted. *'Why is that?'*

Ryan remained silent.

'Because I'm "trying for a baby", so I can't drink. I can't do anything that might risk my baby deciding to slither out of me like water down the fucking plughole.' She waved her arms around, impersonating the water, causing some wine to slop out of her glass and on to the rug.

Before Ryan could make a move to clear it up, Eliza barked, *'Leave it!'*

'It'll stain.'

'I don't care.' Taking a swig of wine, her voice began to wobble. 'I hate that stupid rug.'

Reaching over, Ryan managed to take the glass from her hand, carefully placing it a safe distance away on the coffee table. He took her into his arms, and she immediately slumped. 'Shush. There, there. Shush.' He rocked her. 'I'm here. I'm here.'

'Why did they both leave me?' Eliza asked through her sobs.

'I don't know.' Ryan rubbed her back gently. 'It'll be okay next time.' He was clearly trying to sound positive. 'You'll see. The next one will stay put.'

'I jus' … wan' … a … baby.' Her words were becoming slurred, but their meaning was clear.

'We'll get one.'

'Haven't I punched enough?'

'Huh? What d'you mean?' He tilted her chin upwards.

'*Punished*. I've been punished enough.'

'What for?'

'I should've stopped her. If I'd stopped her, my babies wouldn't have left me.'

'Elz, who are you talking about? Who were you meant to stop?'

'Fucking Ash. Of course.'

'I honestly don't know what you're on about.'

'I should've stopped her. That last time. Standing there in that stupid black coat. She thought she was makin' a statement.

She wasn't makin' a statement. She jus' looked like every other goth down the shopping centre.'

'When?'

'Lullaby ...'

'I don't know what you're talking about, but you mustn't think you lost both your pregnancies as some sort of punishment. It was bad luck, pure and simple.'

'Urghhhhhhh ...' Eliza vomited up the red wine. It almost covered the small rug.

Distracted from their conversation, Ryan immediately began cleaning up the sick and tending to his wife.

18

HANNAH – 2022

As Hannah drove away from Eliza's house, she told Lottie, 'I'm going to drop you off so you can pack up your stuff. I know you don't travel light. I'll be back to throw some things into a bag soon. Okay?'

'Where are you going? Looking for Dave?'

'Yes. I'm going to go and speak to Mr Wilson. I need to know if Dave's been there and what happened. I can't let all this Eliza business distract me anymore.'

'Will you be okay?'

'Yeah.'

'Promise?'

'I promise.'

Lottie sounded worried. 'But ... if Dave's gone missing, maybe—'

'I'll be fine. I just can't keep leaving it and leaving it like this. It's irresponsible to my employee, for one thing.'

'But you called Paul and he thought it was best to wait. He didn't think Dave was in danger.'

'It probably sounded to Paul like I was overreacting. Paul

thinks Dave is still *Chippy*, he thinks he's tough. But I know the real Dave and I'm worried. I just need to know he's okay,' Hannah moaned. Ever since Dawn Barton had died as a result of her inaction, she found herself constantly second guessing what was best. Lottie only had to go missing for a couple of hours, like she had done the day she was with Chen in the meadow, and Hannah was already imagining the worst. And now it would seem that she genuinely cared about Dave's wellbeing too. Who would ever have called that one?

'Okay.' Lottie looked dubious. 'But give me the address and message me as soon as you're safe. If I don't hear from you, I'm calling 999.'

'Don't do that. Triple nine is for proper emergencies,' Hannah replied.

'Well, this could be a proper emergency.'

'Even so. Please don't call that number.' Hannah's expression was stern. 'If you knew how much police time is wasted by—'

'All right, all right.' Lottie held up her hand. 'Well, can I put a tracker on you? Do you have a spare one?'

Rooting around in her pocket, Hannah took out an empty hand with her middle finger extended. 'I guess not.' She shrugged.

'Oh, Han, I actually thought you were going to find one then.'

'Sorry,' Hannah laughed. 'Seriously though, there's probably an app where we can find a friend's phone or something. If you're worried, we could both download it.'

Lottie checked the app store. 'Yes! There is. Oh, it sounds fab. Why didn't we do this ages ago?'

'Because you were never this worried about me before.'

'I know you're big tough Hannah and you can do the same job as any man. At least, that's what you like to think. But I would genuinely like to know where you are today. Can we both do it, please?'

Hannah agreed. 'I don't mind you knowing where I am. But you only get to dial 999 if this app tells you I'm at the bottom of the bloody Solent.'

'Don't say that.' Lottie pulled a worried face.

'Chances are, Dave's fallen so far off the wagon he's having trouble getting back up. I just really need to find him now.'

'You will.'

'And when I do …'

'Uh huh?'

'He's downloading this app as well.'

―――

Hannah pressed the buzzer for Wilson & Cavendish.

The same loud click, and the same female voice politely asking, 'Hello. How can I help you?'

Hannah explained who she was and waited for the secretary to check with her boss if he was free. The couple of minutes it took her to do so seemed like an eternity. Hannah couldn't help thinking that Charlie must have some thugs that he called on when a customer wasn't paying up. What if he'd employed those same thugs to beat up the man who was planning to reveal all about his lucrative little business? Or worse still, beaten Dave up himself. She pictured poor Dave curled up in a ball on the floor, fending off the harsh kicks of Charlie's size thirteen boots.

As before, Hannah heard a long buzzing sound, and the door juddered.

This time she did take the stairs at a run, arriving a tad short of breath at the offices of Wilson & Cavendish.

Mr Wilson offered his sweaty palm and Hannah raised her hand to show she would prefer not to shake. Again!

Mr Wilson gave her a wide smile.

She said, 'I'm pleased to see you smiling. You were so concerned last time we met.'

'Indeed. Well, why wouldn't I smile, after the wonderful job you chaps did for me?'

'That's why I came to see you actually. I wanted to check if my colleague, Dave Chipperton, had been in.'

'Yes, he was here a couple of days ago. I'm incredibly happy with the service.' Mr Wilson glanced at his secretary and ushered Hannah towards the door to his room, saying, 'Let's discuss this in my office, shall we?'

Once inside the office, Mr Wilson took a seat and indicated she should do the same in the chair opposite. 'Coffee, Ms Sandlin?' he asked.

Remembering how good the coffee was at Wilson & Cavendish, Hannah was tempted. But she knew she ought to just get to the point. Shaking her head, she replied, 'I'm fine, thanks.' Giving Mr Wilson no chance to derail the conversation further, she said, 'So, Dave showed you the photographs of your employee loaning money?'

'Indeed he did. He also gave me enough print outs from this damn computer system to prove exactly what that snake has been up to.'

'I'm sorry.' Hannah made a sympathetic face. 'None of that can have been easy to see.'

'Oh indeed, it was horrible. But ... necessary. I asked you a question and you found out the answer. It was hardly your fault that the news wasn't good. I would never shoot the messenger.'

'*Indeed.*' Hannah nodded. Great, now he'd got her doing it too. She thought Mr Wilson would do well to get himself a thesaurus.

'Did you just come as a follow up? Is this like a client survey? Because I was more than happy with the way Mr Chipperton delivered the information.'

'Sort of. I ... umm.' Hannah hesitated. How much to tell him? She most definitely didn't want to tarnish her company's good name by revealing that Dave was missing, especially if his disappearance had more to do with alcohol than it did with that sneaky bastard Charlie. She decided to go with Mr Wilson's assumption and turn it into a client survey. 'I just wanted to be clear on exactly what was said when my colleague came to see you, and perhaps get a follow up. Such as, have you confronted Charlie?'

'Indeed I have.' Mr Wilson puffed out his chest. 'The bugger had nowhere to turn when faced with your evidence.' Realising the language he had used, he added, 'Apologies. I don't like to swear in front of a lady.'

Hannah laughed. 'I've heard far worse.' Mostly from her best friend when she was discussing her now deceased stepdad, Vincent.

Mr Wilson said, 'Even so.'

'How did you leave it? Was he …?' Hannah fished around for a good word. 'Angry or vengeful?'

'I should hope not. That young man had no right to be bloody angry. I told him his job here was terminated immediately.'

'How did he take it?' Hannah asked.

'No choice. I told him to leave this building and never come back. No severance pay. No holiday money due. No reference.'

'And he was okay? I mean, umm, was he annoyed with … with us, Sandlin Private Investigation?'

'Oh, he didn't know where I'd got the information from. He tried to get me to tell him. But, you know, I had your back – I heard some youngsters say that the other day. I wasn't about to disclose who had provided me with the evidence. You're smart, you chaps, no logos on anything. I saw him checking the report over my shoulder. I know he'd like to have worked out who caught him out. But I refused to tell him.'

'Good for you.'

'He seemed to think it was a "bent copper" – his words. He

thought he'd seen one the other day. But I refused to give so much as a hint about you. I simply told him that the investigating company had a copy of everything and that you had a direct line to the police. If anything happened to me, you would hand over the proof to them. Like I say, he had nowhere to turn.'

'And you're sure you don't want to involve the police?' Hannah was becoming concerned that Mr Wilson could be seen to be an accomplice if this all came out. After all, it was his money that was being used for the loans. Plus, she really wanted to see Charlie Bradbury back behind bars.

'Well, you know, I've been thinking about it. I was holding back for his mother's sake. For what it would do to her. But your Mr Chipperton, he told me the sort of people Charlie was lending money to and it nearly broke my heart to think of them worrying about the interest. Single mothers, unemployed fathers. What an absolute ...' Mr Wilson stopped himself. 'Anyway, my loyalty to his mother does not extend that far, so you'll be pleased to hear I handed a copy of everything over to the local police this morning.'

Hannah exhaled. 'I *am* pleased to hear that.'

'I imagine Charlie will have done a moonlit flit if he even suspects that I've gone to the police. Anyway, he won't be chasing any payments. I do think your Mr Chipperton is a smart cookie. He explained that computer system way better than Charlie ever did.'

Hannah felt proud that Dave had handled the situation so well. But, if it had gone as smoothly as Mr Wilson said, and if Charlie had not gone after Dave – where the hell was he?

'I hope that answers all your questions.' Mr Wilson smiled again.

'Yes. It does.'

'I made sure to tell Mr Chipperton how impressed I was.'

'You did?'

'Indeed. I said to him, I said – you sir, you and your company have saved me. If that man had continued unchecked, well I dread to think how much damage he'd have done to my business and my reputation. Imagine being associated with that kind of behaviour. You've saved my life, man. No doubt about it, you've saved my life.'

'Was he pleased to hear that?' Hannah asked.

'Indeed. Got a bit choked up, I think.'

'Really?'

'Oh yes. Just for a moment, you know. Lovely to see such pride in his work.'

Pushing her chair back, Hannah stood up. 'Thank you so much, Mr Wilson. You've given me invaluable feedback.'

'I'll drop an anonymous review to you, for your website. I know how important these things are when you're a new company. Give my regards to Lottie, won't you?'

'I shall. I'm glad you got things sorted.' Hannah reached out and shook his hand. Yes, it was sweaty, but he seemed to appreciate the gesture.

Once outside the building, she sanitised her hands and phoned Lottie. 'I'm fine.'

'You're sure?'

'Absolutely.'

'How do I know you're not being forced to say that?'

'You are a nutter, Lottie Thorogood.'

'If you're really fine, say the name of the guy I can't stop going on about?'

'Seriously?'

'Yes. If you're being held against your will, say the wrong name.'

'Jesus, Lottie.'

'Is that your answer?'

'No! For fuck sake. It's Chen. His name is Chen. Okay?'

She heard Lottie sigh down the phone. 'Thank goodness. Are you coming back to pack now?'

'Not just yet. I've got somewhere else to go. But I won't be long. Then we'll get back to Eliza's and try to sort this whole cousin Ash stuff out. I promise.' Hannah hung up. Turning her car around, she headed out of town.

19

ELIZA – 2022

IT WAS odd doing the housework in Auntie Miriam's house. As much as she told herself it was now *her* toilet she was bleaching and *her* floor she was mopping, it still felt wrong. She almost expected her auntie to pop up and tell her she wasn't doing it right. Housework was never her forte. Cleaning Uncle Robert's study seemed like a huge invasion of privacy. She'd boxed up his stuff, but as yet had done nothing further with it. There were so many records, CDs, books, and magazines. In Eliza's head it would be insolent to even think about selling them or giving them away. Uncle Robert was her elder and somehow governed respect.

Then there was Ash's old room; being in there was the strangest. As she'd already told Scott, she'd removed all Ash's belongings and taken them to the charity shop or put them in the bin. It wasn't so much that Ash didn't command the same respect as Uncle Robert; it was more that Eliza simply couldn't bear to look at her stuff. It creeped her out. Once the room was free of all its former character, she'd tried moving the bed, so it was pushed up against a wall for a change, and she'd painted over the dark walls with a million coats of white. And yet, just standing here now, vacuum in hand, she was instantly transported back twelve years. It was as if the room was saying – you can whitewash me all you like, but I'll never forget. The past would not leave her alone. It beckoned to her, insisting she remember the last evening she'd spent with Ash. If only they'd had the sleepover at hers, or not got together at all. There were so many things about that night that Eliza would do differently if she had the chance.

ELIZA – 2010

'I can wait. I'll wait all night if I have to. But one of you is going to tell me the truth.' Auntie Miriam's lips were pinched, her arms folded across her chest.

'There's nothing to tell you, Mother. You can stand there all night, like a fucking prison guard if you like. But we haven't done anything.'

'Ashley, your pupils are enormous, and so are Scott's. I need to know what you've taken.'

Eliza attempted to calm things down. 'Please, Auntie Miriam, I promise you – it's all under control. They're fine. I'll keep an eye on them. We'll all sleep here, in Ash's room. We'll be okay.'

'How can you say it's under control? Look at poor Scottie.' Auntie Miriam pointed at her young nephew. 'He's off his trolley.'

Scott giggled. 'Off my trolley. Love it! Where's your trolley, Ash? Are you off it?'

'I am. I'm off my trolley too. Or you could say, I'm fucking wasted.' Ash dissolved into fits of laughter.

'Ashley, will you please stop swearing?' Auntie Miriam's dislike of the f-word verged on an obsession. 'Eliza, Scott, I shall be phoning your parents in the morning. There will be no more of these nights out for you three, I can promise you that.'

'Get stuffed. I'm over eighteen!' Ash's tone was cruel.

'I don't care. You're under my roof, you'll do as I say. Do I need to remind you that Scott is only fifteen?'

'No,' Eliza replied. 'We get it. We understand.'

'Or that he's in my care for the night?' Auntie Miriam continued.

'No. Honestly, we know he's too young,' Eliza said.

'He's not too young. He's loving it.' Ash caught Scott's eye and they both burst into further hysterics.

Auntie Miriam made her way swiftly out of the room, calling back, 'I mean it. No more!'

Ash immediately jumped up and performed an impression of her, which caused Scott to laugh again.

'And she said she could wait all night. My mother's got no staying power!' Ash kicked the bedroom door shut.

'Seriously, Ash, this was such a bad idea. Please promise me you won't take any more of those things.' Eliza was already trying to manoeuvre Scott towards the bed.

'You are such a nerd, Elz. And don't even think that Scottie is going to bed yet. The minute my mother goes to sleep, we're heading back downstairs. She's got a bottle of champagne that she's saving to drink on the anniversary of my dad's death, and I think we ought to get it down us tonight.'

'You can't. That's awful. You just said it's for Uncle Robert's anniversary.' Eliza felt panic envelop her. It was almost impossible to stop Ash from hitting the self-destruct button once she started staggering towards it.

'So what? She should drink champagne for his birthday, or their wedding anniversary. Something nice like that. Drinking it on the anniversary of his death is twisted. All we're doing is stopping her from being a bitch.'

'She's not being a bitch. It's just a thing she does.' Eliza was still wrestling with Scott, who was beginning to turn an unhealthy shade of grey.

'Well, now it's a thing she *doesn't*.' Ash smirked at her own joke. 'You up for a little drink, Scottie? Fancy some Moet?'

Scott's response was to vomit rather violently all over Ash's quilt.

'Fucking hell. You're such a baby.'

'I am not a baby.' Scott spewed.

'You two will never change.' Eliza headed towards the airing cupboard on the landing, intent on finding fresh bedding. It was clearly going to be a long night.

———

Eliza woke an hour or so later with a sense of foreboding. She was in Ash's double bed; glancing to her left she could make out the outline of Scott sleeping next to her. They were both still in their clothes. Scott was mumbling in his sleep, and when she placed her hand on his forehead he was unpleasantly clammy. Clearly, the drugs he and Ash had taken did not agree with him. Wondering whether to wake him and check if he was having a nightmare, she simply wasn't sure what to do for the best. Before she could give much more thought to the state of Scott's mind, she had a realisation – Ash wasn't in the room. The last thing she remembered before falling asleep was Scott complaining he was cold, and both of them getting *in* the bed. Ash had been sprawled across the end, at their feet, still moaning about her mother. But now Eliza and Scott were alone. She leant over Scott's sleeping body and whispered, 'Stay here, okay? I won't be long.'

Creeping down to the kitchen in search of her cousin, Eliza jumped over the creaky last step, bumping her head on the coat hooks at the bottom of the stairs, as always. When would she remember those flippin' coat hooks? Why did Auntie Miriam not take them down? If this was her house, she'd pull them off the wall in an instant.

Pushing the kitchen door gently, she chose not to flick on the light. Instead, she left the door slightly ajar, allowing the hall light to guide her way. Ash was sitting at the kitchen table. At first, Eliza thought she was asleep. Her long dark hair was splayed out over the old pine table. But it soon became clear that in fact her head was resting on the table for an entirely different reason. She was sobbing.

'What's up?' With disappointment, Eliza noticed the almost empty Moet bottle on the table.

'Why me, Elz? Why my dad? Who the hell has to lose their dad at twelve years old?'

Scooping her cousin into her arms, Eliza tried to comfort her. 'It totally sucks, it really does.'

'Your dad's not dead, and neither is Scott's.'

'I know.'

'Fergus is a useless wanker, who only comes back when he's out of prison and homeless.'

'I know.'

'Even then, he doesn't come to see his stupid sprog, he comes back because no one else will shag him, but at least he's not fucking dead.'

'Calm down, Ash. You've got to stop swearing. If Auntie Miriam hears you—'

'Fuck her!'

'Ash, please?'

'Six years. Six years since I saw his face or ran out of the witchy woods with him. Six years of being stuck here, with just her.' Ash waved a hand at the ceiling, in the direction of Auntie Miriam's bedroom.

'She loves you.'

'No, she doesn't. She hates me.'

'Don't be silly.'

'She doesn't get me.'

'None of us do!' Eliza laughed.

'He did. Dad did.'

Eliza thought about her Uncle Robert. She couldn't deny there had been a bond between Uncle Robert and Ash that Auntie Miriam was never going to achieve. Nothing Auntie Miriam ever did could compensate Ash for losing her father so young. 'You shouldn't have drunk her champagne.'

'Why not? Maybe I was toasting his death. Just like she does.'

'For her it's a routine. A ritual almost. It's like you with your mourning clothes. She lights a candle in front of his photo, and she plays some of his favourite songs. It means something. You drank it out of spite, or to try to get high again.'

Ash abruptly got up, shoving Eliza away. 'It's nothing like me and my clothes. And you don't know why I drank it. You don't know anything, and he, that vomiting baby upstairs, he's as bad as you are. I've got nothing, no one. Without my dad, I'm alone.'

Eliza could do nothing to stop her; always the physically weaker of the two girls, she allowed herself to be pushed backwards.

'You and the idiot can keep my bed. I'm gonna sleep in Dad's room.'

Eliza knew Ash would sleep on the couch in Uncle Robert's study. It was where Uncle Robert always used to sleep if he'd had a few too many drinks and thought he was going to snore. The room had barely changed in the last six years. It was an extremely masculine room. One wall was completely lined with dark mahogany bookshelves, containing heavy tomes which neither Auntie Miriam nor Ash read, whilst the other walls were decorated in thick flock paper. An outdated Hi-Fi system and a selection of American Classic Rock CDs sat in the corner, no longer played, but still dusted regularly by Auntie Miriam. The study was the epitome of Uncle Robert; you could almost smell his aftershave in there.

A minute later Ash left the kitchen and disappeared down the hall, slamming the study door behind her. What a totally horrible night! Picking up the Moet bottle, Eliza poured the residue down the sink, collected up the cork and every last scrap of foil, and made her way back upstairs. Hiding it all in her bag, she had already decided to ask her mum to lend her the money to replace it. If she could smuggle the replacement into the fridge before the anniversary next week, perhaps Auntie Miriam wouldn't know Ash had drunk the first one.

Unfortunately, as Eliza eased into the bed next to Scott, she woke him up.

He cried out, 'Who?'

Taking him into her arms, she gently rocked him. 'It's okay, you're with me.'

Scott's eyes focused on her, and he gave a weak smile. 'I'm glad it's you, Elz.' A moment later his eyes closed, and his breathing deepened.

Eliza felt relieved. Thankfully, this awful night was over.

20
HANNAH – 2022

HANNAH PARKED at the cemetery and made her way down the stone path. Sadly, she knew only too well the exact location of Dawn's grave. As she approached, she saw a fresh bouquet of white and yellow carnations laid on the grass. Upon inspection, the card attached contained only two words: *I'm sorry*. It was Dave's writing; she'd recognise his scrawl anywhere. It was all the evidence she needed. Driving back to his flat she was determined not to be ignored this time.

Back at Dave's front door, she flipped up the letterbox. 'I know you're in there. You're going to have to let me in this time.'

She waited.

Silence.

'I'm going to kick it in. You know I'll do it. I know exactly where to kick. I don't want to cost you money, mate. But you have to open this door.'

Continued silence.

Hannah played her final card. 'I've been to her grave. I've seen the flowers. I know what happened. Wilson didn't realise, did he? He couldn't know. What he said – about you saving his life. It was a trigger, wasn't it? I get it. But you have to let me help you. You have to come to the door now.'

She waited again, preparing to kick the door at the lock. Luckily, the jeans she was wearing had a bit of give in them and she had on her biker boots.

Noises came from inside the flat. She flipped up the letterbox once more and Dave shuffled into view. He looked bad. Worse than bad. Like death.

He opened the door and stood back. 'Bloody persistent, aren't you?'

'Tenacious.'

'I guess you'd better come in.' He made his way back to the lounge.

Hannah was shocked at how much he'd changed since she'd last seen him. It didn't seem to take him long to go from smart to shite. Dressed in old grey joggers and a stained tee shirt, he smelt of sweat and stale booze. He'd clearly been living and sleeping in the clothes he was wearing for a good couple of days. Could this really be the same man who'd so proudly demonstrated Mr Wilson's accounts package to him, all suited and booted?

Trying not to wrinkle her nose or pull a face, she asked, 'Were you here before, last time I came?'

Dave nodded.

She gave him a gentle punch on the arm. 'You bastard. I've been worried.'

'Sorry.'

'Not good enough.'

'*Really* sorry.' Dave gave a tepid smile.

'You should've told me what Wilson said. And how it made you feel. All of it. You should've called me, and I'd have come straight over.'

'I know. It just hit me like a bolt out of the blue.'

'I get it. He said you saved his life and you immediately

thought of the life you weren't able to save.'

'You mean the life I didn't fucking try hard enough to save.'

'Okay. But you should've told me. I employ you. You don't get to just ghost me for days.'

'I know.' Dave dropped down onto the old, beige sofa, slotting into the groove created by his own backside. Shaking his head, he muttered, 'I'm a waste of space. You're better off without me. Everyone is!'

'And you don't get to decide that either.' Hannah chose a seat as far away as possible from him. 'I do!'

'I just needed some time. I just needed ...' He began to shake, and his head fell to his chest.

'You just needed a drink and to feel sorry for yourself.'

'No!' Dave's head snapped up. 'I don't feel sorry for myself. I feel sorry for Dawn. I feel sorry for her family. You always talk about how *we* did wrong, and *we* should've stopped. I know what you're doing – you're trying to take ownership of your part in it. Well, I'm sorry to piss on your bonfire, but it wasn't you, it was *me*. *All me!* I was so distracted. When I heard those words coming out of that nice man's mouth, it just brought it home to me – you've saved my life, he said. What a joke.'

'Dave, I can't let this ruin you. I have to keep fighting back.'

'Aww, dear sweet PC Sandlin,' Dave sneered. 'Such a fucking good Samaritan.'

Just for a second, Hannah saw the Chippy she had hated four years ago. The man who literally got a hard on when he arrested what he called scrotes. The man who put his own needs ahead of everyone else's and mocked her at every opportunity. Bile rose into her throat, and she instantly wanted to retaliate. Gritting her teeth, she tried to stop the obvious *fuck you* that was eager to escape her lips.

But before she had the chance to say anything, Dave shambled along the sofa and reached out for her. Grabbing her by the arm, he garbled the words, 'I'm sorry. I'm so sorry, Hannah. I didn't mean that. You know I didn't. I'm not him. I promise you.'

'It's okay.' Hannah's anger dispersed. 'This is just a step backwards. You can move forward. I know you can.'

Dave shook his head again. 'What a mess!'

She waited for him to continue speaking. There was no point denying it – it *was* a mess.

'I took the flowers to her grave. I know it's nothing. It's such a small gesture. But I needed to tell her I was sorry, you know?'

Hannah repeated herself. 'You can move forward.'

'D'you think you'll ever be able to trust me?'

'Tell me the truth – did you drive to the cemetery? When you'd been drinking?'

'No. I walked. I promise,' Dave said. 'I couldn't bloody see straight.'

She had to believe him. She couldn't employ someone who would drink and drive. 'Then, yes, I can trust you. Does Shelley know you've had a relapse?'

'God, no. If she knew, she'd stop my time with Noah like that.' Dave clicked his fingers.

Wrestling with her conscience, Hannah said, 'Listen, I'm not going to tell Shelley, but if this happens again, I'm going to have to get hold of her number and say something to her. You understand me?'

'Thanks. You know … sometimes I think I'd have been better off if they'd stuck me in prison. Perhaps I wouldn't feel like I got off too lightly.'

'What good would prison have done you? They're stretched to the limit as it is. You don't need to be inside to realise you did wrong, and that you need to atone for it. You already know it.'

'I guess not. But …'

'Besides which, by your way of thinking, that would mean I ought to be in there too!'

'No. Of course not. You didn't do wrong. Not really. I was

shooting my mouth off, trying to cover up my mistakes. You never—'

'*Stop it!*' Hannah shouted. '*You don't belong in prison and neither do I!*'

'Nice little cell next to Sandy?' Dave tilted his head.

'Now there's someone who *does* deserve to be locked up. That woman is the reason Dawn died. Stabbing her in cold blood like that. I'd be surprised if she's having even half the regrets about her decisions that you are.'

'Nasty little bully.'

'I feel sorry for Bev, actually.'

'Why?' Dave asked. 'She chose to have a psycho for a girlfriend.'

'Oh, come on. She has special needs. She's ...'

'Not the full English?' he suggested.

'Well, I wouldn't compare her to breakfast. But, yes, she's missing the nous that helps a person to make decent judgements. Paul says she's lost without her Sandy. She's been in the station a few times asking when Sandy can come home.'

'Christ. She's got a good couple of decades to wait, hopefully.' Dave raised his eyebrows.

'I know. But Bev never did comprehend the seriousness of the situation. Remember how she was going to take the rap for it?' Hannah shook her head. 'Madness.'

'I guess we can only hope that she moves on. Puts it behind her, you know. And forgets about Sandy.'

'Yes. And you need to do the same. You've got to move on too. You're not helping Noah sitting around here in your sweaty joggers.'

Looking down at his clothes, Dave shrugged. 'I know. You're right.'

'Okay. Have you spoken to your sponsor – Tom, isn't it? Have you told him what's happened?'

'Yeah, he's Tom. No, I haven't. But I will, I promise.'

'Too right you will,' Hannah agreed. 'So when's the next AA meeting near here? Be honest!'

'Later today. Around five,' Dave begrudgingly confirmed. 'But I can't—'

'Yes, you can. There's plenty of time. You get yourself in that shower. You're going to it.'

'I ...'

'*Now!* I insist,' Hannah shouted.

Jumping up and grabbing her face in his hands, Dave said, 'Don't ever fucking stop insisting.'

'I fucking won't.'

'Bossy fucking bitch!'

'That's enough swearing for one day,' Hannah laughed. 'Get in the bathroom. Then we'll have something to eat, and you can call Tom. Later, I'll drive you to the meeting. And I'm going to wait outside!'

He kissed her on the forehead. 'I love you and I don't deserve you.'

'Well, you're right about that.' She pushed him towards the cramped bathroom.

———

The next morning, Hannah was awoken by the words, 'Lottie's made us breakfast. Are you coming down?' Eliza poked her head around Ash's bedroom door, which Hannah had agreed to use as her bedroom for the next few days.

'Give me a second.'

'Well, don't keep her waiting. You don't want it to go cold.'

'It'll just be toast.'

'Oh.'

'It's nearly always toast,' Hannah said. 'Occasionally, bacon butties, but mostly just toast.'

'I told her I don't eat bacon.'

'Then you're one hundred percent getting toast.'

Throwing on a sweatshirt over her pyjamas, Hannah made her way down the stairs. By the time she'd dropped Dave home after his meeting and thrown a few things into an overnight bag, she and Lottie hadn't reached Eliza's place until well after seven. But Eliza had been pleased to see them and she'd made a great fuss of Dixie.

'I've done it as a buffet. Just like those hotel breakfasts in Portugal last year, remember, Han? Where you met that cocktail waitress.'

'I'm not likely to forget.'

'Well, I wanted it to be like that. We can pretend we're on holiday, and that it's not all wet and horrible out there. You come in,' Lottie led them into the kitchen, 'and you take your drink from here.' She pointed at the worktop. 'A nice frothy coffee for you, Han, and green tea for Eliza. Then, you take a plate and help yourself to toast – it's here in the rack.'

Eliza winked at Hannah.

'Finally, you sit yourself down at the table, where you're met with an array of choices.' Lottie flamboyantly waved her hand towards the kitchen table. 'See – a buffet.'

Clasping her hand over her mouth, Eliza muttered, 'Oh God, now I remember.' She stumbled towards the table. Pulling back a chair she fell into it, a shocked expression on her face. 'I know why the jams and stuff were on the table the other night. Sometimes Auntie Miriam would do a big family Sunday lunch, and once we'd eaten, we were allowed to go and play. We'd climb trees if it was Ash's choice or make daisy chains if it was mine. Goodness knows what Scott used to choose – something Ash thought was lame, usually hide and seek, I think. Then, at about five thirty Auntie Miriam would call us in for tea. She was quite particular, and she'd say that we didn't need a big meal, not after such a huge lunch. But she liked to do a little something to send us on our way. She said that way my parents and Scott's mum could pop us straight into the bath and not have to do tea when we all got home. She'd make lots of crumpets and toast and two large pots of tea and she'd put everything on the kitchen table. There were so many things: jams, lemon curd, honey, peanut butter, chocolate spread, anything you can think of. How did I forget that? I used to love the Sunday tea almost as much as the Sunday lunch.'

Lottie was clearly embarrassed. 'I'm sorry, I didn't mean to—'

'No, don't apologise. It's a good thing you reminded Eliza. It's helpful,' Hannah replied.

'Is it?' Lottie asked. 'How?'

'Who else knew about those Sunday tea times, Eliza? Who did you tell?'

'Well, lots of people, I suppose. She probably did that sort of tea for all her visitors, not just us.'

'But obviously Scott would've known?'

'Yes, he and his mum were always there. In the early days, at least.'

'And Ryan? Was she still doing the Sunday teas when you married him?'

'Well ... yes. She didn't have guests as often after she lost Uncle Robert, and even less so when she was older, but sometimes she would still have me and Ryan over for one of her lunch and tea affairs. Ryan couldn't get enough of her gooseberry jam. Of course Scott was never invited again after Ash went missing'

'Hmmm ...' Hannah chewed her cheek

'But it's not either of them.'

'How do you know that?'

'I've already said, Scott's like a brother to me, and Ryan ... well, I told you he was here yesterday, and I gave him some money. He wouldn't have to go to such elaborate lengths to get me to help him out. He knew I'd cave in if he was kind.'

'Exactly, he was here, and you gave him money. And absolutely nothing has happened since. Not a text, which by the way was definitely from an unregistered phone, or a CD on the doorstep, or a ghostly apparition in the garden. And yet you say it's not him.' Hannah joined her at the table, coffee in hand.

'He was so nice to me. We talked about our babies.'

Hannah gave a sympathetic smile. 'I'm honestly sorry to hear about your losses, and I hope Ryan was genuine with everything you both talked about. But you've got to admit, he is clearly a suspect. Nothing has happened since you paid him yesterday.'

'Except it's poured with rain the whole time,' Lottie pointed out.

'It's not him,' Eliza said, adding in a whisper, 'you wouldn't understand.'

Hannah took umbrage. 'You think I don't understand because all you've heard me talk about is a Portuguese cocktail waitress and the woman I met in Costa the other day. But I do understand about loyalty and trust, I promise you. I don't want it to be Ryan, any more than I want it to be Scott. I just don't think it can be Ash.'

'Well then, there has to be another explanation.'

'I hope so.' Hannah put her arms around Eliza. 'I'm not trying to upset you.'

'I know.' Eliza gave herself a shake. 'Anyway, what about this delicious buffet breakfast Lottie's prepared for us. Shall we tuck in?'

'Yes, please do. The toast is going cold,' Lottie said.

'Didn't I tell you it would be toast?' Hannah laughed loudly.

'It's not *that* funny,' Lottie said. 'Honestly, you've been ridiculously happy since you met that woman.'

'Well, pardon me.'

'Tell us more,' Eliza asked.

Hannah shrugged. 'There's not much to tell. She was standing behind me, a bit too close. I mean – none of us are used to that after the couple of years we've all had. I picked up my latte and stepped backwards, right onto her foot. She cried out and I apologised. I was struck by just how good looking she was. Anyway, we ended up chatting. We took our drinks outside and sat for ages on the street, under the awning, just talking about … everything. That's it. Like I told you before, it probably won't come to anything.'

'But you did swap numbers?' Eliza asked.

'Yes, we did.'

'And you have been checking your phone every two minutes since.'

'Yes, Lottie, I have. You know, whenever bloody Chen sends you a text, you go giggly for the rest of the day, so don't think you can take the piss out of me.'

'I don't. I just think it's cute. You and your mystery lady.'

'She's called Mandy, not my mystery lady.'

'Well, I hope she texts you soon,' Eliza said.

'So do I,' agreed Lottie. 'Or else she's going to wear that phone out.'

Lottie was washing up the plates and mugs as Eliza replaced all the preserves. Hannah sat, deep in thought, at the kitchen table.

'What's up?' Eliza asked.

'I was just thinking, you absolutely don't want all this to be down to Scott or Ryan. And I understand why. But realistically, who else could it be? I've been dismissing the possibility that it could be Ash because it just seemed too unbelievable, but maybe I'm wrong. If there's even the slightest possibility it could be her, I need to consider it properly.'

'Okay. So, consider it.' Eliza joined her at the table.

'It's impossible, though. Unless you're going to open up about the night she went missing, I can't even give it house room. I need to know if she's dead or alive, and you're not giving me enough to go on.'

'Scott and I were asleep—'

'Asleep in Ash's bed. Yeah, I know. So you've said. You say it all the time, like a mantra. But guess what, Eliza? I don't believe you.'

'Wh … whhhat?' Eliza blushed.

'There's so much more to that night. I know it, I sense it.' Hannah held her hand to her chest.

'She has Spidey senses,' Lottie remarked over her shoulder, moving on to the drying up.

Eliza seemed upset. 'What good will it do now? What good does raking up the past ever do?'

'It might just help us to determine if your cousin Ash is dead or alive. And by doing so we can either rule her in as a possible suspect for the recent shenanigans, or permanently rule her out. You don't want it to be Scott, and you don't want it to be Ryan. So, come on then, tell me all about how Ash went missing and we'll decide if it's her.'

'I don't know *all about* how Ash went missing.'

'But you do know more than you're letting on?'

Eliza paused.

Lottie and Hannah held their breath.

'Yes, I do know more. But Scott and I promised each other a long time ago – we agreed not to tell. It's not relevant.'

'Can I ask you a favour?' Hannah's voice softened. 'Let me decide if it's relevant or not?'

'Okay.' Eliza nodded.

21
ELIZA – 2022

'As you know, it was twelve years ago. Ash and I were just eighteen. We often used to go out together on a Saturday night and then have a sleepover afterwards. On rare occasions, Ash would let Scott come too. We sometimes stayed at mine and sometimes here. We were never going to stay at Scott's, just in case his dad was back from one of his trips to the Isle of Wight.'

'The Isle of Wight?' Lottie asked.

'It was code. When we were kids, Scott's dad, Fergus was in and out of prison, somewhere or other. His mum used to tell Scott he was working on the Isle of Wight. Whenever we went to Lynton seaside, Scott would watch the ferries off in the distance and say his dad was over there building houses or something. It was a long time before the three of us worked out why his dad was really away.'

'I see.' Lottie nodded.

'Anyway, on that particular night we were all sleeping here. Me and Scott really *were* in Ash's bed. Scott was asleep and Ash had gone to sleep in Uncle Robert's study.' She pointed down the hall. 'Well, at least I thought she'd gone to sleep. It'd been a terrible evening. I was just falling back to sleep, and Scott finally seemed settled. What a crap sleepover; Ash had encouraged Scott to take some pills with her, and he'd been violently ill. Auntie Miriam was fuming and threatening to call our parents in the morning. Ash had then decided to drink almost a whole bottle of champagne that was supposed to be kept for the anniversary of Uncle Robert's death. It had all just been horribly emotional, and I was relieved the nightmare had ended. Then the bedroom door opened.'

Lottie drew in her breath, obviously trying to anticipate what would come next. Hannah's body language was neutral, and her phone was in her hand.

Eliza continued, 'It was Ash, of course. Saying she couldn't sleep, and she was going for a drive.'

'But she was drunk!' Lottie squeaked.

Eliza immediately clammed up.

'Shush.' Hannah placed her hand over Lottie's. 'Let her tell it.'

Eliza continued, 'Yes, she was drunk, and, like I say, they'd taken pills earlier; she was an absolute mess. I pointed all that out. I told her not to even think about driving. But she never did listen to me. She just kept dangling her mum's car keys in my face and saying she was going to go to the woods. When we were kids, we had this thing about finding the witchy woods. It all started as a game we used to play with my Uncle Robert. But, back then, it was fun. It was scary, but in a good way, you know. We hadn't even talked about the woods for years, and suddenly there she was, saying she was going to go and find the witchiest part. Scott woke up and she badgered him to go with her. He wanted to please her – he was always desperate for her approval, although he rarely got it. Poor sod. Anyway, so now I had the two of them saying they were going out in the car. I tried to stop them. I honestly tried everything I could think of to persuade Ash not to go. I said Uncle Robert wouldn't approve. Even that didn't work. I was left with no choice; I had to offer to drive them. Neither Ash nor I had passed our test, but we'd both had lessons, and of the two of us I was the safer driver. Not to mention the fact that I was sober!'

Hannah tapped at her phone, making notes, then said, 'So, you *did* leave the house that night?'

'Yes, we did. Ash and Scott made so much noise going down the stairs I hoped it was going to wake Auntie Miriam, but it didn't. They both stepped on the noisy bottom step without thinking. I even stepped on it too, on purpose, but it didn't wake her up. There was nothing else to do but follow Ash outside. The car was parked out the front there.' Again Eliza pointed, finding it odd that the story she was telling had taken place in the exact same spot they were all now occupying. 'She tried to get in the driver's seat, and I had to beg her to give me the keys. I think she figured I was going to confiscate them. Which of course I was, if I got the chance. But Ash was stronger than me and she was just so bloody determined.'

Hannah nodded, encouragingly. 'Go on.'

'So, somehow, despite my best efforts, we all ended up in the car. Scott was in the back and Ash was shouting at him not to chunder. She said she'd kill him if he ruined her mum's seats and gave the game away. He didn't look brilliant, to be honest. He was so pale. I even suggested he get out and go back to bed, but Ash said that was exactly what a baby *would* do. Scott said he was staying put and Ash shouted that if I didn't drive off soon, she was going to swap places with me. So I started up the car and I drove. I was clutching the steering wheel so tight I could feel my pulse in my hands. I kept expecting the police to pull up behind me. There was nothing else on the road – it was something ridiculous like three o'clock in the morning, and I was driving dead slow because I'd never driven without my instructor before. We would've stood out like a sore thumb. But no police cars came along. Looking back, I've often wished they had.' Eliza paused again, before whispering to herself, *carry on, you need to tell this.*

Lottie seemed to be holding her breath. There was a real sense of a secret being aired.

'Yes. It's okay.' Hannah gave a reassuring nod.

'When we came to Lullaby Woods, near Ayresworth, Ash told me to stop the car in the layby. It was so dark in those woods. I didn't want to go in. I turned around and looked at Scott and I could tell he was absolutely terrified. He was only fifteen; why did she make him go in there?' Eliza's eyes flicked questioningly from Lottie to Hannah. 'Anyway, Ash jumped out of the passenger seat and slammed the door. Then Scott got out of the back. I was fumbling with the keys, trying to find the keyhole in the dark, but before I had the chance to lock the car, she shouted – run for it, and darted on ahead. That was what we shouted when we played the game with Uncle Robert. But back then it was the signal to return to the car. I called her to come back. I just wanted to be tucked up somewhere in a warm safe bed, you know?' Eliza's eyes pleaded with the others, hoping they could understand.

'Of course. Anyone would want that,' Lottie agreed.

'She ran on, and then she started calling our names. We were trying to work out where her voice was coming from, but she was moving about, dashing from place to place. It was hard to know exactly where she was; her voice seemed to bounce off the trees. Then, suddenly she was screaming, just literally screaming her head off. I couldn't tell if it was real. It could've all been part of her stupid plan to scare us, or it could've been that something awful was happening to her.'

'You must've been terrified. What did you do?' Hannah asked.

'We called her frantically. We were running further into the woods. I was holding Scott's hand, like I used to when it was just a game, when we were little. We were both scared that something dreadful had happened. Those screams made me feel sick. I just wanted to find her to see she was okay. And if it *was* all a trick, I was going to grab her and make her go back to the car with us. The ground was uneven and slippery, but we didn't stop running. I remember twisting my ankle on a tree root or something, and then ... Oh, God!'

'What?' Hannah and Lottie both asked.

'Scott's hand slipped out of mine, and within a second I'd lost him too.'

ELIZA – 2010

'*Scott!*' Eliza called her cousin's name, trying desperately to see anything in the impenetrable darkness.

Ash was still screaming. Those horrifying wails that caused Eliza's blood to run cold, the cries moving further into the woods as every second passed.

'Help me. Where the hell are you?' Reaching behind her, Eliza placed her hands on the ground and pushed herself back up to standing, angrily kicking out at the root that had sent her flying. Reaching all around her, she tried to grab onto anything that might be a part of Scott. But there was nothing. He was gone.

Then, as abruptly as they'd started, Ash's screams stopped.

In that instant, Lullaby Woods became still.

Somehow, the silence was even more alarming than the previous cacophony of sound. In the dark, hushed woods, Eliza realised she was now totally alone. All her senses stifled. 'Scott, Ash – where are you?' She waited, still clutching at the air around her, her chest rising and falling with such ferocity she thought she might pass out. This was real fear.

Before, in their childhood game, she would love that moment when Uncle Robert gave the signal, and they all raced back through the woods to Auntie Miriam and the safety of the car. She would throw herself onto the back seat, feeling the adrenaline course through her veins. It was so exhilarating. But now, this absolute blackness and total absence of noise, save for her own heartbeat, this was not exhilarating. This was the most disturbed and lonely she had ever felt.

Not sure what else to do, Eliza tentatively walked forwards. Her ankle was sore, but fortunately she was still able to put weight on it. Thank goodness; imagine if she had seriously hurt herself. What if she was unable to walk – who would save her? Wishing she had a torch, she edged her way on, her arms out in front of her, unclear which way she was heading. Her sense of direction was appalling at the best of times. She probably couldn't even find her way back to the car on a bright sunny day. The best option seemed to be to find Scott or Ash and hopefully one of them would know the way. Her ears strained for any noise that might help her; at this point she would even have welcomed those blood curdling screams again, anything that might indicate she was heading *towards* her cousins and not away from them.

She couldn't be sure, but it seemed like half an hour had passed, and for all Eliza knew she'd been going round in circles. Her ankle was throbbing. She'd called for Scott and Ash loads of times. What the hell had happened to them? Tears streamed down her face, and she was almost ready to drop to the ground and give in to the ever-increasing panic that was clutching at her chest. And then, she heard a car door slam. Running, in spite of the pain in her ankle, she headed towards the sound. It was possibly her one chance; it might not be repeated. She had to follow it before she lost her bearings again. Her feet churned up the mud. A couple of times she slipped. But she managed to keep in her mind the direction that the sound had come from.

Finding herself back on the original path that Ash had run down was a huge relief. There, parked up where she'd left it, was

Auntie Miriam's car. She ran towards it. In the back seat sat Scott. As she opened the car door the light came on and shone down on his head. He was also panting with fear; it was clear he had had an equally terrifying experience. 'Where have you been?' he asked.

'In there, of course.' Eliza pointed to the dark woods.

'Why did you run off and leave me?' Scott sobbed.

'I didn't run off.'

'You did. We were holding hands, and you yanked your hand out of mine. I kept running, but you were gone. Where did you go?'

'I didn't go anywhere. I tripped over. *You* left *me*!'

'Oh shit, I'm sorry, Elz. I didn't realise.'

'I've been searching for you and Ash for ages.'

'Me too,' Scott said. 'Didn't you hear me calling?'

Eliza shook her head. 'No. Did you hear me?'

'Of course not. If I'd have heard you, I'd have come. I've been on my own for ages.' He cried harder.

'You didn't find Ash?' Eliza asked.

'No.'

'Neither did I. This is awful, Scottie. What are we supposed to do?'

'We'll wait. She'll come soon.'

'But what if she doesn't?'

Scott wiped his eyes with the back of his dirty hand. 'She has to come. What else can she do? Once she realises we're not looking for her anymore, she'll stop trying to scare us and she'll come back to the car.'

'Maybe she won't find the car? She could be lost, like we were.'

'She'll find it eventually. We did.'

'I only found it when I heard you slam the door.'

Scott immediately opened and closed his door with a thud. 'Maybe she'll follow the sound.'

'Good idea.' Eliza tooted the horn.

'It wasn't like the old days, was it, Elz?'

'No, it wasn't. It was horrific.'

'I just wanted to find one of you. I hated being alone.'

'Me too.' Eliza tooted the horn again. 'Come on, Ash. I want to go back to bed.'

———

The clock on the car radio told Eliza in luminous green figures that it was four forty-five a.m. They'd been waiting for about an hour. Curled up in a ball on the back seat, Scott had fallen asleep. Eliza made a decision. Gently shaking him awake, she told him, 'I'm going to have to drive back to Auntie Miriam's.'

He rubbed his eyes, smearing more dirt on his face, 'Huh?'

'We have to go.'

'But ... Ash.'

'We have to get the car back before it's light. Auntie Miriam is going to go nuts.'

'But how will Ash get home?'

'I don't know. For all we know she could've walked there by now.'

'What if she's hurt? I mean ... those screams.'

'Scott, she started all this. It was her stupid idea to come here. She wanted to scare the living daylights out of us. Well, congratulations to her, she's succeeded. Now we've waited. We've given her loads of time. I wouldn't even be surprised if she had it all planned. One of her gothy friends probably picked her up in a car five minutes after she ran off. We can't wait any longer.'

Scott considered her words. 'Do you really think she'd be that mean?'

'This is Ash we're talking about.'

'I guess so.'

'Right, so let's get back to Auntie Miriam's.' Eliza turned the key and did a very inexperienced three-point turn in the road.

Whereas before, she had been desperate for Auntie Miriam to wake up and stop them in their tracks, now it was the complete opposite. Eliza was terrified that her auntie would hear the car pull up. As they parked, she told Scott to get out and head inside the house. 'Just get back into Ash's room as quietly as possible.'

'Okay. What are *you* going to do?'

'I'm going to try to park on the exact spot Auntie Miriam does. I don't think this is right – she'll look out of the window and see that the car has moved. We can't have her knowing we've been out in it.'

'I want to wait for you.'

'No, Scott. Please, do as I say. Just get back inside. I'll be there in a minute.'

He agreed, albeit grudgingly.

'Don't slam any doors,' she instructed.

'Okay.'

'And remember the bottom step.'

'*Okay!*'

Eliza watched Scott walk towards the house, and as soon as he was clear of the car, she moved forward and attempted to manoeuvre it back into the correct parking spot. Auntie Miriam did it all the time; she had the knack.

Two minutes later, she stood back to look at the car; it was about right. Hopefully, Auntie Miriam wouldn't realise it had been moved. As she locked it up, she noticed her trainers. 'Bugger!' Mud. She unlocked the car and checked the floors. As suspected, both the driver's mat and the back seat floor were covered in muddy footprints. She was going to have to hope there would be an opportunity for her to clean up tomorrow.

Thank God she'd spotted it though. Nearly busted! Eliza popped around the side of the house and used the hedgehog-shaped boot scraper in the garden to get the worst of the mud off her trainers. Leaving them by the back door, to be cleaned in the morning, she headed inside. The house was still in darkness; they'd made it home just before daybreak. She checked Uncle Robert's study, half expecting to see Ash sitting on the sofa with a sarcastic expression on her face. The room was empty. What was she playing at? Deciding not to switch the hall light on and risk waking her auntie, Eliza nipped up the stairs and joined Scott in Ash's bed. He was already asleep.

———

They were awoken a few hours later by Auntie Miriam's voice. 'Who on earth has walked mud up my stairs?'

Eliza's eyes sprang open. 'Scott, did you clean off your shoes last night?'

'You told me to get into Ash's room as quick as possible. You never said anything about my shoes.'

'Shit!' Of course, what fifteen-year-old boy thinks about cleaning his shoes?

'Scott. These are your footprints! They're way too big for the girls.' Auntie Miriam arrived in Ash's room with a flurry of waved arms and an angry expression. 'What were you up to?'

'He felt ill. He went outside to get some air, didn't you, Scott?'

'Y... eah,' Scott stuttered.

'Well, you're an idiot. Get up and vacuum my stairs.'

'But it's not even nine o'clock. And it's Sunday.'

'I don't care. Get that mud out of my house.'

Eliza jumped up. 'I'll do it for him. I'll do your car too as a special treat to make up for the mess in the house.'

'Thank you. But it ought to be Scott.'

'I don't mind, honestly.' Eliza rushed down to the understairs cupboard to grab the handheld vacuum, making sure not to limp in case that led to questions. 'I love using this little gadget!'

Auntie Miriam followed her down the stairs, avoiding the mud. Pushing the study door open, she said, 'I assume that daughter of mine has slept in here.'

The room was still empty.

22

HANNAH – 2022

'WITH ALL DUE RESPECT, Eliza, how can you possibly say *that* was not relevant?' Hannah asked.

'Because ... well, because Ash would've gone there by herself anyway, if I hadn't offered to drive her, and if Scott hadn't agreed when she asked him to go with her. She would still have gone. She would still have run off into those woods and she would still be missing today. Nothing we did actually changed anything. That's why we agreed to say we were asleep in bed.'

'But her mum knew. You said yourself, she noticed the mud on the stairs, and she always blamed Scott.'

'Yes, she did. She had her suspicions; she always knew those muddy footprints meant something. She was never the same around him after that. She said the apple hadn't fallen far from the tree. I should've told the truth, but Scott wanted to keep quiet.'

Hannah shook her head in disbelief. 'But he was younger than you. Still a child. Why didn't you overrule him?'

'Honestly, we just kept thinking she would come home, and it seemed stupid to drop ourselves in it.'

'But you were the adult,' Hannah said. 'You owed it to Scott to speak up.'

'Don't you think I know that? If I could go back …'

Lottie asked, 'Are we seriously the first people you've ever told that to?'

'I don't know. I think I told Ryan once, when I was drunk. After we'd lost the second baby. I was waiting to start trying again. I knew it was okay to have a drink, so I had a *lot* of red wine, and I must've told him that Scott and I were with Ash in the woods when she went missing. He never mentioned it when we were together and it was all so hazy, but he said something about it yesterday. So …' She shrugged. 'Anyway, like I say, I don't think us being there changed anything. She would've gone to the woods, and she would've left home that night. She obviously had it all planned.'

'You're referring to the money that went missing?' Hannah asked.

'How do you know about the money?'

'My contact at the station gave me the basics. There was a large sum of money in the sideboard, and it went missing at the same time as Ash.'

'Yes. Exactly. It was two thousand pounds. Don't you get it? It wasn't an accident that she went missing that night. Whether we had stayed in her bed or gone with her, she would still have left. She was always threatening to leave this house. She hated her mum, and she hated being here without Uncle Robert. It was meant to happen.'

'You can't know that.' Hannah shook her head. 'There are too many variables.'

'I do. I know it because it's obvious. Neither of us could find her. She probably went straight to the road on the other side of the woods, waited for it to get light and hitched a lift. God only knows exactly how long Scott and I were wandering about searching for her, and each other – it was all so pointless. I wish she'd just gone off on her own. Why wake us up and drag us into it? Why make it a part of my nightmares for all these years?'

'She sounds like quite a selfish person to me,' Lottie said, adding, 'I don't mean that in a nasty way. I was self-absorbed once too. I can recognise it in others.'

Eliza said, 'Perhaps if Uncle Robert hadn't lost his fight with cancer, she might have been a nicer adult. We'll never know.'

'But eighteen is incredibly young to go off completely alone and start afresh. Even with a handful of cash and a mother you can't stand,' Hannah said.

'Hang on.' Eliza frowned. 'You just pointed out that at eighteen I was an adult, old enough to confess to going to the woods with her. You can't have it both ways.'

'Actually, you're right. Eighteen *is* an adult, as far as the law's concerned, but it's nothing really. Just a step away from childhood. I apologise. It seems both you and Scott have paid a high price for that night. We've all done things we regret. I'm no exception, and I was way older than you when I made my biggest mistake.'

'So, does that rule her in or rule her out vis-a-vis the messages I've been getting?' Eliza asked.

Hannah thought for a second. 'I'd say it rules her in. I know her mum had her declared dead, and I understand why. But nothing you've said today tells me she's not still alive and kicking.'

'What about the screams? Maybe something happened to her that night,' Lottie said. 'What if she was killed by some passing mad axe man in Lullaby Woods?'

'If that were the case, her body would've been found years ago, wouldn't it?' Eliza asked.

'Yes, imagine how many dog walkers have been through every inch of those woods in twelve years?' Hannah replied. 'It's not possible for her to have been killed in there. Unless ...' She paused.

'*Unless* what?' Lottie asked.

'Someone could've moved her body.'

'You mean the mad axe man?'

'No, Lottie. Not the friggin' mad axe man. Sometimes you can be as daft as a brush.' Hannah rolled her eyes.

23
ELIZA – 2022

SCOTT HAMMERED on the front door, demanding Eliza open it.

As soon as she did, he barged his way in. His hair was a mess; he'd clearly been running his fingers through it. *'Right, tell me again, to my face this time, because I cannot fucking believe this!'*

'Stop it, Scottie. It's not as bad as you're making out.'

'Actually, it doesn't get much worse than this.'

'She's not going to tell anyone.'

'Eliza, you said she's a policewoman. She's probably told all her copper mates by now.'

'She's not in the police anymore, she's a private investigator.'

'I just don't get it. I told you to ditch her card. What d'you need a private investigator for anyway?'

With a sigh, Eliza replied, 'I had no one to turn to. Ryan's too busy with his new marriage and I pushed all my friends away when I got so down about the babies. I didn't want to bother Mum and Dad with it all. I just thought Hannah would be able to help.'

'But why the hell did you tell her about that night? We've never told anyone. We agreed.'

'I know. But we were so young. What seemed like the right thing to do then, doesn't now. What else can I say?' Eliza shrugged.

'You should've checked with me first. We are gonna be in deep shit now.' Scott slapped himself on the forehead.

'Why?'

'We were with her when she went missing and we *never* told anyone. The police asked us loads of times and every fucking time we repeated the same thing – we were asleep in Ash's bed. We lied to the police. D'you honestly think she's going to let that go? She won't be able to stop herself. She'll dob us in.'

'*For what?* We didn't do anything wrong, Scott. Besides which, you were still a child when you lied to the police. You'll be fine.'

'Oh yeah, they'll look at my dad's record and they'll say – he must be the same.'

'She's not going to tell the police. I promise you.'

'So, what is she going to do with that little gem of information that you so kindly handed her?'

'It's going to help her to investigate Ash's disappearance a bit more, that's all.'

'But you just said on the phone that you'd hired her to work out which wacko left a CD on your doorstep and broke into your kitchen.'

'I did. And she's investigating that too. But she's been itching to look into Ash's disappearance, and, honestly, what harm can it do?'

Scott shook his head. 'I told that nosey bitch that Ash was dead when we met her. You've got no idea what you've done. Or what trouble this could cause.'

'Auntie Miriam's gone now; nothing Hannah finds out can harm her.'

'I wasn't thinking of Auntie Miriam.'

'And nothing she finds out can harm *us* either.'

'What if she actually isn't dead? What if she wants her house and all the money back? You're well screwed if that happens.'

'I'll deal with it. I don't even want this house anymore.' Eliza threw her hands up.

'Good, can I have it?'

'No, you bloody can't.' Eliza gave a tiny smile. 'Nice try though, Scottie.'

'Where has the PI gone now? Why isn't she here?'

'She had to go home and meet some guy, Dave something. He works for her.'

'A likely story.'

'It's true. And Lottie's taken the dog out.'

'Bear?'

'No, her dog. A spaniel.'

'So they're both staying here, and one of them has brought her dog. You are such a soft touch.'

'Like I say. I didn't know who to turn to. You weren't around, and I wasn't going to spend another night on my own after I saw that figure in the garden.'

'Right, fine. Well I'm here now. You can tell those two to sling their hooks.'

'No!'

'Why not?'

'I like having them here. I was at school with Lottie, she's funny, and Hannah is … well, she's marvellous. They're going nowhere until I find out who was in my kitchen the other night.'

'You couldn't leave it, could you? You had to tell someone. I knew you would.'

'Scott, I kept it in me for *twelve years*. You can't imagine how it feels to let it out.'

'I've often wanted to let it out too, but I'm not a snitch.'

Eliza took his face into her hands, remembering the relief

she'd felt when she'd found him sitting in the back of Auntie Miriam's car that night. 'Scottie,' her voice softened, 'I love you so much. It was a horrific thing to go through, especially for you. I'm honestly sorry that you're angry about me telling Hannah and Lottie, but I promise you, it doesn't make any difference. Our being in those woods was irrelevant. Hannah understands that.'

ELIZA – 2010

Eliza waited for news of Ash. The days passed, and still no phone call and no Ash. What the hell was she trying to do to all of them? How had it been more than a week already since that awful night? Eliza had never expected it to get to the point where her auntie decided to call the police. Worse still, she and Scottie had been summoned to Auntie Miriam's house to tell the police everything they knew about the last time Ash had been at home. She longed to call Scott and talk to him, but there was no credit on her phone, and she had no money to go to the newsagent and top it up. The home phone was in the hall; her parents didn't see the need for a cordless one. So any conversation she had would easily be overheard by them, and that seemed like an awful idea.

She understood why the policeman had asked her and Scott to meet him at Auntie Miriam's. He wanted to get an idea from all of them about what had happened. But why had he said he was going to need to speak to them separately? It made them seem like suspects or something. When faced with a copper, would Scott continue to say the same as her?

Whenever Auntie Miriam or Eliza's parents had asked them, they had stuck rigidly to their story that they'd both been asleep in Ash's bed at the point they assumed she'd left the house. Not mentioning Lullaby Woods had been difficult, and on more than a few occasions over the last week she'd come close to slipping up. But Scott had insisted it was best not to tell anyone what had happened, and even though she was the older of the two, she had stupidly agreed to go along with his plan. It had been hard enough to lie to Auntie Miriam and her parents, but when the police had asked to speak to them, Eliza had started to panic. This was a whole different ballgame.

Eliza had just a couple of minutes alone with Scott before she suspected they were about to be whisked off to separate rooms.

'I've changed my mind, Scottie. I think we ought to tell them we were with her.'

'After we've literally been saying the opposite all week. No way.'

'But it's getting serious now. Why did I let you persuade me to lie?'

'You never tell coppers what really happened, Elz, that's the rule.'

'That's your dad's rule, but it's not ours.'

'D'you think they're going to believe that we both searched for her in the woods and neither of us could find her?'

'But it's the truth.'

Scott shook his head. 'They won't believe us.'

'I think they will.'

'Please, Elz. For me? Please, just keep saying we were asleep in her bed. It's what we've told everyone else.'

'Yes. And Auntie Miriam doesn't believe it for a minute.'

'She will. She has to. We just have to keep saying it.' Scott stuck out his little finger. 'Pinky promise, you won't tell them.'

Eliza considered for a second. She so wanted to come clean. At the very least it would give the police an idea of where Ash had really been the night she'd gone missing. But Scott's eyes were brimming with tears, and she knew how scared he was of the police. Reaching out, she linked her finger with his. 'Pinky promise.'

Auntie Miriam entered the room. 'Eliza, the policeman wants to speak to you next. You can wait here, Scott.'

24
HANNAH – 2022

HANNAH WAS HAVING another meeting with Dave. This time they were at Hannah's home.

'Well done on the debugging. I swear you know that equipment better than I do,' Hannah smiled.

'Hmm.'

'What?'

'I know what you're doing.'

'What am I doing, Dave?'

'You're humouring me. You're giving me simple tasks to do. Something to keep me off the booze, but nothing too taxing.'

'I might well be giving you some simpler tasks, but I can assure you I am not humouring you.'

'Breaking me back in gently then.'

'What's wrong with that? If you'd been ill, I'd do the same.'

'But I wasn't ill.'

'It doesn't matter whether you were physically ill, mentally ill, or just plain off your game. I chose to keep you on and I'm choosing to give you jobs I know you can handle. And you *are* better than me with the debugging equipment – it's a fact.'

Dave took the coffee she handed him. 'Thanks. For this, and for keeping me on.'

'No problem. By the way, that,' Hannah sniffed the air, savouring the rich Colombian aroma, 'is a bloody decent cup of coffee. Not a hint of bitterness. I want the same next time I come to you.'

He gave her a salute. 'Yes, Gov.'

'I like the sound of that name.' Consulting her list, Hannah said, 'I had an email from Branscombe's this morning; they need background checks done on a couple of new employees. I'll sort that. I can do it whilst I'm watching over Eliza.'

'How's that going? Have you managed to convince her to let you investigate the cousin's disappearance yet?'

'Kind of.'

'I knew you would,' Dave laughed. 'Hannah Tenacious Sandlin.'

'Well, to be honest, it's pertinent, you know. The CD, the jams – all that nonsense is connected to Ash. Until I determine if she's alive or dead, I can't take the harassment case forward.'

'Funny old world, isn't it?

'You mean the jams on parade?'

'Yeah, the jam on the kitchen table, the ghost in the garden, all of it. You and I know it's probably all about money.'

Hannah agreed. 'It's almost always all about money. But Eliza doesn't think like us. She told me some stuff last night that she'd been keeping from me, stuff about the last time she was with her cousin, and she honestly thought it wasn't important.'

'Example?' Dave asked.

'Oh, let's just say, she wasn't actually asleep in anyone's bed when Ash went missing.'

'Ohhh ... I'm intrigued.' Dave smiled. 'Tell me more?'

'Okay. Strap in!'

A few minutes later, Dave was up to speed with Eliza's case. 'Well, I'm not going to lie. The whole thing sounds crazy to me. Screaming in the woods in the early hours of the morning. No wonder that Scott bloke is screwed up.'

'I know. I don't like him, and I don't trust him, but Eliza seems unwavering in her belief that he's a good guy. Plus, the more time I spend with her the fonder I am of her, and the more determined I am to solve her case.'

'Is it creepy sleeping in Ash's room?' Dave asked.

'Nah. You know me; I can sleep anywhere. Besides, it's just a room. There's nothing left in it except a spare bed.' Hannah stood up. 'Right, I'll let you get off. Enjoy your visit with Noah.'

'Will do.' Dave joined her, ready to leave. 'You're sure you want to take those two background checks? I don't mind doing them.'

Hannah appreciated how hard he was trying. She knew he had to keep busy; it was his only way of coping. But she didn't like to give all the work to him. It was still *Sandlin* Private Investigation, after all. 'No, I'll be fine. Like I say, I'll probably go back to Eliza's place and work from there. I've got what I need on my laptop.' As she left, she repeated, 'Great work on the debugging, Dave. Thanks for everything.'

Dave looked her dead in the eye. 'No, *thank you*!' So many unspoken words passed between them.

Giving him a squeeze, she replied, 'We just have to keep living our best lives and doing what we can to help others.'

He nodded, his eyes slightly teary. 'I know. I can't go back and change anything.' Without even mentioning her name, they were talking about Dawn again.

'You're right.' Hannah looked away. She hated to see his guilt.

'Are you heading back to Eliza's straight away?' he asked.

'Soon. I'm stopping off at Mum and Dad's first. My gran's there today.'

'Say hi to Jacqui and Ken and give Granny Annie a hug from me.'

'You've never even met her, Dave. I think a hug might be a tad forward at this stage. Besides, only the elite few get to call her Granny Annie. She'd be Mrs Penn to you.'

'Shame. I bloody love that name.' Dave laughed. 'Your gran sounds like quite a character!'

'She is. I can't wait to see her. It's ages since I last spoke to her.'

'Well, I'll let you get on then.' Dave made his way to the front door.

Hannah followed him. Once there, she asked, 'Everything else is okay, isn't it? I mean … you know … you're staying off the booze?'

'Back on the twelve steps and keeping in touch with Tom.'

'Moving forward?'

Dave gave a gentle smile. 'Yes.'

'Good news. Say hi to Noah.'

'Will do. You just watch your back, okay. That Scott sounds well dodgy. You don't go through something like that at fifteen and come out all right. If you need me, let me know.'

'I will do. But I'm pretty tough, you know. I reckon I'm tougher than that little weasel anyway.'

'I reckon you probably are,' Dave agreed.

25
SCOTT – 2022

MAKING HIS WAY HOME, Scott was still fuming at his cousin. Telling those fucking women a secret that they'd sworn to keep – what the hell was she doing? Didn't she think *he'd* wanted to tell people too? Didn't she realise it killed him to keep it all inside? It was probably that investigator. Yes. She'd no doubt probed and questioned and wheedled it all out of Elz. If Eliza had to tell someone it would've been better to have told Ryan or one of those simpering idiots she used to work with. Telling a private investigator was just about the worst thing she could've done. A PI was only a small step down from a copper, and Scott had been taught not to trust them. You never, ever tell them what really happened. That was the rule. He'd stuck to it for twelve years, and now Eliza had ruined it!

SCOTT – 2010

'Are you sure you're telling me everything?' the policeman asked Scott.

'Tell him the truth.' Auntie Miriam seemed to have lost

weight already. Never a particularly large lady, in a week, she had become almost skeletal.

'That *is* the truth.'

'Last Saturday night you went to sleep in your cousin Ashley's room, and she went to sleep in the study?' the policeman said.

'Yes.'

'*Scott!*' Auntie Miriam shouted.

'What?'

'Look at the policeman; you keep staring at the floor.'

'I don't know what you want me to say.' Scott felt his face become uncomfortably hot. 'I've told him everything. I fell asleep. When I woke up, I was in Ash's room, Eliza was asleep next to me, and it was morning. That's it. There's nothing else.'

'Except your cousin Eliza says you went outside during the night to get some air because you felt sick.'

'Oh, yeah.'

'So, why didn't you mention that to me as well?' The policeman's tone grew stern.

Scott's eyes returned to the floor, 'I just forgot that bit. All right?'

'You got up and put your trainers on, then you went outside to be sick, you got your trainers covered in mud and you came back into the house?'

'Yes!'

'I have to say, lad, your auntie's garden is incredibly neat. I can't see anywhere you'd get that much mud on your shoes out there.'

Scott faltered, then mumbled, 'I think I trod in one of her flowerbeds.' He waited for his Auntie's usual response of – Oh, Scottie! But none came.

'Did your cousin Ashley mention anything to you about wanting to leave home?'

'Yeah.'

'What did she say?'

'She said it all the time. She always said she wasn't going to live here once she was an adult. And she's an adult now, isn't she? She didn't like it here.' Realising he was upsetting Auntie Miriam, Scott apologised. 'Sorry. But that *is* what Ash said. Loads. Since she was like fourteen or something.'

'Do you think your cousin has run away from home?'

Scott shrugged. 'I dunno. I guess so.'

'Did she seem like she was planning it the night you and Eliza slept here?'

'Maybe.'

'And there's nothing else you'd like to add?'

'Add to what?'

'To your statement.' The policeman sounded impatient.

Scott shook his head.

'If you think of anything, you must tell us. Do you understand?'

'Uh huh.'

'Tell your parents or tell your auntie and we'll come back and see you. Okay?'

'There won't be anything. There isn't any more to tell.'

The policeman spoke to Auntie Miriam. 'I think that's about it, ma'am. The money that's gone missing, coupled with the frequent declarations that your daughter planned to leave home, seem to confirm that this is nothing more serious than a runaway teenager.'

'Nothing more serious! Officer, this *is* serious. I don't know where my daughter is. I've called everyone I can think of. I've tried telling myself she's just run away to scare me. But she's been gone for over a week now. That's why I called you!'

'You have confirmed that your daughter has gone missing before, though.'

'Yes, for one or two nights, never this long.'

'But in all honesty, ma'am, I doubt she had a couple of thousand pounds in cash before. I think she'll be back when she's spent it. You mark my words; she'll walk back through that door any day now. And, may I add, for future reference, it's not a good idea to keep that amount of cash in the house.'

'I am aware it was not a wise move, but, as I've explained to you, it was a part payment for the builder who's working on the patio for me.'

'Nevertheless, I wouldn't be doing my duty if I didn't advise you.'

'Your duty is to find my child!'

'I understand that, but your daughter is no longer officially a child. If she left this house of her own free will, which I think we're all agreed she did, then there's little we can do. Ashley mentioned to several people that she planned to leave home as soon as possible ...' the policeman coughed gently, '... and I reckon the large sum of money prompted the decision to go when she did.'

'In the middle of the night!'

'As good a time as any, and probably when she found the cash.'

'I wish I hadn't told you about the money going missing. It doesn't change anything. It could have nothing to do with Ashley.'

'I think it's a fair assumption. You say you placed it in the sideboard on the Thursday. On the Saturday, your daughter took drugs, drank alcohol, and went off in the middle of the night. Then, on the Sunday, you realised the money was missing. I find, ma'am, that on the whole, the most obvious explanation is usually the correct one.'

'My daughter is many things, but I don't think she'd steal from her own parent.'

'No one ever does think that.' The policeman stood up and made his way to the lounge door. 'As I said to your nephew and niece, if you think of anything else about the night in question, do call me. I honestly believe she'll be back when the money runs out.'

'Well, I hope you're right.' Auntie Miriam joined him in the doorway. As she passed Scott, she gave him a look he'd never seen before. She had always been kind and caring and he had felt very at home in her house. But today, well, today she seemed to despise him.

Having seen the police officer out, Auntie Miriam returned to the lounge and said, 'I know you're lying to me. That mud did not come from my flowerbeds. They're all as pristine as they were before. You know more than you're letting on, and I shall never forgive you if something terrible has happened to my child.'

'I don't—'

Auntie Miriam interrupted him. 'Don't bother lying any further. When you're ready to tell me how you traipsed all that mud up my stairs, I'm ready to listen.'

Scott stared blankly at her.

'I think it's best you go home now; Eliza has already been collected. If you need to have any more contact with the police, please do so from your own home. Don't come back here.'

'Why would I want more contact?'

'If you decide to tell the truth. Who shall I call to pick you up? Your mum? Or is your dad out … I mean, is Fergus back at home?'

'Yes, he's on parole.'

'Why in God's name does your mother keep taking him back?' Auntie Miriam shook her head.

'I think she loves him.'

'It was a rhetorical question.'

'What?'

'Forget it. I'll call him now. We can only hope he doesn't end up back inside, I suppose.'

'He won't. He's promised me.'

'His promises mean nothing.' Auntie Miriam bristled. 'He promised me he hadn't stolen my watch, or Robert's grandfather's medals.'

Scott chose not to comment. He'd been with his dad when Fergus had taken the medals to the pawn shop.

'I feckin' hate that woman.' Fergus hit the accelerator and drove erratically away from Auntie Miriam's house.

'She thinks I'm lying about last Saturday, Dad.'

'What about it?'

'About being asleep when Ash went missing.'

'And? Are ya?'

'No. Of course not.'

'Well, that's good enough for me.' Fergus nodded.

'Thanks.'

'It's best if ya just keep away from her from now on. No point going back there. D'ya hear me?'

'Yeah.'

'You do as I say.'

'I will.' Scott shrank down in his seat, his arms folded over his chest.

'She makes out she's so full of feckin' airs and graces. Her husband was your mother's brother. Raised by the same parents, for Christ's sake. She's no grander than us. We're family. She'd do well to remember that fact.' The volume of Fergus's voice rose.

'Yeah.'

Fergus thumped the steering wheel. 'She ought to have more respect.'

'I know,' Scott squeaked, avoiding eye contact.

'Why did the police want you there, anyways? It's got nothing to do with you, surely?'

'Just to check. You know ... what we all remembered about the last time Ash was at home.' Scott's gaze moved down to his feet. He noted the remnants of mud on his trainers. 'I wish you could've been there.'

'I told ya, I'm not breathing the same air as some feckin' scumbag copper.'

'Well, Mum then.'

'What good would she be? She's about as sharp as the knife me old ma used for butter.'

'Well, she might know what to say to the police for me.'

'Know what to say! She couldn't empty a boot if the instructions were on the heel.'

'Aww, don't say things like that about her, Dad.'

His dad gave him *that* look. 'I'll say what I like, son.'

Scott flinched.

Fergus continued with his rant. 'The stupid woman can't do anything right. I told her I wanted ya called Shaun, didn't I?'

'Mum always says you left when I was born, so she called me what *she* wanted.'

'She had no right. I came back, didn't I? She's an eejit, your mother is.'

'Dad ... please.'

'I jus' told you, I'll say what I like. Now, don't go on. You know how I hate your constant whining.'

'Sorry.' Scott knew when it was best to stop.

'Good lad.' Fergus's outburst was over for now. 'Coppers didn't mention the money then?'

'N ... n ... no,' Scott lied.

'Grand. See, your auntie's got so much money she still hasn't noticed it's gone. Told ya, didn't I? Stuck up bitch.'

'Yeah, you did.'

'Right so.'

Scott made a point of examining his fingernails, now scared of saying anything, in case it was wrong.

Putting his foot down, Fergus jumped a light as it turned red. 'You did well there, son.'

Scott continued to say nothing. He wanted to be pleased; a compliment from his father was exceptionally rare. But deep down he knew he'd done nothing to be proud of.

Fergus drove on. 'We'll get fish and chips tonight, boy.'

On the outside, Scott was every inch the teenage boy on his way to collect a fish and chip supper with his father.

Inside, however, his mind was racing. Running over and over the events of the previous Saturday night.

Finding the money had seemed like such a windfall. Eliza had gone downstairs to check on Ash. She'd specifically told him to stay put. But when she hadn't come back, he'd become curious; he thought he could hear an argument and maybe crying. Was Ash upsetting Eliza? He needed to check. He headed down the stairs, luckily remembering the bottom step and the coat hooks at the last second. Against the odds, he made it noiselessly into the hall. The door to the kitchen was ajar. Scott pressed his body to the wall and listened to Eliza and Ash. Ash was swearing a lot. She was asking why her dad had died and Eliza's hadn't. Then she said something mean about his dad. Something about Fergus buggering off the minute Scott was born and only popping back to shag his mum. That made Scott angry. He hated the way Ash spoke about his dad. He hated her and yet he loved her too. If only she would once look at him the way she looked at Eliza, like she actually wanted to spend time with him. He'd taken the bloody pill earlier to try to impress her, and that had all ended badly. Why did he have to vomit? Perhaps Ash was right, and he *was* just a baby. He heard Eliza criticising Ash for drinking the champagne. Maybe he ought to go in and offer to drink it with her, if there was any left. That would make him seem grown up, wouldn't it? Better still if he drank something stronger. Perhaps some of that horrible whisky his uncle used to drink? Scott snuck into the study to find the drinks cabinet.

There it was, an old-fashioned teak sideboardy thing, with the tiniest of locks on the front. The key was always left in the lock. He gingerly turned it and the door sprang open. He reached inside, his fingers feeling for the heavy crystal decanter that he knew would contain the foul liquid. His stomach churned at the thought of it. Would he even be able to force it down? He had to. Ash might be impressed. As he moved the decanter forward a small, brown envelope fell onto its side. Picking it up, he realised it was not sealed. When he opened it, he was shocked to find it contained money. Twenty-pound notes by the looks of it. Lots of them. He thought for a second, knowing that the right thing to do would be to place it back behind the whisky decanter and lock the door. But, as he was forever being told, Scott was Fergus's son, and he simply couldn't help himself. Before he knew what he was doing, Scott had shoved the envelope full of money into his jeans pocket and returned the decanter to its original position. Closing the door of the sideboard gently, he turned the key.

Barely two minutes had passed, and yet so much had changed. Scott had become a thief; he had become his father. He heard Ash tell Eliza that she was going to sleep in the study – he didn't have long. He crept back up the stairs.

Once back in Ash's room, he hid his newly acquired wealth in his backpack. By the time Eliza returned, he was back in bed. Pretending to wake up with a jerk when she got in next to him, he allowed her to cuddle him. When Auntie Miriam found the money was missing, she would probably just assume she'd misplaced it. As his dad often said – that woman had more money than she ought to.

The next day, when he'd left Auntie Miriam's and gone

home, he had shown his dad the money. It was one of the few times Fergus had been genuinely pleased with his son.

———

Two weeks after the fish and chip supper, Scott's dad left his mum again. Choosing a new woman to shack up with, he took the £2,000 with him. Fergus's motto was always – finders keepers.

26
HANNAH – 2022

'I THOUGHT you promised to be here early afternoon; it's getting on for three o'clock,' Lottie whined.

'I said I'd *try*. And I'm sorry. Don't nag me, please,' Hannah replied.

'I'm not nagging. But you knew I was nervous about this fete.'

'If you're that bothered, we won't go. I don't want you to be upset.'

Lottie shook her head. 'It's not that. I *do* want to go. But I've been thinking about it all day. It's good they're starting up the fetes again, but ... you know – Mulberry House!' After a second, she asked, 'Come to think of it, where have you been? Working?'

Hannah paused. 'Uh huh. Just something I needed to do. I didn't realise I'd overrun so badly.' Taking Lottie into her arms, she said, 'Listen, I'm here now. There's still plenty of time – it doesn't finish until five p.m. If you'd like to go, I am more than happy to escort you, fair maiden.'

'All right. All right. I forgive you.'

'So, what's the deal?'

'Well ... if we're going, we'll need decent boots,' Lottie said. 'I know that meadow, and it'll be a total bog after all the rain we've had recently.'

'You'd think they'd put the stalls on that posh bit of lawn near the house or over on the concrete,' Hannah said.

'They probably will,' Lottie agreed. 'But ... I just have a feeling we're somehow going to end up in the meadow.' She shrugged.

'Yes, we probably will.' Hannah gave a supportive smile.

'I can't believe they're going ahead, to be honest. It's been so wet. I'll bet the stream is fit to burst ...' Lottie's eyes closed for a second.

Hannah saw a shot of pain in her friend's expression. Aware of the need to change the subject and rid her of the distressing memory, she asked, 'Can I borrow your brown wellies, Lottie?'

'The brown *wellies*? They're Dubarry boots, not wellies!'

'What's the difference?'

'About three hundred quid.'

'Has the shop got big windows?'

'I bought them online.' Lottie frowned. 'What are you on about?'

'Must've seen you coming!'

'Ha ha!'

'Well, it's either the Dubarrys or my new biker boots. You know I would never own a pair of wellies.'

'You may borrow my old hunter boots,' Lottie offered. 'We can swing by home and get them on the way.'

'Thank you, madame.' Hannah grinned, glad to note that Lottie's countenance had returned to a thing of beauty.

'Erm ... what do you need to borrow wellies for?' Eliza entered the kitchen.

'We're going to the fete. You know, at Mulberry House,' Lottie replied. 'We were just saying, it'll probably be boggy.'

'Oh, your mum and dad are doing those again?'

'Not exactly ...' Lottie faltered, looking to Hannah for guidance.

'Someone else lives there now. The new people have reinstated the fete.'

'Can I come too?'

'Of course. We were just about to ask you,' Lottie said.

'I'll go and put some jeans on. Not sure these trackies are the right thing for a fete at such a grand house.'

Once they were alone, Hannah said to Lottie, 'At least you won't see Vincent there.'

'I will, though. I'll see him everywhere. By the stream, comforting my mum. By the fire circle.' She cringed. 'That's what I've been thinking about all day.'

'Sorry.'

'The only good thing is, he may not be the only ghost I'll see. I'm hoping to get glimpses of my mum, picking flowers, or organising the WI ladies.'

'Absolutely. I'm sure it will bring back some good memories for you too. It's been such a long time since you were there.'

'Can you do me a favour?' Lottie asked.

'Name it?'

'If you get a chance today, if you're on your own with Eliza, can you tell her all about my parents? I hate that she thinks they're still alive, but I can't bring myself to tell her.'

'No problem. But are you sure you want me to tell her *all* about your parents?'

'Well, maybe not *all*. Definitely not how Chen is connected. Maybe just tell her they're dead and how it happened.'

'Okay. No worries.' Hannah gave Lottie a squeeze. 'Right, let's collect those snobby wellies and head over there. Are we taking Dixie?'

'Would I be awful if I left her here? I know she'd probably love to reminisce.'

'It's up to you,' Hannah said. 'She won't know where we've

been. Bagsy I don't have to give her a bath when we get back if you do take her, though.'

Lottie looked sad. 'She's so cosy, asleep in her basket. I'm going to leave her here. I think it'll be too upsetting for me to see her in the meadow.'

Hannah asked, 'Did you take her with you that day you went back to Mulberry House? You know, after that scumbag threw you out.'

'No. I was a coward that day, too.'

'You're not a coward. You just need to think about your mental health. Remember what your counsellor says?'

'I know. I should do what feels right for me and not worry about what's expected.'

'Precisely.' Hannah hugged her friend. 'It all takes time. You might not ever get over it, but you'll learn to live with it.'

Lottie nodded. 'Right, let's get those wellies.' She gave her dog a kiss goodbye and called up the stairs for Eliza to hurry up.

They entered Mulberry House via the side gate. Hannah asked if Lottie recognised the lady taking the money on the door, but was told she must be the new owner because she wasn't familiar at all.

As they strolled around, Lottie pointed out all the stalls she remembered from her childhood. Suddenly, she exclaimed, 'Oh my gosh, splat the rat!'

'What the hell …?' Hannah shook her head.

'They drop a soft toy down a tube, and you wait with your baseball bat poised at the bottom. The idea is, to win a prize, you must send the rat flying before it hits the ground.'

'I could've done with that baseball bat the night Ash broke in,' Eliza said.

'Or whoever it was. You don't know it was Ash.' Hannah put her straight.

'Well, whoever. I would've felt a lot safer with a baseball bat than I did with a bloody umbrella.'

'You have Hannah now. She's tougher than any old baseball bat.' Lottie smiled, affectionately.

Once they'd seen everything on offer, they wandered into the meadow, as Lottie had predicted, and made their way over to the stream. Hannah could see that Lottie was becoming emotional. 'Are you okay?' she asked.

'I think I just need some time.'

'Of course.'

'Can you ... you know? Lottie gestured towards Eliza.

'Sure. You take a minute; I'll fill her in on the gaps.'

It didn't take long to explain to Eliza that Lottie's dad had slipped by the stream and died as a result of the fall, and that her mum had gone on to marry a bastard who was wanted for several counts of obtaining money by deception. 'Then, just three years after the marriage, her mum sadly decided to take her own life.'

'How awful.' Eliza looked shocked.

'Worse still – Mulberry House and all Lottie's inheritance went to that predator her mum had married.'

'Oh, no! I never knew. I've probably said a whole bunch of inappropriate things.' Eliza clasped her hand over her mouth.

'I don't think you have. But honestly, you weren't to know anyway.'

'Poor Lottie.' Eliza shook her head, and asked, 'But doesn't she have money now? She owns the house you two live in, doesn't she?'

'Her stepdad had a flash of conscience and left half his money to her. She inherited it when the slimeball died of a heart attack. We think he probably left the other half to his sister.'

'Wow. I guess getting half back was something.'

'Absolutely. You know what, I think she's better off away from here anyway. This place holds so many incredibly sad memories for her. Where she's standing right now is where she found her dad dead.' Hannah looked over at her friend. 'She's told me loads of times that she's a better person now than she was when she lived here, and I believe her. Half the money was enough for her to rebuild her life.'

'Her stepdad sounds like a right git.'

'He was. The first time she ever mentioned him to me she called him a ...' Hannah lowered her voice. 'Well, let's just say it starts with a c and isn't considered polite.'

Eliza drew in her breath sharply. 'We got immediate expulsion if we used that word at our school.'

'I think she had every right to use it, though. He was a nasty piece of work. Having said that, searching for him was the most exhilarating thing I'd done since I left the police; it was the thing that got me out of a dark place. Finding Vincent Rocchino somehow saved us both.'

Eliza smiled. 'You two are brilliant.'

Hannah watched as Lottie turned away from the stream. She wiped her face with the back of her hand and made her way over to them.

'Okay?'

'Not too bad.'

'Seen your ghosts?'

'Yes.'

'Which ones?'

'Mum, over by where the pool used to be. She worked hard on those flower beds. Dad, in the stream, of course, and ...'

'Yes?' Hannah urged.

'Well, I saw that stupid little cun—'

Placing her hand over Lottie's mouth, Eliza cried, 'Don't say it, you'll get expelled!'

Lottie laughed. 'Once a St Bede's girl, always a St Bede's girl! Well, anyway, I saw him everywhere, but it's okay. My counsellor and my best friend are helping me to deal with it all. So, fuck him!'

'I think that one would've just got you suspended,' Eliza laughed.

'Yes, I think it would,' Lottie giggled. 'Besides, being here has made me decide one thing.'

'Which is?' Hannah asked.

'I reckon I'm ready to think about getting another horse. I mean, I chose my house because it was close to a livery yard. Maybe it's about time I started looking out for one.'

'Yes. That'd be amazing for you.' Hannah was pleased; it was a step in the right direction. Another way of Lottie claiming part of her old life back again.

'So, what now?' Eliza asked.

Hannah said, 'Coffee!' at the exact same time as Lottie asked, 'Can we see the fortune teller?'

'I'll get the drinks. You two join the queue,' Eliza offered.

Hannah and Lottie waited in the queue outside the pop-up tent of *The Great Shazam – Fortune Teller*.

'We're next,' Lottie pointed out, needlessly.

'If she says I'm pregnant, I want my money back.'

'Hannah, it's just a laugh. It says on the sign, all the money raised is going towards the conservation area by the village pond. They're trying to encourage wildlife back there. That's what it's really for.'

'Why did I let you talk me into this? My dad would piss himself if he knew I was queuing up for this.'

'Ken's not a believer in psychic mediums, then?'

'Not one bit. He'd be joking about this for years to come.'

'Well, like I say, it's just a bit of fun. You'll see.'

Mystic Shazam called them inside. What was clearly a bog-standard bell tent had been temporarily transformed into a Bedouin tent by the simple placement of an array of colourful sarongs and scarves on the floor, walls, and ceiling. The lighting was subdued and provided by fake candles, clearly for insurance purposes – those scarves looked awfully flammable. There was a strong aroma of incense from a can. The only furniture in the room was a small round table, also draped in a scarf, and two camping stools.

On one of the stools sat Mystic Shazam, who was draped in yet more scarves and sarongs. She wore a large number of cheap rings and a pair of silver dangly earrings. Her jewellery appeared to be not so much family heirlooms, but more last-minute acquisitions from Clare's Accessories. Attempting a mysterious voice, she asked, 'Who wants to go first?'

'She does.' Hannah gave Lottie a gentle shove in the small of her back.

Lottie paid the £2 fee and sat on the other stool, opposite Mystic Shazam, placing her hands, palms upward, on the table as instructed.

Mystic Shazam took hold of her hands and studied them intently, turning them this way and that. 'Ahh yes, I see a lot of happiness here. A young girl canters on a pony, through the meadow. That same child is blowing out candles and opening a pile of presents. Oh, hang on, first, a mother awaits a baby. She waits so long. She almost gives up hope. But here she is, here's the daughter she longed for. Such happiness and smiles. There is sunshine and joy.'

'Lovely,' Lottie said.

'But, no, the sunshine has gone, and clouds are forming. I see great sadness. A stream. There is sadness surrounding a stream and there is loss.'

'Not so lovely!'

'But, my dear,' Mystic Shazam squeezed Lottie's hands, 'you are beautiful, and you look well. You have a great life ahead of you.'

Hannah knew her face must be a picture. Her mouth hung open, and for a rare moment she was totally lost for words. Eventually she asked, 'How could you know? The stream? The pony?'

Lottie laughed. 'Thanks, Sharon. It's good to see you again.'

Mystic Shazam reached forward, giving Lottie a hug. 'You too, Charlotte. And you truly do look well. I'm sorry to mention the stream – I was just … you know, trying to be mysterious.'

'Explain, please?' Hannah demanded.

'This is Sharon from the village. She used to be the cleaner at my primary school. She's known me since …'

'Since your mother patiently waited for you.'

'Of course, yes. Since before I was born. Do my friend now, Sharon?'

'Okay. Swap over.'

Begrudgingly, Hannah settled onto the stool. 'This one will be a bit harder for you, Mystic. Seeing as you don't know me from a box of rotten eggs. Let's go!'

Mystic Shazam took hold of her hands and studied them. Hannah gave a cynical snort.

'I see lots of women around you.'

'Now that is good news, isn't it?' Lottie smiled.

'Shush, don't help her.'

'Woman like you, I see that. No men,' Mystic Shazam continued.

'Yes, I do look very gay.' Hannah rolled her eyes.

'Except … Wait, there is one man in your life. He really cares about you. He's so funny, isn't he?'

'Debatable!'

'He's a sceptic. Like you. He would find this whole thing ridiculous.'

'Yes. Right. All the points go to you, Sharon, for earwigging our earlier conversation about my dad. Anything else?'

'There's one particular woman. She has long dark hair. So dark.'

Lottie's head snapped around. 'What?'

'Black hair, I'd say.'

'Sharon, what d'you mean? Why did you say that?' Lottie seemed concerned.

'She likes you. She likes you a lot.'

Hannah grinned. 'Oh good. Well, that was worth the two quid.'

———

They left the tent and Hannah immediately began searching for Eliza. 'Now I definitely need a coffee.'

'Hang on. Stop a minute, Han. Aren't you curious?'

'About what?'

'What she meant. Who she was referring to.'

'No.'

'Do you think she knows about Ash?'

'Lottie, you told me yourself, not five minutes ago, that Mystic Shazam is Sharon from the village. She's about as mystic as a glass of water. Why would you even think she knows I'm investigating Ash?'

'Long dark hair. Black hair, she said.'

'Yes. Mandy.'

'Mandy? Your mystery lady. She has long black hair?'

'Yes.'

'You've seen her again?'

'Umm ... we've exchanged a couple of messages and ... I met up with her for lunch earlier. That's why I was late. Sorry.'

'You cheeky cow. Why didn't you tell me?'

'I don't know why I didn't tell you about the text messages. I guess I just didn't want to jinx it.'

'And ... what about the fact you met her today? Why say you were working?'

'*You* asked *me* if I was working. It was easier to just say yes. Besides, she asked me not to tell anyone that we'd met up.'

'Why?'

'She doesn't want anyone to know that we're seeing each other.'

'Doesn't she want to meet me?'

'It would seem not. Not yet at least. Look, Lottie, it's early days. I like her, she likes me. You'll meet her when she's ready. Okay?'

'I let you meet Chen.'

'You let me interrogate him! That's not what I want for Mandy.'

'All right.' Lottie nodded, but it was clear she was unhappy. 'But that still doesn't explain how Sharon knew about her. Maybe she is mystic.'

'And maybe,' Hannah flicked her shoulder, 'she's just more observant than you are.' Dislodging a long dark hair, she watched it blow away in the wind. 'Mandy has the kind of hair that gets everywhere!'

Eliza joined them, bearing gifts of tepid, instant coffee and custard tarts. 'Sorry, Hannah, I suspect it's not your usual blend.'

Hannah sniffed the contents of the takeaway cup. 'Bloody

hell, judging by the length of the queue I thought I was going to get a lovely latte.'

Eliza shrugged apologetically. 'They didn't do green tea either.'

Hannah took a sip and Eliza asked, 'Is it awful?'

'It tastes like the salty tears of an old fisherman.'

'Oh God!' Eliza laughed.

'Thanks for queueing up, though.'

Lottie took her share of the picnic, saying, 'You missed your turn with the fortune teller.'

'Was she any good?'

Lottie and Hannah exchanged a look.

'No. She was crap!' Hannah replied. 'But I wasn't really expecting much, to be honest.'

'Oh well, no harm done.'

'Where shall we go to eat this delicious offering?' Hannah asked.

'All the picnic tables were taken. I couldn't see anywhere else to sit,' Eliza answered.

'We could go to the fire circle. I'll bet no one else has gone over that way,' Lottie suggested.

'Sounds intriguing.' Eliza said.

'Are you sure?' asked Hannah. 'If you've got any doubts, we can just stand here and drink this; you don't have to go anywhere you're uncomfortable with.'

Lottie smiled. 'Thank you, Han. You're good to me. But I'll be okay. Follow me.' She strode off across the meadow as if she still owned the place.

Lottie was right. No one else had found the fire circle. The grass had been allowed to grow around it, and due to the dip in the meadow it wasn't visible from the house. They sat themselves down on what turned out to be soggy logs, and ate their custard tarts in silence.

After a couple of minutes, Eliza declared, 'Well, this is, in fact, an enjoyable treat. You were right about the coffee, Hannah. One hundred percent salty tears. But who knew an egg custard could taste so good?'

'I'm guessing they were made by one of my mum's friends, Doreen from the WI. She was always good at baking,' Lottie agreed. 'Especially pastry.'

Eliza stalled a second before tentatively saying, 'I'm sorry to hear about your parents, Lottie. Hannah told me they've both passed away. I hope I didn't say anything to upset you before I knew.'

'Of course not. You weren't to know they'd both died since we left school.'

'Good. I've been worried. After we lost Ash, people made stupid comments all the time that upset me. I always felt like people were gossiping.'

Hannah blushed. Wasn't that exactly what she and Lottie had done the first time they'd seen Eliza and Scott in the café? She thought it best to steer them away from the subject, just in case Eliza remembered. 'It's difficult to drop news like that into the conversation.' Turning to Eliza, Hannah reassured her, 'You didn't upset Lottie, I promise you. I think she just trusts you enough now to want to share it with you.'

'How do you feel about being back here, Lottie?' Eliza asked.

'Not too bad. It's kind of nice that all these people are in my garden.'

'I'll bet you loved seeing all the visitors here when you were a child, didn't you?'

Lottie looked towards Hannah. 'Shall I tell her, or will you?'

Hannah laughed. 'Lottie was a spoilt little princess back then. I have no doubt whatsoever that she hated sharing her meadow with the hoi polloi, and that would've included you and me.'

'Wow.' Eliza shook her head with surprise.

'Yep. She was horrible.' Hannah laughed even louder. 'But we love her now.' She shuffled along the soggy log towards her friend.

'All true!' Lottie smiled. 'I was embarrassed about what a cow I used to be, but Hannah and my counsellor have taught me to let it go.'

'Like I said to Hannah, you two are brilliant. There's something special about you guys,' Eliza smiled.

'Thank you,' Lottie replied. 'Hannah and her family are the best thing to ever happen to me, and I am not exaggerating when I say that.'

Tepid drinks poured away, and tarts consumed, the trio collected up their rubbish and walked back towards the fete.

Hannah noticed Lottie staring over at the house. 'Let it go,' she whispered.

'I have.'

Hannah's phone vibrated in her back pocket. Pulling it out to take a peek, she was delighted to see a message from Mandy.

'Why are you grinning like a Cheshire cat?' Lottie asked.

'Mandy's free this evening. She wants to meet up again.'

'*Again?*' Eliza asked.

'Yes, this sneaky woman has been exchanging texts, and they met for lunch today,' Lottie replied, prodding Hannah.

Ignoring the silly faces the other two were pulling, Hannah asked, 'Would you mind if I got you to drop me off at ours on the way back?'

'Can't you just invite her to Eliza's to meet us?' Lottie pouted.

'Now then, watch it. That spoilt princess is creeping back,' Hannah said. 'I told you she doesn't want to meet any of my friends yet.'

'But why?'

'I don't know. Let's be honest, she's only met *me* a couple of times! She says she doesn't go out much. I get the impression she doesn't like being in a crowd.'

Rolling her eyes, Lottie said, 'We're hardly a crowd.'

'Maybe she's shy. Anyway, it doesn't matter. I'm happy to keep her all to myself for now.' Hannah smiled to herself, then asked, 'Will you be okay to stay with Eliza tonight?'

'I guess so.' Lottie shrugged.

They'd reached the side gate. Rubbish in hand, Eliza went on the hunt for a bin.

'Anything else you want to see before we go?' Hannah asked Lottie.

'I think I've seen enough,' Lottie replied in a slightly sullen voice. 'Anyway, they're starting to pack up now, and you need to get going.'

'Please, Lottie, don't make me feel bad. I really like Mandy. We just want to get to know each other, that's all. She's not my usual type. This feels more ... grown up.'

'Let's just leave it. You go and be with Mandy and I'll keep Eliza company.'

Having found a bin, Eliza re-joined them.

Hannah told her, 'Listen, I won't meet Mandy if you're at all worried.'

Eliza considered the offer. 'I don't mind. If Lottie's there I won't feel alone. Can we call you though, I mean, if anything happens?'

'Of course. Listen, your safety is my priority. You're still my client. If either of you are worried about anything, you call me, and I'll come running. Okay?'

Eliza nodded. 'That's fair enough, don't you think, Lottie? Everyone gets a night off sometime.'

'I guess so.' Lottie gave another shrug.

'Great. Drop me at our place. I should have plenty of time for a shower before she arrives.'

'You gave her our address?' Lottie asked.

'Yes. She's only coming over for a drink. You don't mind, do you?'

'Whatever. It's your home too.' Lottie shrugged a third time.

'Mind you don't knock your head off doing that.' Hannah laughed. 'Oh, yes, and no hanging about round the corner to take a peep at her. I know all the tricks, remember.'

27

ELIZA – 2022

Two things happened simultaneously as Eliza and Lottie entered the house – Eliza's phone pinged to announce a text message and Lottie noticed that the back door was not shut. Running to the kitchen to say hello to her dog, she realised that the door was banging on its hinges, and let out a scream. Dixie's basket was empty.

Reading the text, Eliza groaned.

'She's not in the kitchen. Help me search, please!' Lottie called. 'I'll look in the garden. Can you check upstairs?'

Eliza arrived in the kitchen and shook her head.

'Why not?'

'There's no point. Someone's taken her.'

All the blood drained from Lottie's face. 'What d'you mean?'

Eliza read from her phone – *It's Ash. I have your dog. I need £25K or you won't get it back.*

'*No!*'

Eliza felt awful. This was all her fault. 'I'm so sorry.'

'What if she's hurt Dixie?'

'She wouldn't. I'm sure of it.'

'I hope you're right.'

Eliza offered, 'I'll pay. I'll get Dixie back for you.'

'The money doesn't matter. I'll pay. I just don't want her to be hurt. Please, text her back, tell her we'll pay. Just tell her to take care of Dixie.'

Eliza grabbed her phone and sent a reply to the effect that she would pay as soon as possible and asking how to get the money to Ash. Instantly a text came through with directions to a clothes recycling bin. She was told to put cash in a carrier bag and place it next to the bin. Then she was to walk away and not look back. The text also said that if she called the police, the dog would be killed.

'I'm going to be sick.' Lottie paced the floor, her hand clasped over her mouth.

'She would never kill a dog. She wasn't like that.'

'What if it's not her, though? It could be anyone. It could be someone who hates dogs.'

'We need to tell Hannah,' Eliza said.

'Yes, of course. But …'

'What?'

'She's got Mandy coming round.'

'Oh, forget that. She said we could interrupt if we needed her, and I'd say we need her now, wouldn't you?'

'I hope she won't mind.'

'Lottie, she loves Dixie, and she loves *you*. She *will not* mind.'

'Okay, *I'll* call her.' Lottie dialled and put her phone on speakerphone so Eliza could listen in. Hannah answered in three rings. After a brief explanation, she agreed to come straight over. 'Are you sure? What about Mandy?' Lottie asked.

'Don't be silly. I'm coming now. She's not even here yet. I'll call her on the way and tell her I have to cancel. Keep calm and tell Eliza not to reply to the text until I get there, okay?'

'Oh!'

'For God's sake. Has she already replied?'

'We just wrote that we'd pay, but please don't hurt her.'

'Lottie, why did you do that?'

'Because I *will* pay!'

Leaning towards Lottie's phone, Eliza shouted, 'Hannah, it's me, Eliza, I'm going to pay. I got us into this.'

'Honestly, she's my dog. I'll pay.' Lottie moved the phone away from Eliza.

Hannah shouted at the pair of them, 'Will you two moneybags stop arguing over who's going to cough up twenty-five grand? Neither of you needs to pay. Just wait until I get there.'

Lottie hung up and burst into tears. 'My poor baby.'

Again, Eliza tried to apologise. 'I should never have asked you to come and stay here.' She could see that Lottie was not only upset but also angry. Lottie had already been through so much; this was the last thing she needed.

With nothing to do but worry, the pair paced the floor until Hannah arrived, some ten minutes later. Bursting into the kitchen, she asked to see the text. After she'd read it, she asked, 'Is this the sort of thing Ash would do, threaten to kill a pet?'

'No. Never! She wasn't like that.'

'Right. So it's not her. It's someone trying to exploit you for money. It's the same person who tried to convince you that Ash was meddling in your fridge and leaving you CDs. We'll see how this bastard likes it when the police hear about this.'

'No. She says it in the text – we're not to involve them. She said she'd kill the dog,' Eliza cried.

'I can't make you call them. But I think it's your best bet. I don't think kidnap cases work out well when the police aren't involved.'

'Oh no!' Lottie sobbed.

'Well, think about it,' Hannah said. 'What's to say they'll even bring Dixie back once they've got the money?'

Lottie replied, 'Surely it's worth a shot. I can't bear the thought they might hurt her.'

'If you really don't want to involve the police, I'll follow you to this clothes bin and try and nab them myself.'

'That sounds like a better idea. You can do it, Hannah; I know you can.' Lottie's face was wet with tears.

Eliza reached for her phone, ready to text that she would collect the cash from the bank the minute they opened in the morning. As she picked up the phone, it began to ring. She automatically looked to Hannah for advice.

'Who is it?' Hannah asked.

'Scott.'

'Do you want him to know about this?'

'*Of course*. He's my cousin.'

'Okay. So answer it then. Tell him.'

Eliza answered. 'Scott, the most awful thing has happened.'

Hannah and Lottie stood helplessly in the kitchen listening to Eliza explain the situation.

'Someone's taken Lottie's little dog and they're asking for a ransom. They said they're Ash, but she wouldn't do that, would she?'

'But how did they get in?'

'I don't know. The back door was open again.'

'I thought you were being more careful.'

'I *was*. I'm sure I've been locking it since that night.'

'What did they ask for?'

'Twenty-five thousand.'

Scott whistled. 'Have you got that?'

'Yes. I'm sorting it.'

'Really?'

'Yes. If my bank is going to take too long, Lottie will get it. Listen, the money isn't the problem. It's what they might do …' Eliza dropped her voice to a whisper, 'to the dog. They said they'd kill her if we didn't pay.'

'*Fucking hell!*'

'I know. It's all my fault.'

'I'm coming round,' Scott said.

'Okay. If you want to. But I don't think there's much you can do here.'

'It'll be all right, Elz. I'm sure it will.'

'They said no police. But Hannah thinks we should tell them. What d'you think?'

She heard Scott gulp. 'You know what I think of the police. Surely there's a better way?'

'Hannah says she'll help me, but …' Eliza paused. 'She said there's not always a good outcome if the police aren't involved. So maybe I should just …'

'Hold on. I told you, I'm coming round. Don't do anything hasty. Wait for me, okay?'

'I will. But I've got Hannah and Lottie here. I'm not alone.'

'They don't know you like I do, Elz. They're not family. Just wait for me. I'll be half an hour tops.'

'Okay. Scott …'

'Uh huh?'

'I love you.'

'Love you too.' Scott hung up.

Lottie asked, 'What does *he* think he can do that Hannah can't?'

Eliza sensed anger and desperation in her voice. 'Nothing. Honestly. He's just coming to support us.'

'Every second we wait for him to come round is a second that bitch could be hurting my dog!'

Putting her arms around Lottie, Hannah whispered, 'Try to calm down. I know you're angry. But it's not Eliza's fault.' To Eliza, she said, 'Having said that – if your bloody cousin isn't here in half an hour, he can get stuffed.'

Realising that her anxiety was not a priority right now, Eliza said nothing.

Almost exactly half an hour from hanging up on the call, Scott appeared on the doorstep. In his arms he held Dixie.

Throwing herself at him and snatching up her dog, Lottie shouted, *'Dixie! Thank God.'* She turned the dog around and around in her arms, asking, 'Did they hurt you, darling?'

Eliza was confused. 'What the hell, Scott?'

He replied, 'I found her outside. Just strolling down the street on her own.'

Hannah gave him a sideways glance. 'How did you know she was Lottie's dog?'

'Eliza told me she was a spaniel. I know my dog breeds.'

'Did she?' Hannah turned to Eliza. 'Did you?'

'I don't know. I can't remember. Anyway, what does it matter? She's back. Thank you so much, Scott.'

Lottie was holding onto her dog so tightly Eliza feared that Dixie's eyes might pop out. She said, 'Lottie, let her go a bit.'

'Oh yes, sorry, sweetie. I'm just so pleased to see you.'

'Well, that's saved you a few grand, hey cuz?' Scott said.

Lottie immediately turned on him. 'It wasn't about the money, you absolute cockwomble. Ash was threatening to kill her.'

Ignoring the insult, Scott asked Eliza, 'Do you think it really was Ash?'

'No. Ash was no angel, but she wouldn't kill someone's pet. This had to be someone else. Someone twisted in the head.'

'The main thing is, she's safe. And now we need to get her the hell out of here!' Lottie said.

'Shall we take her over to my mum and dad's?' Hannah asked. 'I'm sure they'll be happy to have her. Just until all this is resolved.'

Lottie agreed. 'Absolutely. The sooner the better.' She headed towards the door.

'Wait,' Scott said. 'What d'you mean by *resolved*?'

'Someone's playing Eliza for a fool. They're messing her about and I'm going to find out who they are,' Hannah replied.

'But it's sorted. I found the dog. You're taking it to your place. Forget it.'

'No. It's far from sorted. Maybe they got nervous and let the dog go. Maybe they changed their minds about this, but there will be something else and we need to stop it,' Hannah insisted.

Eliza had to agree. 'She's right. This is never going to end by itself, Scott. Either it's Ash and we need to know that, or it's someone else and they have to be turned over to the police.'

'It will end. I'll make it end. You don't need these people, Elz. It's always been just us. Ever since …'

'I do need them, Scottie. This is driving me crazy.'

'Fine! I've never been enough for you, have I?' Turning to Lottie, Scott spat the words, 'You're fucking welcome!' With that, he stormed out, slamming the kitchen door behind him.

All three watched him leave the room.

Hannah mumbled under her breath, 'She was just strolling down the street on her own, was she, *Scottie*?' To Eliza, she said, 'Will you be okay if I just go with Lottie to my mum and dad's?'

'Yes. I'll be fine. Scott will stay with me.'

'Great!' Lottie said, sarcastically.

'I know you don't think much of him, but he's family.' Eliza felt the need to defend her cousin.

'She won't be alone. That's the main thing,' Hannah said to Lottie. 'Anyway, my mum replied to my text – she says yes, of course we must bring Dixie over. Plus, my gran is at their house tonight. She came for dinner, so we'll get to see her as well.'

'Granny Annie. Oh brilliant.' Lottie gave a watery smile, the first since they'd got back from the fete.

'I know,' Hannah agreed. 'I only managed a flying visit with her the other day.'

'Granny Annie is proper family!' Lottie glared at Eliza.

'So is Scott!'

'Oh yeah, bloody marvellous. We've seen what your family are like. Taking my beautiful dog and threatening to kill her!'

Hannah took control. 'Stop it! We don't know who took Dixie. We have no idea if it was Eliza's family. She's genuinely sorry. Can't you see that? I know you're upset, Lottie, but please, we need to stick together. We need to support Eliza too.'

'*You* can. She's *your* client. I don't have to.' Lottie's face grew red.

'Lottie! This isn't you.'

'You care more about her than you do about me. You care more about Mandy too.' It seemed Lottie could hold it in no longer. With a loud wail she cried, 'I'm so sorry. I don't mean to be horrible. It's just … Dixie … she's my baby. She's been with me for so long. I thought someone was going to … I thought …'

Eliza rushed at Lottie, taking her into her arms. 'You have every right to be upset. I'm the one who should be sorry.'

With a shrug, Hannah said, 'Oh sod it, I'm in too.' Wrapping her arms around them both, she reassured Lottie, 'And don't be daft. You know how much I care about you. Don't you go worrying about Eliza or Mandy or anyone else. I will *always* put you first.'

'I know. I know. I'm so lucky,' Lottie blubbed. 'It's just the shock.'

'Of course it is. It's been horrible. Come on, beautiful. Let's get Dixie over to Mum and Dad's.'

After they'd gone, Eliza popped the kettle on. In need of tea to calm her shattered nerves, she decided that perhaps camomile might do the trick. Opening up the pantry she searched the now mostly tidy shelves for the herbal tea bags. Damn, no camomile;

she could've sworn she had some left. Rummaging around in search of something calming, she spotted an old biscuit tin. It was towards the back of one of the shelves she hadn't got around to sorting yet. It was rather rusty, and she sincerely hoped it didn't contain actual biscuits. How soft would they be by now? Perhaps it was a sewing kit, or something like that. Eliza prized off the lid.

The contents were instantly recognisable. A few of Ash's missing posters folded neatly into four. She unfolded one. Ash's face stared back at her. Just how she had looked that last night. Auntie Miriam must've wanted to keep a few but couldn't bear to look at them. How many had they printed off? Fifty? A hundred? Something like that. They'd stuck them to telegraph poles, billboards, and buildings. Tired of sitting and waiting, Auntie Miriam had insisted that someone must know where her daughter was. By then it'd been two weeks since the night Ash had left them.

ELIZA – 2010

Sticking a drawing pin into the tree, Eliza moved onto the next one. She wondered what would happen if the pin worked itself loose and fell on the ground. What if a fox or a bird ate it? No. She couldn't risk it. Retracing her steps, she swapped the pin for a piece of Sellotape. The posters wouldn't stick well, and the first sign of rain would ruin them, but she simply had to try.

Having stuck about fifteen to various trees in Lullaby Woods, Eliza headed over to Auntie Miriam's to see if there was anything else she could do. On the bus ride over, she wondered if anyone had seen the posters yet. Her auntie had insisted on putting her own phone number on the poster, despite the police warning her that it was better to say *please contact local police if you have any information.*

When they'd been planning what wording to have printed, Eliza had said that she was worried her auntie would be called by all the children in Kingshurst, having a joke. But Auntie Miriam had simply said, 'When you have children of your own, Eliza, you'll understand my desperation. What does it matter if someone calls me and says something stupid or rude to me down the telephone?'

'I don't want them to do that to you, though.'

'I couldn't care less if ninety-nine people call me and do this, what is it you call it, prank calling. As long as the hundredth person tells me where my child is.' At this point, Auntie Miriam had dissolved into tears and Eliza had decided not to mention the telephone number again.

———

Now at Auntie Miriam's, Eliza made her aunt a tea and insisted she take it sweet.

'I'm really not keen on sugar in my tea, love. I never had it when Robert was alive. I liked to look good for him. I don't see the point in switching now.'

'It's for the shock.'

'I'm not still in shock.'

'Eliza pushed the mug towards her auntie, maintaining, 'I think you are. It's just not getting any easier, is it? We all thought she'd be back within a few days. Now it's been more than two weeks. How long do we have to keep imagining the worst?'

Auntie Miriam took the mug. Sipping at the hot, sweet liquid, she said, 'I don't know. It's like torture. Every time I think that it's been, as you say, over a fortnight since I last saw her, I think – how can that be? How am I just going on living when I don't know where my daughter is?'

'There's no other option, Auntie Miriam. She'll come back. I know she will. Even Ash wouldn't want—'

'But what if she *can't* come back? She could be lying dead somewhere, and no one is telling us, or worse, she could be ...' Placing her mug on the kitchen table, Auntie Miriam pulled a tissue out of her cardigan sleeve. After blowing her nose, she said, 'I can't bear it, Eliza. I honestly just cannot bear thinking about all the things that could be happening to her.'

'This can't go on forever. I promise you; she'll be back.'

'How can you know that? What makes you so sure?' Auntie Miriam looked a little suspicious.

'Because ... because ...'

'What!'

'Because Ash has gone missing before and she's always come back. She must know this is killing you.'

'She's never been gone anything like this long before. One night. Two at most. Then she'd come back. She'd march through that front door and slam it shut. She'd shout – I'm back, but I don't want to talk to you. And I'd be angry. Of course, incredibly angry. But at least I knew she was safe. This time, there's no such reassurance.'

'Scott says that maybe—'

'I have no desire to know what that boy says. Unless he's actually going to tell me the truth. Which I very much doubt. He is his father's son. There's no hope for him.'

'Honestly, he thinks she'll be back soon too. We speak about her all the time.'

Picking up her mug, Auntie Miriam deposited its contents down the sink. 'Sorry, I can't drink that.'

'It's okay. I just wanted to help.'

'You've been a great help, so have your parents. You got those posters made for me and you've all put them up. I'm sure they're going to be the key.'

Before she realised what she was saying, Eliza had already opened her mouth to speak, 'I put some more up today, in the ...' Realising her error, she chose to stop there. Damn it, she'd just been so keen to tell her auntie that she was trying.

'In the?'

'The woods.'

'The woods?'

'Yes. Lullaby Woods.'

'Why?'

'Hmm …' Eliza thought for a second. 'Well, lots of people walk their dogs in Lullaby Woods. Someone might know something.'

'I suppose so. But … it's hardly local.'

'It's not that far.'

'Remember Robert, the witchy woods?' Auntie Miriam smiled.

'How could I forget? It was terrifying … but brilliant.' Eliza smiled too.

Auntie Miriam filled the kettle. 'I'm going to have a tea without sugar; fancy one?'

'I've got some green tea. Hang on.' Eliza began rummaging around in her bag.

'*Green!* Whatever next?'

'It's good for you,' Eliza smiled. 'Antioxidants. Want to try it?'

'No, thank you. I'll stick to PG Tips. I do find those monkeys amusing.'

'I think they've decided it's cruel to use them in the ads.' Eliza said.

Auntie Miriam tutted. 'Nonsense, they looked like they were having fun.'

Changing the subject, Eliza said, 'All we need is one person to read a poster and remember seeing Ash. It'll happen. I'm sure.' She gave her auntie a hug.

'Thank you.' Auntie Miriam moved away as the kettle boiled. 'What would Robert say? If he knew that Ashley was missing. Dear God, it would kill him all over again.'

'He would be so worried.'

'And that's another thing. I really thought she'd be back for the anniversary.'

Eliza shrugged. 'Ash will be back. I know it.' She tried to sound convincing, but she wasn't even sure if she believed it herself anymore.

28
HANNAH – 2022

HANNAH COULDN'T BEAR to think of anyone hurting Dixie. Lottie would possibly never have forgiven her. She'd been reminded of an important point – she must never underestimate a situation. All this time she'd believed that this person was low level danger. She thought of them as Ash for ease, although she struggled to believe that Ash was really behind it all. Whoever they were, they'd been messing with Eliza's mind, they'd been winding her up, but Hannah had stupidly thought they would never cross a line. Now they had. Today they'd crossed way over that line, and Hannah Sandlin PI was fuming.

Delivering Dixie safely into Jacqui's arms, Lottie asked, 'Want a cuddle?'

Jacqui's answer was to snatch up the little dog. 'Hello, darling.' She kissed Dixie on the nose.

Ken appeared in the hallway. Putting on his shoes, he said, 'I'm glad to hear you got Dixie back. What a palaver. You both okay?'

Hannah and Lottie nodded.

'Well then, I can't stop – the dartboard at the legion is calling my name. Can you hear it?' He cupped his hand to his ear.

'Yes, Dad. We can,' Hannah replied.

'You don't mind me leaving?' Ken asked. 'I'll stay if you need me.'

'Absolutely not. We're all fine,' Lottie assured him.

Passing behind them in the hallway, Ken poked Hannah in the ribs. 'We had omelettes for tea. You know what they say about omelettes, don't you?'

'What do they say?' Hannah asked, already preparing herself for a lame joke.

'You can't make a duck egg omelette without quacking some eggs,' Ken replied.

'Get out of here, you fool.' She batted him on the backside.

Rolling her eyes at her husband, Jacqui said to the girls, 'Gran's in the lounge. She can't wait to meet this little one.'

'Thanks, Mum, we'll take her in as soon as this comedian gets out of our way,' Hannah replied, giving her dad a playful shove down the hallway.

As the door closed behind a whistling Ken, Jacqui asked, 'Are you really okay?' This question was directed towards Lottie. Hannah didn't mind; Dixie was *her* dog, and she was clearly the most shaken by the day's events.

'I'm just so relieved. When I think …'

'Best not to dwell on it.' Jacqui put her arm around Lottie. 'Just be glad they decided to let her go. Although setting her down in the street on her own is a ridiculously dangerous thing to do.'

'Hmm … that's if you believe the version of events as told by that waste of space known as Scott.' Hannah shook her head.

They walked into the lounge where Granny Annie was watching TV.

'Hi, Gran. Twice in one week – what a treat,' Hannah exclaimed.

Looking up from the TV, Granny Annie caught sight of the dog. Her face instantly broke into a grin. 'Winston!'

'No, Gran, this is Dixie.'

Jacqui tried to explain. 'You remember, I told you, Mum. She's Lottie's little spaniel. She's going to be staying back here for a while.'

Granny Annie reached out, her arthritic hands attempting a grabbing motion. At the same time, she tried to rise from her chair.

'Sit down. I'll bring her to you.' Jacqui placed Dixie on her mum's lap and flicked off the TV.

Granny Annie buried her face into the dog's fur. 'My beautiful boy.'

Lottie and Hannah exchanged a glance. They both knew Granny Annie was becoming confused. Recently she'd shown signs of the usual forgetfulness of old age, but this seemed more than that. Whoever Granny Annie thought Dixie was was incredibly real to her.

Hannah sat down next to her gran and rested her hand on her arm. 'You know this is Dixie, don't you? This is Lottie's dog. You know Lottie, yes?'

Granny Annie removed her face from the warm burrow of Dixie's fur. 'I thought ... oh, of course. It couldn't be ... How silly.'

Jacqui said, 'My dad was allergic to pets, so we never had one when I was growing up. But I know Mum had a dog when she was a child. I think that's who Winston was. Right, Mum?'

'Yes. An awfully long time ago,' Granny Annie said.

Hannah asked, 'Tell us more about him, Gran?'

'It wasn't fair.' Granny Annie returned her face to Dixie's soft fur for a second, before saying, 'I was eleven. It was winter, 1949.' She settled down into her chair and the rest of them got comfy. 'I remember being excited about Christmas coming and that it would soon be a new decade.'

'The fifties. It sounds so long ago,' Jacqui mused.

'Yes, it was.' Granny Annie resumed her story. 'Anyway, amid all that excitement, my parents made a decision, and no matter how much they explained it, sending Winston to live in another house made no sense.'

'They sent him away!' Lottie exclaimed.

'Yes. I tried arguing. I said he was our dog. We'd had him since he was a tiny puppy. But my mum said he couldn't be around children anymore. I told her Winston could be around *me*. I'd take care of him.'

'What did she say?' Lottie's chin quivered.

'Just that we couldn't keep talking about it. Mr and Mrs Farmer had agreed to take him. He'd be okay there. He wouldn't ... you know.' Granny Annie clamped her false teeth together noisily.

'Bite anyone?' Hannah guessed.

'Exactly. I told my mum that he wouldn't bite anyone at our house. Not *again*. I wouldn't let him. I'd stay by his side the whole time.'

Lottie shrugged. 'No good?'

'No. She just said – we've already talked about it, Anne-Margaret. I knew my goose was cooked when my mum used my full name. It meant she was at the end of her tether.'

'But ... who had he bitten?' Hannah asked.

'My little brother, Frankie. My mum just kept saying we cannot keep a dog that bites children. Mr and Mrs Farmer were in their sixties. They didn't have any children. Mrs Farmer had an aged mother who lived with them, but she was always in bed with her chest.'

Hannah smiled gently to herself. 'As opposed to what? In bed without it?'

Granny Annie continued. 'My mum tried to remind me what the other option was …'

'Oh no!' Lottie was distraught. Her eyes, like Granny Annie's, were full of unshed tears.

'Exactly. I put my hands over my ears, and I shouted – I do not want to talk about that!'

'So what happened next?' Lottie asked in a whisper.

'Frankie appeared at the top of the stairs, nursing his bandaged arm, and asked what all the shouting was about. I told him – it's you, all the shouting is about you! He asked me why. Of course my mum tried to reassure him. She said – it's not about you, Frankie, darling. Go back to bed. Keep your arm rested.'

'I suppose it must've been awful for her to see her little boy bitten,' Hannah wondered aloud.

'But it was his own fault. He was forever messing poor Winston about.' Granny Annie said.

'Oh, I see.' Hannah nodded.

'Frankie held his bandage high in the air and said that Winston could've killed him. I told him not to be ridiculous. Winston was a loving dog.'

'But nothing worked with your mum?' Lottie asked.

'No. How could poor Winston compete with little Frankie? I hated to admit it, but Frankie was cute. He was a rotter, but he had the cutest face. He could give a little gappy smile and deny all knowledge of how the vase got broken, or how the biscuits had been eaten. He just had one of those faces. Winston had done nothing wrong, at least not in my eyes. But my mum would never trust him again. If the choice really was to either send him away to live with the Farmers or to put him to sleep, then essentially there was *no* choice.'

Hannah knew Lottie wanted to grab her dog off Granny Annie's lap, but she was clearly containing herself. Hannah was grateful to her for allowing Dixie to remain where she was. To her gran, she asked, 'So, you had to let him go?'

'Yes. I remember, I looked up those stairs at my little brother, and I shouted – I'll never forgive you for this, Frankie. He just stuck out his tongue and went back to his room. After that day, I never saw Winston again.'

Lottie jumped up and gave Granny Annie a hug. 'I'm so sorry. How awful for you.'

'But you did forgive your brother, didn't you?' Jacqui asked.

'Oh yes, I forgave him. He was hard to be mad at, to be honest. But he never did calm down.'

'He died young, didn't he?' Jacqui said.

'Yes, he did. We used to call him our James Dean. He lived fast; he lived for the thrill of life itself.'

'Do you mind me asking how he died?' Lottie asked.

Jacqui replied, 'A motorbike accident, wasn't it, Mum?'

'Yes. Took a corner too fast. Silly boy.' Granny Annie wiped her face with the back of her hand; the tears that had been threatening to fall were now making their way down her papery cheeks. 'I miss him too, him and Winston.'

'Do you have any photographs of Winston, Gran?'

Granny Annie shook her head. 'No, not even one. Come to think of it, I hardly have any of Frank either. We just didn't take them back then.' She shrugged. 'People take more photographs of their food these days than we did of our nearest and dearest'

'It sounds like Frankie was very young when he teased the dog. Personally, I think the adults should've stepped in sooner. You can't really blame a child that young, can you?' Lottie said.

'Well, that's arguable. Anyone knows – if you tease something every day of its life, sooner or later it will turn on you.' Granny Annie rummaged in her handbag for a tissue.

There was a moment of silence as they all reflected on the fates of poor Winston and Frankie. Suddenly Hannah gave a shriek. 'Oh my God. I need to go.'

'Why?' Lottie looked concerned.

'Damn. I wish I could blue light it.'

'What's the rush?' Jacqui asked.

'I need to get back to Eliza's house.'

'Why?' Jacqui seemed worried about her daughter's sudden departure.

'If I'm right, she's in danger.' Hannah got up, hastily kissing her mum and gran on the cheek. 'Lottie, you'd better stay here.'

'What are you on about? Eliza's okay. She's not on her own.'

'That's the problem.'

'What d'you mean?'

'Because, Lottie, I think I know what happened to Ash!'

29
ELIZA – 2022

Eliza paced the kitchen, her gaze repeatedly returning to the space on the old, tiled floor where Dixie's basket had been. She couldn't believe that a couple of hours ago she'd been at Mulberry House, eating custard tarts and laughing at Hannah's description of the coffee. What a dreadful turn of events.

Scott was still stomping about in the lounge. She could hear him flicking through the channels on the TV. He didn't stay on any one programme for more than a few seconds. She could tell he wasn't really watching anything, just trying to calm his anger. He had not liked the accusing way Hannah and Lottie had treated him. He was always so keen to stress that he and Eliza were family and that should be all that mattered. Should she try to put things straight between them?

Before Eliza could decide whether to approach him or leave him to cool off, her phone began ringing. Checking to see if it was Hannah, she was annoyed when Ryan's name appeared on the screen.

'Ryan, what do you want?'
'Well, hello to you too!'

'Listen, it's all turning to rat shit here, to be honest. So, if you've called for more money—'

'Far from it.'

'Pardon?'

'I'm calling with good news. But, first, what do you mean – it's all turning to rat shit?'

Eliza decided not to elaborate. 'Oh, nothing. Just ... you know, not a great day for me.'

'I'm sorry. Can I do anything to help?'

A thought flitted across her mind that yes, he could, he could leave his bitch of a wife and come back to her, he could make love to her, and they could discover she was pregnant and miraculously she could carry the baby to full term. But she didn't say that, because there was Otto now, and besides, she could never trust him to love her completely and solely ever again. So, instead, she just replied, 'No. It's fine. I'll sort it. Tell me your news?'

'I've got a new job.' There was pride in his voice.

'Already?'

'Yep. Not only that but it's a step up. I'm going to be overseeing the whole quality department at Frazer Halmer's Electrical. I'll be on way more money than before, Elz.'

'That's brilliant. Your eye for detail and dedication is paying off. I'm pleased for you.'

'Thank you. Also, Frazer Halmer is much larger than WB, so hopefully less chance of getting made redundant in the future.'

'When do you start?' Eliza asked.

'Next week. That's why I'm calling. I won't need the money you gave me. I'll be earning, and what with the pay rise and the redundancy money I can get the mortgage straight. I'd like to send the money back to you. Just let me have your bank details.'

Eliza gave it some thought. 'You know what? Keep the money.'

'No. I can't.'

'Of course you can. Put it in an account for Otto or something. Take him skiing. Whatever you want to do.'

'Really?'

'Yes.'

Well ... if you're sure. Thank you – from Otto.'

'I *am* sure. Good luck with the new job.'

'Thanks, Elz.'

Eliza ended the call. What was ten thousand pounds? Nothing now. Otto was kind of cute, and it wasn't his fault that his mother resembled a horse.

As soon as the call ended, Scott walked into the kitchen, his face like thunder. 'You gave Ryan money?'

'That was a private conversation actually.'

'Well, then you need to learn to speak more quietly!' Scott pushed his face close to hers. 'You did, didn't you? You gave your ex money?'

'Yes, I ... I did,' Eliza stammered.

'How much?'

'It's none of your bus—'

'*How much?*'

'Oh fine, I gave him ten thousand. He was made redundant, and he was struggling with the mortgage.'

'Nice.'

'He just offered to give it back. He's got a new job and he doesn't need it. But ... well, I figured he could use it for Otto. I was prepared to give twenty-five thousand pounds to keep someone's dog safe today – I think I can give Ryan's child ten.'

'But not me?'

'Please. You know why I can't give you money. Auntie Miriam said I wasn't to do it.'

'Auntie Miriam blamed me over you for one reason only – you cleaned your fucking shoes! If I hadn't walked mud up the stairs, she would've left her money to both of us. You said yourself it's not because I wasn't her blood, it was purely because she thought it was my fault.' The volume of Scott's voice rose. 'But you were there, you were in the woods, and you were just as much to blame as me.' His face, still far too close, was now twisted with bitterness.

ELIZA – 2010

Eliza sipped her green tea. It made her feel grown up to drink it. If she was honest, she wasn't that keen, but she felt sure if she stuck with it, it would grow on her.

Opposite her, Auntie Miriam sat drinking her PG Tips with a desperate expression. 'I just refuse to believe that Ashley got up by herself and walked out of this house that night. And that she's not coming back. It makes no sense whatsoever to me.'

Eliza nodded, afraid to say anything for fear of tripping up again.

'If I had someone to blame it would be so much easier to understand,' Auntie Miriam whispered.

Who *was* to blame? Eliza wondered. Surely only Ash herself.

30
HANNAH – 2022

As she opened the front door, Hannah heard shouting in the kitchen. Scott was saying that Eliza was just as culpable as he was.

Charging her way into the room, Hannah barked, 'But she wasn't, was she, Scott?'

Both Eliza and Scott jumped. Scott had been shouting so loudly that Hannah had been able to enter the house undetected.

Scott spun around. 'What the hell are you talking about?'

Hannah saw his angry stare instantly transfer from Eliza to herself. 'Eliza isn't to blame for Ash's disappearance. She never has been. It was something my gran just said that made me realise. If you tease something every day, eventually it will turn on you.'

Scott's eyes darted from side to side.

'You turned on her, didn't you, Scott?' Hannah continued. 'You turned on Ash because she pushed you too far. You killed her, didn't you?'

Scott shook his head. 'What the fuck?'

'What are you saying?' Eliza sounded horrified.

'Your auntie blamed him, and she was right to do so. It had

nothing to do with who wiped their feet. She just knew. It was instinctive.'

Scott made a dismissive sound and began slouching towards the kitchen door.

Although considerably shorter than him, Hannah stood up to Scott. Stepping to block his exit, she said, 'You did it, didn't you?' She glared at Scott, defying him to try to move her and appearing braver than she felt.

Scott paused, saying nothing. Again, his eyes darted around the room; he was a caged animal seeking an escape. Hannah could tell he was considering all his options.

Eliza leapt again to her cousin's defence. 'I remember you, how you looked that night, Scott. Sitting in the back of the car waiting for me. A frightened, lanky, fifteen-year-old boy, with dirty hands and a tear-stained face. You've always said that you couldn't find Ash. *Always!* For twelve years you've stuck to your story. Surely Hannah must be wrong.'

After a long pause, Scott's shoulders slumped, and he finally spoke. In a resigned voice, he said, 'I did so much to try to please her. I took those shitty pills. I went in the car with you guys. I even went into the woods. And she *still* teased me. She *still* belittled me. Right up to the end she treated me like crap.'

'And so ... you what... you killed her?' Eliza asked incredulously.

Hannah and Eliza waited for his answer. The question hung in the air like a fog.

After a deep breath, Scott replied, 'Yes. Yes, I did. I killed Ash.' He lowered his head and gradually released all the air from his lungs. All the bravado was gone. Once again Scott was just a dirty-faced teenage boy.

31
SCOTT – 2022

No longer thinking of running, the adrenalin began to leave Scott's body. The time had come. He knew he only had one shot to make his cousin appreciate the truth. If he was going to finally tell her, then she simply had to see it from his point of view. 'What you need to understand is ... none of it was meant to happen.'

SCOTT – 2010

At the sound of Ash's screams, Scott and Eliza started frantically calling her. They were running further into the woods. Eliza was holding his hand, like she used to, when it was just a game, when they were kids. The ground was uneven, but they didn't stop running. And then ... Eliza's hand slipped out of his.

Scott ran on blindly, determined to find out why his cousin was screaming. Reaching out he felt for Eliza. But ... she was gone.

'*Elz! Elz! Grab my hand.*'

His instruction met with silence.

'*Elz!*' Scott's hand was flailing about, grabbing for her. How had he lost her? She'd been right there. Where had she gone? He stopped running, bending forwards to catch his breath.

Ash's screams stopped abruptly, and Lullaby Woods became silent.

Scott stood up tall, cupped his hands over his mouth, and shouted, *'Eliza! Ash! Come on. This isn't funny.'* His heart was hammering in his chest. Like it used to when they played the game with Uncle Robert. But this was not a game. Somehow, he'd lost both the girls. He might be nearly six foot tall and the biggest of the three, but he was still a kid inside and there was no doubt about it, he was shitting himself right now.

When there was no reply from either of his cousins, he walked on. By now he wasn't sure if he'd turned himself around. Was he walking towards the place where he'd heard Ash scream or back to the place where he'd last felt Eliza's hand in his? It was impossible to tell. The woods were just so dark. He wished it had been a clearer night. The cloud cover meant that there were hardly any stars, and right now he couldn't even find the moon.

He walked on, hating to be alone in the woods. Every sound made him jump and caused an adrenalin spike in his body. This was worse than any of the horror films he had agreed to watch with Ash when he was about twelve or thirteen – more attempts to prove he wasn't a baby!

As he was so alone, he allowed the tears to fall freely from his eyes. No point trying to man up as he usually did when Ash set him a challenge. He constantly spoke to himself, muttering, 'It'll be fine. I'll be okay. I'll find them soon.' He had to believe it. The alternative, that he might be wandering here in the dark alone for the rest of the night, was too awful a prospect. The effects of the pill he had taken earlier had worn off and he was left with a feeling of low-level nausea and a groggy head.

Every so often Scott would hear the cry of an animal, a fox's screech, an owl's hoot. Each one caused him to flinch. After a few minutes of walking, he didn't know where, he found himself in a clearing. Whispering, 'Please, Eliza, please, Ash – be here.' He searched the area. A moment later the cloud cleared, and for the first time the moon came into view. Not quite full, it was, however, large enough to shed a decent light on his surroundings. To his left was a slope. He thanked God that he hadn't stumbled down there in the dark. Shit, it was way too steep for him to have managed. He would most definitely have lost his footing. He was incredibly grateful to the moon for appearing when it did. He stood still and silent in the clearing, listening for the voices of his cousins. They must surely be calling him as well.

Without warning, something prodded him in his lower back, and a voice said, 'Boo!'

Scott's heart leapt into his mouth. Spinning round, he shouted, 'Whoa! What the …? Why did you do that?'

Smirking, Ash asked, 'Did I scare you?'

'Of course you did!'

'Oh, come on, Scott, don't be such a baby. It was just a joke.'

'How the hell is scaring me in the middle of the woods a joke?'

'We used to like being scared in the woods.'

'That was different. Uncle Robert was there, for a start.'

Ash shrugged. 'How was I supposed to know you're still a little boy? I thought you were a man now.'

Scott stared down at his cousin. Dressed all in black, with her long dark hair covering much of her face, she was barely visible. He could make out the whites of her eyes and her teeth when she spoke. Also, just occasionally the moon would shine directly onto her pale face, and he was able to see her sneering expression. A rage began to grow in his belly. Why the hell had he let this ridiculous girl control him for so long?

Through gritted teeth he asked, 'What's all this for, Ash? Why do it? Why bring us here?'

She replied in a calm voice, 'I don't know. I just felt like it. I like it out here in the woods. It's dark and cool. It's—'

'Why don't you just shut up?' Scott interrupted her. 'You always want to be mean and moody. D'you think anyone is impressed by this act of yours? We all get that your dad died, and we get that it pissed you off. But all this mourning rubbish is starting to wear really thin.'

Ash reached up and shoved him in the chest as she shouted, 'How dare you mention my dad? Pissed off, pissed off, is that what you think I was? You're a fucking idiot. You have no idea what it felt like when my dad died. Why would you? Your dad's the worst kind of arsehole going. He's useless. He can't stay out of prison for more than five minutes. And your mum's no better. What a stupid woman. She takes that fat wanker Fergus back every time he comes sniffing around her fanny like a dog on heat.' She grimaced. 'It makes me heave to think of them shagging. And what did they produce? You! They made the biggest baby on the planet.'

Scott was breathing deeply, in and out through his nose, trying to control his rage. Drawing himself up to his full height and towering over Ash, he shouted, 'I have told you so many times, I am not a baby.'

'Oh yeah, you don't look like one. I'll give you that. You get to be tall and broad. You get to have a strong man's body. You're lucky. But in here,' she reached up again and poked him on the forehead, 'you will always be a baby.'

'*Shut up!* I'm warning you.'

Ash laughed sarcastically. 'I heard you, Scott. I heard you saying "It'll be fine. I'll find them soon. I'll be okay". Such a baby.' She shook her head, dismissively.

'That was way back there.' He pointed into the woods.

'I know.'

'You've been following me. You knew I was scared, and you did nothing!'

'It was amusing. You sounded funny.'

'You're a psycho.'

Ash gave an indifferent shrug. 'Whatever you say ... baby.'

'I'm warning you. Don't ever call me that again. Or you'll regret it.' Scott wasn't sure why he was making these threats. Not once in his life had he hurt a girl. He'd had the odd playground fight as a child, but only with boys. He wasn't keen on violence. Especially not towards women. His father had often been angry – he mostly used his voice rather than his body, but occasionally he could get physical. Scott didn't like it one bit. So he was surprised to feel his own hands clenching into fists as he said again, 'I promise you. You will regret it.'

Pushing her face up as close to his as she could reach, Ash emphasised the word with a hiss, *'Baby!'*

They stood for a moment: Scott's fists tightly clenched by his sides; Ash still on tiptoe, wearing a totally fearless expression.

Scott shook out his arms and released his fists. He whispered to himself, 'I'm better than this.'

Ash stepped away from her cousin with such an expression of self-satisfaction it almost made him sick. 'I knew you wouldn't do anything.' Turning her back on him she muttered, 'Not just a baby, but a coward too.'

Before she could take another step, Scott bent down and picked up a large stone from the ground. Originally intending to throw it into the trees as Uncle Robert used to do, hoping the sound off in the distance would scare Ash, he was amazed to find his hand gripping it tightly as a fury swept through him. It was like an uncontrollable force. Tapping Ash on the shoulder, he quietly uttered her name. As she turned, her eyebrows raised quizzically, he struck her hard on the side of her head with the stone.

He wasn't sure what he was expecting. He thought perhaps she would cry out. Maybe even that she would fight back. What he had not planned for was that she would drop to the ground like he'd seen people do when they were shot on TV. One minute she was gazing at him, that questioning look on her pale face, obviously wondering why he had used her name so gently, the next she was a crumpled heap of black on the ground. Scott could just make out a nasty gash on her left temple. He was horrified to see blood dripping down her face and into her hair.

'Ash! *Ash!*' He shook her.

Her head juddered from side to side as he tried and failed to rouse her.

'Oh fuck, oh fuck, oh fuck.' If he thought he had been scared before, that was nothing to how he was feeling now. 'What have I done?'

A cloud moved in front of the moon and the clearing returned to darkness. Scott's breath was coming so fast he thought he was going to vomit. Forcing himself to make it deeper and more even, he tried to think straight. This wasn't his fault. She'd made him do it. He would explain that to Auntie Miriam and she would understand. He knew, even as he had those thoughts, that they were nonsense. He'd killed someone. He was going to jail. This was worse than anything his dad had ever done. Just a short while earlier he'd been worried about taking Auntie Miriam's money, and now this! No one would believe him if he told them it was an accident. The truth was it *wasn't* an accident at all. He'd done it. He'd hit her. Why had he hit her on the side of her head? It was a dangerous place to get hit. He remembered that now. *Too fucking late!*

Scott couldn't go to jail. He'd seen programmes about it. In the prison films he'd watched, men got raped in the showers. Scott began to shake.

As the cloud briefly cleared, he spotted the steep slope next to where Ash lay. Could he? Should he? If he could get her body to roll down the slope it might just appear as if she had slipped and hit her head on a rock on the way down. Sick to his stomach, he gave her a kick to move her closer to the edge. She made no sound. He had been hoping for a sigh or a moan, something to tell him his suspicion was wrong, and that she wasn't dead. But no. All he heard was the sound of the foliage moving as the dead weight of Ash edged closer to the slope.

He stood for a good minute contemplating what he was about to do. If he did it, it would be horrific. But if he didn't? *I don't want to get raped in the shower!*

Working himself up to it, he counted to three in his head, then, with all his strength he pushed her body down the slope. At first, he thought she was only going to roll once or twice. It seemed as if she had come to a halt, caught up in some prickles, and he worried that he would have to clamber down the slope and push her again. But luckily, she slowly continued rolling, and, picking up momentum, tumbled down the steep slope. Unbelievably, she didn't hit any trees on the way down. She just kept going until she was out of sight. Whoever found her at the bottom of the slope would assume the head injury had occurred on the way down. Noting the way the body bounced, he was sure of that.

As soon as he lost sight of Ash's body Scott headed in the opposite direction, now intent on finding Eliza. Stopping once to dispose of the stone he had hit Ash with, and once to finally vomit, he pressed on through the woods, calling Eliza's name.

More by luck than judgement, he came to the path they had originally taken into the woods. At least, he thought it was the right path. He wasn't one hundred percent sure, until he saw, like a beacon of hope, Auntie Miriam's car, parked at the end of the path by the side of the road. Relieved, he ran to the car, hoping to find Eliza waiting for him. She wasn't there, but thankfully the car was unlocked. Climbing into the back, he slammed the car door shut and collapsed in his seat.

His face was wet with tears and his throat felt closed. All he could think about was Ash's body tumbling down the slope, like a sack of potatoes. How soon would someone find her? Would anyone find the stone he'd used? He'd thrown it away a long way from the slope, in the hope it would never be associated with his crime. What was Auntie Miriam going to say? Bile rose into his throat. He knew he could never tell a living soul what he'd done. He wished he could tell Eliza; she would hug him and tell him it wasn't his fault – Ash should never have kept calling him a baby. But what if she didn't? What if she looked at him like the cold-blooded killer he was? He could never take that risk.

In the middle of his thoughts, the driver's door was yanked open and Eliza appeared. Much like Scott, she was grubby and panting heavily. Her hair, which was usually neat, was more of a bird's nest now. She'd clearly caught her ponytail on some low hanging branches. She had a wide-eyed stare, and Scott could only guess what a terrible time she'd had in the woods. Obviously not as bad as his, though!

A conversation followed in which it was established that Eliza had not run off and left him, she had tripped on a root and had fallen. She thought *he* had left *her*.

Scott was amazed to hear she'd been calling him the whole time. He wished with all his heart that he'd heard her before he'd run into Ash.

Eliza asked him, 'You didn't find Ash?'

'No.' It was the obvious thing to say, and it just came out of his mouth. The first of many lies. So much easier to say he hadn't found her than to describe what was playing out over and over in a loop in his head right now.

Eliza said, 'Neither did I. This is awful, Scottie. What are we supposed to do?'

Scott found himself replying, 'We'll wait. She'll come soon.' Another lie.

32
HANNAH – 2022

Eliza and Hannah stared at Scott. Hannah had thought maybe he might admit to it, but she had not expected so much detail. She suspected that telling it was cathartic for him. She looked at Eliza, checking she was okay.

Her mouth was agape. 'You can't mean it, Scott. You can't have done that.'

Scott shook his head. 'I'm so sorry, Elz. You have no idea how many times I've wanted to tell you.'

'*No!*' Eliza began to cry. 'If you did that, it means every conversation we've had about her in the last twelve years has been bullshit. I can't ... I just can't.' Eliza dropped her head into her hands.

Scott approached her from behind and, putting his arms around her, said, 'I couldn't tell you. I couldn't risk it. I was so scared of prison.'

'You realise you've just admitted it was you who took the money as well?' Hannah said.

'Yes.'

'That was a huge reason why the police were convinced she'd gone off of her own free will.'

'What you don't seem to get, Miss fucking PI, is the fact that I was petrified. I waited for someone to find her body. Someone out walking their dog or playing with their kids. I watched the news, expecting to see her. I imagined her body all decomposed, but still dressed in mourning. I was scarred for life from that night. If I told Eliza, and she hated me, it would've killed me.'

'But nobody did find her,' Eliza whispered. 'Never. In twelve years, no one found her body. Does that seem possible to you?'

Scott took his arms away from Eliza and sat down at the kitchen table. 'You know, I've never understood how she wasn't found. The only thing I can figure is that the ground at the bottom of that slope is damp, all year round. It's pretty swampy. I reckon she sank.'

Placing her hand over her mouth, Eliza gagged.

Hannah said, in her most official voice, 'I'm going to have to report this to my ex-colleagues.'

Scott nodded. 'I guessed as much.'

'I think the law will go easy on you, given you were a child at the time, and the fact that as yet there's no body.'

'*As yet?*' Eliza asked.

'They're going to have to carry out a full investigation. They'll want to search this muddy area that Scott's describing.'

Eliza turned to Scott. 'What about all the other stuff? The stuff that was done to *me*. Was that you too?'

He shook his head, passionately denying it. 'I promise. That wasn't me.'

'Should I believe him?'

Hannah shrugged. 'I don't know. I think we'll let the police decide about that too.'

Scott seemed determined to prove his innocence regarding the recent shenanigans. Dropping to his knees in front of his cousin, he begged her, 'Please, Elz. I would never do that to you. I know how scared you were, and I promise you …' He stopped, clearly trying to regain composure.

'Don't promise me anything. Your promises mean nothing. You've just confessed to me that you *killed* Ash.'

'But, Eliza, you know me.'

Looking her cousin up and down, Eliza shook her head. 'I have absolutely no idea who you are.'

'Listen.' Hannah tried to position herself between them. 'This is clearly a highly emotive subject for both of you. Eliza, you're trying to take in something momentous right now – you need to process it. And Scott, you've told us something that's been buried deep inside you since you were a child. You need to give yourself time too.'

'Scott, when we agreed to tell everyone that we were asleep when she left the house, you claimed it was the best thing for both of us,' Eliza said. 'You convinced me that us being in the woods was irrelevant. I even told *you* that, didn't I, Hannah? But it wasn't best for both of us at all. It was a cover up. It was for *your* benefit.'

Scott remained speechless, tears trickling down his face.

'How many times recently have you insisted Auntie Miriam should've shared her money between us? How often have you moaned that it was unfair she denied you any inheritance? And all the time, you … all the time you killed her daughter!'

Clearing her throat, Hannah said, 'You have to remember the mitigating circumstances that Scott has described. He was a child. She taunted him. I don't mean to be rude about the deceased, but Ash sounds like a right bitch. It's like my gran said, she just teased you once too often, Scott. And I think I'm right in saying that you're remorseful. That event has shaped your whole life.' In a strange way Hannah felt a little sorry for Scott. Not only the dishevelled man who knelt before his cousin today, but also the frightened fifteen-year-old boy who was callously driven to an indescribable act of violence all those years ago. Something that under normal circumstances he would clearly never have contemplated. In fact, it was worse than simply feeling a little sorry – Hannah pitied Scott, like one would pity a beaten dog or a pig on its way to the slaughterhouse. The pity churned her stomach.

Scott replied, 'Yes, I regret it, you're right. And yes, it's ruined everything.' He began speaking in a monotone voice, as if in the confessional box. 'I thought they'd find her. First on the Sunday. I expected someone to report the discovery of a body in the marshy part of the woods. I waited all day for the knock on the door. Then, when nothing happened, I thought it might take a few days. Once we got into weeks, I was totally confused. How was no one finding her? I've been over it a million times. How she dropped to the floor, how she didn't make a sound when I nudged her, how her body rolled down the slope. When we had her declared dead, I thought I would be able to move on. I thought it would stop haunting me. But it never has.'

Eliza paced the kitchen floor. 'All those times you moaned that you should've got half of Auntie Miriam's money. Bloody hell, Scott, how could you say that?'

'I don't know.' Scott was pale and shaking. 'It was just ... well, so much time had passed since that night and no one had ever found her, so I started to think ... maybe she was still alive somewhere. Maybe I didn't kill her after all?'

'You thought she was alive. But you couldn't stop thinking about how you'd killed her?' Eliza shrugged. 'Confusing, Scott, real confusing.'

'Schrödinger's cousin,' Hannah muttered.

Scott had risen from his knees and was following Eliza around the kitchen. 'I'm so sorry that I never told you. It's not an easy thing to say, you know?' He asked Hannah, 'Will you come with me?'

'To the police station? Of course I will.'

'No. To Lullaby Woods. I can show you where she disappeared.'

'Well ...' Hannah considered. 'It's a job for the police now.'

'Please. Maybe if I show you, you'll be able to work out that she's not really dead and that it's all okay.'

'I highly doubt that,' Hannah scoffed.

'Please?'

'When d'you want to go?'

'Right now.'

Hannah shook her head. 'No way. It's going to be dark soon.'

'We have enough time. Please, I need to show someone.'

Hannah thought for a second and then sighed. 'All right. Show me this slope and I'll see what I think could've—'

Eliza butted in, 'You can't go there with him. He's dangerous.'

'Him! He's about as dangerous as a summer cold. I'll be fine.'

Clearly upset by her comment, Scott pleaded with his cousin. 'Don't say that, Elz. You know me. I'm not dangerous.'

'I didn't think you were dangerous that night in the woods, far from it. And I'm sure Ash wouldn't have thought it either. But look where that got her.'

'That was different. I'm not like that. I just want to show Hannah where it happened. See what she thinks. Maybe there's a reasonable explanation for it all.'

'Don't be ridiculous. Of course there isn't. You said yourself that you …' Eliza swallowed, 'that you kicked her body and it just rolled down the hill. You said she didn't cry out. I think I'm going to be sick.' She sat down on one of the hard kitchen chairs and dropped her head between her knees.

Scott hesitated. Hannah assumed he was weighing up whether to try to comfort her or to stay back. She shook her head at him. 'Leave her to take it all in. Come on. If we're going, we'd better head out now. Like I said, we don't have long to see the crime scene.'

'It's really not a crime scene,' Scott argued.

'I'll call it that for now. Thank you very much.' Hannah walked towards the coat hooks in the hall to grab a jacket. 'Good. I thought I'd left this one here.'

'Wear my wellies,' Eliza called out. 'It'll be muddy.'

'I need a piss first,' Scott said.

'Get up there then.' Hannah ushered him up the stairs, grabbing Eliza's boots. She gave Scott a second to get into the bathroom before following him upstairs. Placing her ear to the door, she called out, 'I can't hear anything. Hurry up, we're losing the light. It'll be dark in those woods in less than an hour.'

Through the bathroom door, she heard his muffled reply, 'Coming now.'

Pinging off a couple of text messages, Hannah went back downstairs to check on Eliza, who, thankfully, seemed calmer and less likely to vomit.

'Are you sure you'll be okay in the woods with him?' Eliza asked.

'Yes. Honestly. Scott seems to want to confess it all. He's probably relieved after all this time that he can finally get it off his chest.'

'Shall I come with you?'

'No. I'd rather not have to worry about you as well. Same reason I told Lottie to stay put with my mum and gran. I'll call you both as soon as he's shown me this infamous clearing in the woods.'

'What will happen to him next?'

'I'll take him to the station, and he can make his confession. After that it's all down to the SIO on the case; it will depend on what the police find at the site.'

Scott entered the kitchen. 'Ready?'

'Yes.' Hannah replied, picking up her car keys. 'Off we go to Lullaby Woods.'

Eliza shuddered.

'I thought you knew where the clearing was.' Hannah spoke through clenched teeth; her patience was wearing thin.

'I do. It just looks different, that's all.'

'It can't have changed that much,' Hannah said. 'It's not like they've put a bloody Starbucks in the middle.'

Scott was still wandering aimlessly, constantly turning his head from side to side. 'I just thought it was ... umm.'

With no other option than to wander around behind him, Hannah was close to giving up. 'Have you been back since that night?' she asked.

'Yeah. A few times. Not to begin with, obviously. I couldn't drive then. But over the years I've been back about three times. I have found the right spot before.'

'Right. Well, I don't think you're going to find it tonight. It's getting way too dark for me to see this flippin' slope anyway. Why don't we head back to the car, and I'll take you to the station? Someone from there will bring you back here tomorrow, no doubt.'

'*No!*' Scott shouted. 'I need to find it. I need *you* to see it.'

'Why *me*?'

'You're a PI and you might be able to solve it somehow.'

'There is no solving it. You did it. You can't deny that now.'

Scott marched off down a path between two large trees, his trainers slipping and sliding as he hit a muddy patch. 'I think it's this way.'

Hannah rolled her eyes. 'That's about the fifth time you've said that in the last ten minutes. I only came because I thought you'd lead me straight to it!'

'Honestly. This feels right to me. It'll be a couple of minutes now – tops.' He disappeared.

'Bloody idiot,' Hannah mumbled, following the path he'd taken. 'Wait for me!' she called after him.

Reaching a clearing where the light was a bit better, she saw him standing off in the distance. He was staring down a steep slope. This was obviously the place.

He looked distraught and Hannah tried to think of something to say. Something that would ease his guilt. She knew all about guilt and how it can eat away at your soul, if you let it. Opening her mouth to call out some useful words of wisdom, she was shocked to feel a large hand clamped over her mouth from behind. At the same time the person placed their other hand over her eyes. Plunged into darkness, Hannah felt as if she'd been dropped into an ebony ocean.

She tried to struggle, but the person who had grabbed her was exceptionally strong. Turning her around, they began dragging her backwards. She could do nothing to resist. Trying to dig her heels into the ground made no difference whatsoever. She attempted to inhale, but was horrified to discover that the person had such large hands that the one covering her mouth was also blocking her nose. Was that intentional? Were they simply going to suffocate her, right here in the clearing in Lullaby Woods? She tried a few more times to take a breath, but found it impossible to get any air past the hands that imprisoned her. They were huge. A thought occurred to her: *my dad would say, hands like shovels*. An image of her dad flashed through her mind. Was she going to die here? Was she never going to see her mum and dad again? Or Lottie? Was this how Dawn had felt when she lay in the street, the life blood draining out of her?

Hannah continued to wriggle, simultaneously trying to prize away the hands that held her captive. If only she could make a gap in the one over her mouth and nose, just enough to get some air. She felt she might be about to lose consciousness, and if she did, it would be curtains.

Finally, the hand that was pinching her nose so tightly shut moved, only a tiny fraction, but enough to allow her to take in some air. She drew in a long breath. Never before had air felt so good, even taking into account the smell of stale sweat that now assaulted her nostrils. She continued to try to prise the hands off her face, all the while being sightlessly dragged backwards.

Then, the person with the shovel hands and the strong arms spoke. 'This feckin' bitch needs to stop wriggling.'

Hannah had no intention of complying. If she was going down, she was going down fighting.

He spoke again. 'She should never have stuck her nose in. For feck' sake, who ever heard of a woman private dick? The clue's in the name.' He laughed at his lame joke, adding, 'She ought to know her place.'

Hannah got lucky with her aim and managed to stamp down on one of her captor's feet. But she wished she was wearing her biker boots instead of the stupid wellies Eliza had suggested she borrow, because it clearly didn't hurt him enough to help her escape plan. In fact, by the way he tutted, she suspected it just irritated him.

Then she heard him say, 'When I'm done with her, I'm gonna kick some lumps out of you too. Why the feck did you come and free the dog?'

On the other side of her, close by, she heard a familiar voice say, 'You went too far. I only agreed to the small stuff, the texts, the CD, that sort of thing. I never said you should take someone's dog. That was too much.'

Her captor shouted back, 'Don't you tell me what I can and can't do. You've messed it all up. She knows too much about it. We'll get nothing out of Eliza now. Not a feckin' penny. You're an eejit.'

'I'm sorry. It was just … the dog. You can't threaten to kill a dog.'

Hannah could feel her captor's hot stinking breath on her neck. He was angry; that much was clear.

The other person asked, in a fearful voice, 'What are we going to do now?'

'I wish my wallet was as thick as you. What do you think?' Hannah's captor replied.

'You don't mean …?'

'It's nothing you haven't done before, boy.'

'*No! Dad.* Please?' Scott sounded terrified.

A thought occurred to Hannah. *So this is Fergus!*

'Listen, you little gobshite, she knows too much. You told me in your text that you'd confessed what you did. It's right there on your phone. How long before the coppers start saying I was an accessory after the fact? I'm not going down for your mistakes.'

'I can't do it. Please. We mustn't. It's wrong.'

'You asked for my help. You said it was urgent.'

'I know.'

'Feckin' came straight here, didn't I?'

'Yes, you did … but …' Scott stammered. 'I can't.'

'Didn't stop you doing it when it was that little freak, did it? You were happy to kill her. No right or wrong back then.'

'I wasn't. It was an accident. You know I regret it.'

'You think I've got time to keep hearing you bang on about your regrets. Get away with you. Because of your soft heart and your stupid big mouth, it's all ruined. Why couldn't you just do as you were—' At the same time as Fergus abruptly stopped speaking his hands fell away from Hannah's face.

She blinked, surprised at the view in front of her. She had been dragged over to the edge of the steep slope. Next to her stood an extremely startled Scott. On the ground at her feet lay the man who had clearly held her captive. The infamous Fergus. He was large and appeared to be somewhere in his mid-fifties. He had an ugly, inflated face with several scars, each of which told its own story, and a deep forehead. The rest of his head was crowned with ridiculous, fair curls, which would be more at home adorning the head of a toddler. His hands were undeniably large and calloused. He also wore a startled expression.

Spinning her head around to see what could've happened to cause such a change in their positions, Hannah was delighted to see Dave. Standing back slightly from the group and holding a hefty tree branch in his right hand, he jeered. 'Gotcha, ya bastard!'

In the next moment, one of the four departed the scene.

Attempting to make an escape, Fergus got up shakily to his feet. A second later he blacked out. As his pale grey eyes rolled back into his head, he fell backwards, plummeting down the slope. Immediately he began to roll. Down and down the steep decline, his body gathering speed as it went. Then – he was gone.

Clearly traumatised by what he'd just seen, Scott cried out, *'Dad!'*

Hannah watched him relive an event that had been so horrific it had ruined his life. And now his father had suffered the same fate.

Immediately, another departure occurred. Taking advantage of the fact that both Dave and Hannah were staring down into the murky abyss, the place that was now possibly a grave to not only Ash but Fergus as well, Scott turned and ran.

'I'll go after him,' Dave shouted.

'No, don't bother,' Hannah replied. 'When I texted you, I also texted Paul. The police should be here any minute. He won't get far on foot.'

Dave glanced down the slope again. 'Maybe I hit him a bit too hard. But I had to be sure.'

'Better safe than sorry, I guess. Although it was a pretty big piece of wood.'

Paul laughed. 'I couldn't find anything smaller.'

'Well, he wasn't messing about. Thank goodness you found me.'

'The app thing you put on my phone is brilliant. I was able to pinpoint you exactly.'

'And you saved my life.' Hannah hugged him. 'I honestly think if you hadn't turned up, I'd be down there too.'

'Never any question of me not turning up, boss.'

'I reckon you'll make employee of the month for this.'

Dave chuckled.

'And, I mean it, you genuinely did save my life.' Hannah smiled. Off in the distance they heard sirens and saw the blue lights of their ex-colleagues. 'Looks like they're here.'

'Fancy going to tell them the full story?' Dave asked.

'I think we ought to.'

33
ELIZA – 2022

Eliza fussed around making sweet tea. Handing a steaming mug to Hannah, she said, 'Drink this – for the shock.'

'Sit down,' Hannah instructed. 'If anyone deserves to be in shock it's you, Eliza.'

'Yes,' Lottie agreed. 'You must be so upset. Scott promised you it wasn't him.'

'I know, but after finding out he killed Ash, I couldn't trust a word out of his mouth.' Eliza stirred more sugar into everyone's mug.

'Enough already with the sugar.' Hannah placed her hand over her mug. 'I don't like tea at the best of times. Please, just let me finish telling you exactly what happened.' She patted the seat next to her.

Eliza sat down. 'How come the police didn't find Scott?'

'He just gave them the slip. They searched the woods, but it was pitch black in there by the time they arrived. They should've thrown a bigger number at it, in my opinion.'

'Sorry?'

'Sent more coppers,' Lottie volunteered.

'Very good. You're learning,' Hannah said. 'To be honest I thought they should've brought the canine unit. Those dogs definitely would've found him.'

'He won't get away though, will he? Where would he go?' Lottie asked.

'He has some dodgy mates. He might go and stay with them,' Eliza volunteered.

Lottie asked Hannah, 'Will Eliza get a family liaison officer, like they do on the telly?'

'Unlikely,' Hannah replied. 'Technically no one's dead, and FLIs are short on the ground.'

'Shame.'

'I don't need anyone else, not if I've got Hannah,' Eliza said.

'They're good people. They do an important job. I've known them to make a huge difference to a case, don't get me wrong. But, like I say, they're for serious incidents, and as much as this feels serious to you, Eliza, as it stands right now, no one has been murdered.'

'I guess everything will change when they find Ash's body,' Lottie said.

'Absolutely,' Hannah agreed. Her phone vibrated and she checked her messages. 'There's been a report from a patrol car that they've seen a man walking along the road by Lullaby Woods. More news to follow from Paul when he has some.'

'He's good to keep you in the loop, isn't he?' Lottie said. 'I mean, he probably doesn't have to.'

'No, of course he doesn't *have* to. But Paul's all right. He knows he can trust me with the information, and he's rewarded for his trouble. Besides, if it wasn't for me, they'd have nothing. It's ironic – Paul gave my tip off to my old boss, McAlpine. Paul said he was well impressed. Bloody hell, what I would've given a few years back to impress that man.' Hannah sighed.

They all took a sip of their hot sweet tea.

Grimacing, Hannah reached for her phone, which had once again vibrated. 'Another text just in,' she announced.

Eliza waited, watching Hannah's face. How would she feel if the police had picked up Scott?

After a couple of seconds, Hannah let out a whistle. '*Jesus!*'

'What is it? Have they got Scott?'

'That's the weird thing,' Hannah replied. 'It turns out the description of the person seen didn't match Scott at all. Apparently, it was a much older man, staggering about, with blood on his face.'

'Wow, so Fergus survived the fall,' Eliza said.

'It sounds exactly like him, even down to the blood on his face, courtesy of Dave and that enormous branch he was wielding. Unfortunately, Paul says he's disappeared again. They really need daylight to catch those two buggers.'

Eliza said, 'So, if Fergus could survive, maybe …'

'Exactly,' Hannah agreed.

'You know what I'm thinking?'

'Of course. I'm picking up what you're putting down,' Hannah said in a fake nerdy voice. 'If he survived, maybe Ash did too.'

'Exactly!' Eliza smiled at Hannah's attempt to cheer her up.

'It's not just about the fall, though,' Hannah reminded her. 'It's possible that the blow to the side of Ash's skull was fatal in itself. Scott seemed to think it was.'

'Yes. But if it wasn't …?'

'Another thing is that Paul says the road this guy was seen on is the same strip of road where the witness reported seeing a young woman get into a lorry all those years ago. It's conceivable that if Ash wasn't killed by Scott or the fall, she may have finished up on the same piece of road.'

'Oh my goodness!' Lottie looked fit to burst. 'Maybe you've solved both mysteries, Han.'

'We'll know more when they're able to search the area tomorrow.'

'And Dave saved the day?' Lottie grinned.

'Yes,' Hannah agreed. 'The police weren't far behind, but I still think I might have carked it before they got to me if it wasn't for Dave.

Eliza shivered. 'Fergus has always been a wrong-un. I hated him as a child. There was something about him. He was just nothing like my parents or Auntie Miriam and Uncle Robert. Scott's mum was stupid; she let him drift in and out of their lives. I swear she should've installed a revolving door for him.'

'Ridiculous woman,' Hannah scoffed.

'Totally. When Fergus was in prison, Scott would start to gain a bit of confidence, he seemed happier. Then bloody Fergus would return, and he changed back. That man was a tyrant.'

'It doesn't sound like an enviable childhood,' Lottie said.

'Not only that, but poor Scott also had Ash to contend with. I always felt as if he had no one to look out for him, except me. That's why I gave him the benefit of the doubt. I suppose I was mad to believe him when he promised he wasn't doing all the stuff to scare me. Especially after he confessed to killing Ash. I guess I just wanted to believe him.' Eliza's heart was heavy.

Hannah put her hand on top of Eliza's and squeezed. 'I don't know if it helps at all, but from what I heard, I think Fergus was the driving force behind their campaign. I reckon Scott must've told him stuff. I think he gave his dad the details he needed to make it seem like it was Ash. He obviously *did* remember your Uncle Robert's favourite song that was played at the funeral. And I don't doubt he helped come up with the idea for the jams etc. But I wonder how much of it he actually wanted to do. The Fergus you've described, and the one I heard in the woods, is an extremely dominant man; one who has a definite hold over Scott.'

'But Scott lied to me. He said he thought he'd seen Ash by the

Co-op, wearing one of her big coats. But at the time he said that he was already convinced she was dead. It wouldn't surprise me if he went to the charity shop and bought her stuff back so they could scare me with it.'

'Pasty-faced loser!' Lottie muttered.

'Huh?' Eliza asked.

'Nothing.' Lottie sipped her tea.

Pushing her mug away, Hannah sighed. 'Sorry, Eliza, I can feel my teeth falling out as I drink that.'

'Okay.' Eliza took the mug and absentmindedly moved it to the draining board.

Both Hannah and Lottie said simultaneously, 'Rinse it out.'

Eliza laughed. 'What's up with you two?'

Lottie explained. 'We used to do office cleaning. You wouldn't believe the number of people who leave tea and coffee in a mug overnight. It's incredibly hard to get the ring out of the mug.'

Eliza smiled. Pouring the tea down the sink, she ran some warm water into the mug and left it to soak. 'Fair enough. There you go.'

'I think maybe we ought to try to get some shut eye,' Hannah suggested. She asked Lottie, 'Will you head back to our place, or would you rather stay here?'

Lottie considered. 'Well, Dixie's safe at your mum's for the time being, so ...' Turning to Eliza, she asked, 'D'you mind if I sleep here for another night?'

'Of course not. We'll all be okay together.'

———

The slight squeak of Eliza's bedroom door gave her a start. Her eyes sprang open. In the doorway stood a broad figure.

'Scott?' she whispered.

'I'm afraid not. You're close, but no cigar.'

As Eliza flicked on the bedside light, she caught sight of the knife.

'Keep your mouth shut and listen,' Fergus barked.

'How did you get in here?' Eliza asked.

'A little something I picked up years ago.' With an ugly grin, he held up a front door key.

Way too late, Eliza realised she should've changed the locks when she moved in. 'Always did help yourself to other people's stuff, didn't you, Fergus?'

'That's *Uncle* Fergus to you.'

She shook her head. 'I don't think so.'

'Fair enough. Call me what you like.' Fergus shrugged. 'I didn't come here to play happy families anyway.'

'What *did* you come here for?' Eliza asked.

'To offer you a deal.'

'I don't usually do deals at knifepoint.'

'This?' Fergus gestured to the knife in his hand. 'This is just an insurance policy. It's my way of making sure you hear me out and don't call that feckin' bitch private investigator of yours.'

'Right. Well, it's not something I'm comfortable with.'

Fergus lowered the knife, but it remained a threatening presence in the room. 'Like I say, just listen to me and this won't get used.'

'Go on then. Say what you came here to say.'

Fergus rubbed his head and winced. It was clear Dave had made a good old dent with his improvised cosh. 'It's a one-time deal. You give me a decent sum of cash and I promise to disappear. No more scary nights for you. No more wondering if I'm going to turn up in your room. I swear to God, you pay me, and I'm gone for good.'

'Well, that does sound like a pleasant situation. You gone for good. I only wish you'd done it years ago. Scott would've benefitted from a little less time with Daddy.'

Fergus gave a snarl. 'My son has a healthy respect for me,

which is more than can be said for the rest of the cunts in your family.'

Eliza rolled her eyes. 'Charming.'

'All of 'em. Your ma and pa. That friggin' saint, Robert. They all thought I was scum. And don't get me started on Miriam. The way that woman used to speak to me, I could've …' He clenched his fists.

'Auntie Miriam was a shrewd judge of character. That's why she left nothing to Scott.'

'That bitch ought to have shared it between you pair. Scott was Robert's nephew.'

'She left nothing to him because she knew deep down what he'd done. Maybe she thought he was rotten through and through, just like you,' Eliza sneered.

'He was Robert's blood. She should've remembered that.'

'Hannah told me that you know what Scott did to her child.'

'I do.'

'How long have you known?' Eliza wondered aloud.

'Long enough,' Fergus replied.

'Did he tell you at the time?'

'No, a few years later. Stupid boy got drunk and blubbed like a wean. Not long after that he took me to the place in the woods. Nothing much to see there, to be honest.'

Eliza could barely believe the impudence of the man. 'And yet you still think he should've got half the inheritance?'

'It would've saved a lot of heartache for everyone.'

'You mean it would've saved you and Scott having to try to trick me out of my money by pretending Ash was still alive.'

'Ah, but some of that was a good crack.'

Ignoring the gleeful expression on his face, Eliza asked, 'Which one of you dressed up in black?'

'Now that would be a young lady I know from the pub. Charlene. She was happy to take part in a prank for the price of a couple of Strongbows. Great girl.' Fergus winked.

'But it wasn't a prank, was it? I'm told it was attempted extortion.'

'Don't be daft. It was a prank, pure and simple.'

'What I cannot believe,' Eliza said, 'is that Scott was complicit with your plans.'

'He was what now?'

'He agreed to it. He helped you. It breaks my heart that he did that.'

'You should've shared the inheritance when you first got it. He wasn't asking for the feckin' house, nothing like it. You could've given my boy a decent pay off and avoided all this.'

'Well, as nice as it is to catch up with you, Fergus. It's the middle of the night ...' Eliza reached for her phone on the bedside table.

Immediately Fergus raised the knife, snarling, 'Keep your feckin' hands where I can see them.'

She placed her hands back on top of the duvet. 'I was just wondering what time it was.'

'Like you say, it's late. Let's get to the point, shall we?'

'Which *is*?'

'I'm gonna need a one-off payment of fifty thousand pounds. Get that to my bank and you'll not see me again.'

'And Scott?'

'What about him?' Fergus asked.

'What does he get?'

'I'll settle his debt for him. Stupid boy will no doubt get himself into shite with someone else, but I guess I could help him out just this once.' Fergus had the audacity to appear chuffed with his own generosity.

'You, *Uncle* Fergus, are all heart.'

'Right. So, we have a deal?'

'A deal? Hmm ...' Eliza considered.

'Wouldn't you like to know I was well and truly gone? That I wasn't going to turn up here and scare yous all.'

'It sounds appealing.'

'I'll even give you back the front door key.'

Eliza placed her hand on her heart. 'A true gent.'

'Right, so put my bank details into ya phone. As soon as ya pay up, you'll find your life will be a lot less stressful.'

'Sounds wonderful.'

'Doesn't it? Right, no messing me about though. I'll come back if you cheat me. You know me.'

'Oh yes, I know you well. May I?' Eliza gestured for her phone.

'Go on.' Fergus said. 'Easy now.'

'Now would be a good time,' Eliza said.

'What?'

A voice behind Fergus spoke. 'I am armed, Mr O'Connell. I'm going to ask you just once to drop the knife.'

Fergus's expression told Eliza that he could feel the barrel of the gun prodding him in the back.

'What the …?' He tried to turn around.

'Drop the knife or I'll shoot.'

Eliza watched as Fergus made his decision. With a creased brow, he appeared to run through all possible scenarios in a second. Deciding he didn't wish to be shot in the back, he dropped the knife.

Stepping around him, Hannah kicked the knife under the bed.

At the same time, Eliza pressed the panic button hidden behind her bedside lamp and an ear-piercing screech was omitted. Smiling, she said, 'That umbrella sure does come in handy.'

Fergus, spying the metal-tipped umbrella in Hannah's hand, snarled, 'Ya feckers.'

As he lunged at Hannah, the sound of heavy boots could be heard thundering up the stairs. A moment later, three of Hannah's ex-colleagues came crashing into the bedroom. Grabbing Fergus, they wrestled him to the ground. Within seconds he was handcuffed and being read his rights.

'You'll find his weapon under there.' Hannah nodded towards the bed.

With a courteous nod towards Hannah, the police officers retrieved the knife and manoeuvred an incensed Fergus down the stairs.

'Why did you wait so long to press the button?' Hannah asked.

'I had to know how much of it was Scott's idea.'

'Still, I thought you were never going to give me the signal.'

'I knew you were there, and I knew your colleagues were in the lounge waiting. I just needed to find out about Scott.'

'And?' Hannah asked. 'How do you feel about him now?'

'I don't know. I guess I want to forgive him. I know he would never have done any of the things he did to me if Fergus hadn't made him.'

'You're a good person, Eliza.'

'I don't know about that. Maybe I ought to have paid off his loan when he first asked me. Then none of this would've happened.'

'But you were doing what your auntie wanted. She didn't want him to have any money, and as it turns out she was right about him.'

'I guess so.'

A voice from down the hall called out, 'Han, is it safe yet?'

Hannah called back, 'Yes. You can come out now, Lottie. I expect Eliza is about to make us all another mug of her delicious, sweet tea.'

'Well, I am in shock,' Eliza agreed.

'At least you got the chance to ask your questions.'

'Yes, I did.' Eliza threw back the covers. 'And thankfully I was in my joggers and a t-shirt. Imagine the indignity of having that conversation in my PJs.'

Hannah agreed. 'We were ready for him. Although it turns out we didn't need to leave the back door unlocked.'

'Cheeky bastard, taking that front door key.' Eliza screwed up her face.

'There was never any question he wouldn't come though, was there?' Hannah said.

'No,' Lottie agreed. 'Because he's a fucking greedy bastard. I hate men who try to get money out of women.'

Hannah reached for her friend and hugged her. 'And that's why I told you to stay in your room and lock the door. You've had enough dealings with swindlers to last you a lifetime.'

'Tea then?' Eliza suggested.

'Oh, go on,' Hannah agreed.

As they made their way down the stairs, all bending their heads to avoid the coat hooks at the bottom and stepping over the squeaky step, Lottie said, 'So that's your Uncle Fergus banged up again. Just Scott to find. Let's hope he's not good at hiding.'

Eliza smiled gently to herself, remembering a much smaller Scott.

ELIZA – 2002

'You can come out now, you baby. We finished the game ages ago,' Ash called out.

The girls waited. Still Scott remained in hiding.

'Seriously, Scottie. We can't find you. We give up and we don't want to play hide and seek any more,' Eliza shouted up the stairs.

'Let's just leave him. The idiot can stay in his hiding place all day for all I care.' Ash shrugged and headed towards the kitchen.

'Scottie, we're going outside to climb trees. You can come too.' Again Eliza tried to make her voice as loud as possible.

'You said he's not allowed anymore. Not since he acted like a total wally and broke his stupid wrist.' Opening the large back door, Ash made her way into the garden. 'Just forget him.'

'Scottie, can you hear me? Come out when you're ready. But we're not looking anymore.' Eliza knew how good Scott was at hiding. If he wanted to, he could make himself impossible to find.

34
HANNAH – 2022

Because she had given back the key to Eliza's house when they'd moved out, Hannah rang the doorbell.

Within seconds, Eliza opened up, excitedly. 'Oh, it's just you.'

'Cheek!' Hannah held aloft two brown paper bags; a delicious waft of Chinese food accompanied her. 'I got everything we wanted.'

Lottie appeared in the hallway. 'Did you remember the crispy seaweed?'

'Yes, my dear,' Hannah replied.

Stepping aside, Eliza said, 'Then you may come in.'

They made their way into the kitchen and began unpacking the food.

'So, umm … where's Mandy?' Lottie asked, clearly attempting to sound casual.

'She's driving herself here. She'll be along soon. I promise.'

'I thought you were picking her up?'

'No. Just the food. She likes to drive herself.' Hannah decided not to go into the details surrounding Mandy's need for a quick getaway.

'Fair enough.' Eliza took four plates out of the cupboard.

'Just don't tell my mum and dad you've met her, for God's sake,' Hannah warned. 'They've never met any of my girlfriends and I know they'll go ballistic if they find out you two met her first.'

Throwing an assortment of cutlery and napkins onto the table, Eliza said, 'We won't tell, will we, Lottie?'

Lottie zipped her lips.

'I'm so nervous.' Hannah ran her fingers through her hair.

'Why? It's just us.' Lottie reminded her.

'I know. But I want you to like her and I want her to like you, and …'

'*And* what?' Lottie asked.

'You do have a tendency to say stupid things.' Hannah winced, before adding, 'Sorry, Lottie, but you *do*. It's not even that they're stupid as such, just that you say whatever pops into your head. Years of privilege, I guess.'

'In the words of Ken Sandlin – I resemble that remark,' Lottie joked.

'Just promise me you won't bombard her with questions, will you?'

'Of course.'

With her head in the fridge, searching for the wine, Eliza agreed. 'We will be calm and casual.'

The doorbell made them all jump. Just for a second, they stood looking at each other, all expecting someone else to answer it.

'Go on then, Han,' Eliza instructed. 'She's *your* girlfriend.'

'Of course.' Hannah ran her fingers through her hair again, this time to spike it up, and puckered her lips. 'Here I go.'

Opening the door, she was delighted to see Mandy. Somehow, she just got prettier every time Hannah saw her.

'Hi, you,' Hannah said.

'Hi, you,' Mandy replied.

They kissed.

'You're sure you're ready for this?' Hannah asked.
'Of course. It'll be fine.'
'I'm glad you're so confident.' Hannah gave a small smile.
'What've you told them about me?' Mandy asked.
'Not much, just, you know, how we met and stuff. Oh, and that you're beautiful.'
'Thank you.'

Hannah just knew that in the kitchen Lottie and Eliza would be sitting in silence, straining to hear Mandy's voice. 'Was I meant to tell them … you know, was I supposed to tell them everything?'

'That was up to you.'
'I just thought you'd tell it better.'
'Okay.' Mandy took a step forward. 'Am I allowed in?'
'Of course, sorry.'

Mandy stepped into the hallway. She looked around, taking it all in.

'Shall we go through?' Hannah asked.
'Yes, let's.'
'They're in the kitchen. I'll lead the—'

Mandy had already begun walking down the hall.

Hannah watched as her girlfriend pushed the kitchen door open. She made sure to be close behind, wanting to see the reaction of both Lottie and Eliza.

'Hi.' Mandy stepped into the room. Surveying the food on the table, she sniffed, saying, 'Wow. That smells delicious.'

Hannah studied Lottie's face. It was so important to her that her friend liked her girlfriend. She need not have worried. Lottie's face broke into a smile. 'Oh, my goodness, it's so nice to finally meet you.'

Hannah switched her gaze to Eliza. What would she think?

Making a similar sound to their old friend Henry Hoover trying to gobble up a sock, Eliza inhaled deeply.

Hannah waited.

A moment later, Eliza stood and offered her hand, 'Wow, you're even more beautiful than I thought you would be. I'm Eliza.'

Mandy took her hand and shook it, replying, 'I'm Mandeep, but my friends call me Mandy.'

Eliza gestured for Mandy to sit down, and they all chose a seat. After a couple of awkward minutes when they not only tried to serve themselves food from all the takeaway tubs, but began the slightly artificial chat of getting to know each other, things settled down and the self-consciousness in the room evaporated.

'Whereabouts are your family from?' Eliza asked.

'My mother was born here in Kingshurst, but her parents were from Pakistan, and my father was born in Pakistan, but moved to the UK when he was a teenager.'

'Would you say you're a fairly westernised family?' Lottie asked, glancing at Hannah to see if the question was all right or if it was *stupid*.

'We're a funny mixture really. Like all families who have their origins outside the UK, we have a lot of traditions that we've passed down for generations, but equally, we've all lived here for so long that we are also westernised.'

'I love your nose ring, and your jeans are gorgeous ...' Lottie stopped, checking Hannah's reaction again.

'Thanks. I must admit I'm a sucker for a designer sale,' Mandy laughed.

'I have no idea what you see in our Han then,' Lottie smiled. 'She wouldn't know a designer outfit if it jumped up and appeared in her night vision goggles.'

Mandy reached for Hannah's hand. 'I like her just as she is.'

Hannah's face turned pink. *This woman!*

Tying up her shiny, black hair in a scrunchy, Mandy tucked into her food.

'So, if you don't mind me asking, why the need for secrecy?' Eliza said.

Mandy paused, her fork halfway to her mouth. Shaking her head, she said, 'It's silly. As much as my parents are westernised, they do still have some traditions that they like to stick to. I saw the way things were heading when my eldest sister was about sixteen. They started talking about all the charming young sons their friends had. My sister put her foot down and declined an arranged marriage, thank goodness! So that set the tempo. They've never insisted any of us marry someone we are not in love with. But I knew before I was even sixteen that no one's *son* was going to be right for me. I knew what I wanted, and this crazy chick here with the spiky bleached hair and the biker boots is it.' Mandy grabbed hold of Hannah's hand.

Lottie cheered.

'But explaining that to my mother and father is hard. They're old fashioned. I'm not saying they're homophobic. More that it wouldn't even occur to them that I wouldn't like boys.'

'How have you managed to dodge a wedding for so long?' Eliza asked. 'I mean, no offence, but you're ... over thirty, yes?'

'Correct. I'm thirty-four.'

'So ...?'

'They just think I'm the fussiest thirty-four-year-old in town.'

Lottie got up from the table and made her way around to the back of Hannah's chair. 'I'll bet if they met our Han, they'd like her. She is amazing, after all.'

'Yes. I am starting to see that for myself,' Mandy agreed, blushing. 'But I'm not ready yet to face introducing her to them.' Turning to Hannah, she added, 'And you're okay with that, aren't you?'

Hannah felt Lottie's arms around her and thanked her for the reassuring hug, before saying, 'Yes, of course I'm prepared to wait. Like I told you before, I'm not in any rush for you to meet my mum and dad either. We'll take our time.'

Giving one more squeeze, Lottie moved on to Mandy. Giving her a hug from behind, she said, 'Now it makes sense why you didn't feel ready to meet us before. But I'm so glad you decided to.'

'Thank you, Lottie,' Mandy smiled. 'I'm glad you understand. I've never been one for nights out and parties. It's not easy being one person at home and a different person outside it.'

'Well, you can just be yourself with us,' Lottie assured her.

'You are as precious as Hannah said you would be.'

Sitting back down at the table, Lottie beamed at the compliment and helped herself to more crispy seaweed. They ate for a few moments in what had become a comfortable silence.

Eventually, Eliza asked Hannah, 'No news from Paul on Scott then?'

'No. He's still on his toes.'

Turning to Mandy, Lottie said, 'Do you know about Eliza's cousin?'

'No. What does on his toes mean?'

'It means he's missing. Oh my God, Eliza has so much to tell you.' Lottie leant forward, an excited expression on her face.

An assortment of leftover Chinese food was scattered in tubs over the kitchen table, and they were well into their second bottle of wine, except Mandy, who was driving. The conversation had been flowing freely for a good hour.

Turning to Hannah, Mandy said, 'I just cannot believe that two nights ago you were accosting criminals armed only with an umbrella. You really are incredibly brave.'

Hannah caught the look of pride in Mandy's big brown eyes and felt her insides melt. 'Oh shucks. T'was nothing!'

'I'm glad you didn't tell me before, though. I would have been so worried if I'd known what you were going to do.'

'It's like I always say – it's work, that's all. Besides, it's Eliza's family, and it wasn't my place to tell you it all. It was *her* story.'

'You were very professional.' Eliza nodded. 'But I don't mind Mandy knowing about it now we've met.'

'I thought Scott might turn up here,' Lottie said, rising and beginning the task of clearing the plates.

'Leave them,' Eliza offered. 'I'll do them later when you're gone.'

Lottie sat back down. 'If you're sure.'

'I am. Anyway, I need to tell you something, well … show you something.' Eliza said, intriguingly.

'What?' Lottie and Hannah asked together.

Eliza rose from her chair and headed over to the pantry. The middle shelf contained some new spices she had recently bought. Tucked behind the oregano was a piece of paper. Clearly taken from an old notepad, the edges were torn and the paper itself was slightly yellow. She handed it to Hannah. 'This note arrived this morning. It's Scott's handwriting.'

'Bloody hell, it's practically illegible.' Hannah moved the paper further away from her eyes, as if she were a middle-aged man surveying the wine list in a dimly lit restaurant. You could hear a pin drop as she read.

Sorry. I know what I did was wrong. You didn't deserve that. All I can say is it wasn't my idea and I wish I'd stood up to my dad and refused when he first said it.
Elz, you were always the best one out of the three of us. It's right that your the only one left.

Love from Scott.

X

'Hmm ... the wrong *your* again,' Hannah noted.

Lottie asked. 'What does he mean?'

'About me being left. I don't know. I hope it doesn't mean anything sinister.'

'You say you got it this morning?' Hannah turned the note over, examining it.

'Are you looking for clues, Sherlock?' Lottie asked.

'It was here when I came home from the shops. It was just lying on the doormat,' Eliza said.

'So, he's been here.' Hannah handed the note back.

'I guess so.'

'Have you tried calling him?' Mandy said.

'Like ... a thousand times.' Eliza shrugged. 'He's obviously ditched his phone.'

'It's quite a nice message, I suppose,' Lottie mused.

'D'you think?'

'Well, he's still a bastard. But he's a sorry one.'

'I just wish I knew what he meant.'

'Well, it doesn't sound like he's planning on being found by the police any time soon, does it?' Hannah shrugged.

'No.' Eliza bit her lip. 'I hope he's not going to do anything ... you know.' She chose her words carefully, aware of how Lottie's mum had died.

'He might just mean that you're the only one left in Kingshurst,' Hannah said.

'Hopefully, yes,' Eliza agreed. 'Anyway, I called the police and they said I could drop it into them tomorrow. I guess there's not a lot they can do with a note.'

Lottie said, 'Nothing that Miss Marple here couldn't do, that's for sure.' Spotting the fortune cookies, she added, 'Hey, why don't we let these little things tell us what the future holds for us?' She picked one up at random and cracked it open.

Pulling out the piece of paper, she read, *The greatest achievement in life is to stand up again after falling.* Wow. That could not be more apt.' Her eyes brimmed with tears. 'I was hoping it was going to say Chen was on his way home, but this'll do me. Do yours.' She handed a cookie to Eliza.

Eliza opened it and read the fortune. *Someone you care about seeks reconciliation.* That's unbelievable.' She picked up her wine glass and drained it. 'It makes me feel bad for Scott.'

'Mandy?' Lottie passed the last cookie across the table.

'No. There are only three.' Mandy shook her head.

Hannah said, 'Yeah. It's weird that they give you an odd number like that.'

'You have the last one.' Mandy handed it to Hannah.

'Well, okay. But how will you possibly plan your life without one?' she joked.

'I'll cope,' Mandy smiled.

'Yes, you will, because it's all bollocks.' Cracking the final cookie open, Hannah said, 'Help. I'm being held captive in a Fortune Cookie factory.'

Mandy looked a little startled, but Lottie roared with laughter. 'Bloody Ken, again! He does that every year with the Christmas Crackers.'

'What does it actually say?' Eliza asked.

This time Hannah read what was on the piece of paper. 'Ahh hem.' She cleared her throat, theatrically. *'Investigate everything. Knowledge is power.'*

'It doesn't?' Lottie squeaked.

'Honestly.' Hannah handed the piece of paper to her friend. 'Look.'

'Wow. These fortune cookies are amazing.' Lottie gave it back. 'Keep that.'

'I actually think I will.' Hannah nodded. 'Maybe they're not bollocks after all. Definitely more impressive than The Great Shazam!'

A second later, Mandy's phone beeped. Checking it she tutted. 'It's my father, just wondering where I am.'

'Do you live with your parents?' Lottie asked.

'Yes. I had my own place. Then my mother became ill, and I stupidly sold up and moved back in to help with her care. My sisters are all married; it seemed the right thing to do at the time. But now ...'

'Now you're stuck there,' Lottie volunteered.

'Yes. I should think about moving out now she's better, but my father is a good deal older than her, and I just know if I leave, something will happen to cause me to have to move back again. I know it's pathetic.' Mandy absentmindedly fiddled with the buttons on her shirt.

'Not at all. Han lived with her parents up until recently. We understand. Don't we, Hannah?'

'Of course,' Hannah agreed.

'I know. But it means I get these silly – Where are you, Mandeep? texts all too often. I'm going to have to head off; he won't stop texting now until he's seen me.'

'Okay.' Hannah rose from the table. 'I'll see you out.'

'I can give you a lift if you like,' Mandy offered. 'You *and* Lottie. But I don't want to break up the evening.'

'It's fine. A lift would be great. Saves us calling a taxi. We'll pick up my car tomorrow,' Hannah told Eliza.

'You'll let me know if you hear anything about Scott, won't you?'

'Of course. By the way, the police still haven't found anything in Lullaby Woods, and I've heard a rumour they're thinking of stepping down.'

'So, they don't think Ash is in there after all?' Lottie asked.

'Well, certainly not in the part Scott led me to. You know, without a body, he isn't even wanted for manslaughter. Ash is still just missing, presumed dead, and all Scott can be charged with as it stands is his part in your extortion, Eliza.'

'I'd like to be able to tell him that she isn't in there.' Eliza looked deflated. 'Especially after reading this.' She waved her fortune in the air.

Hannah agreed. 'It might be a bit of a weight off his mind. I'm not saying what he did was okay; obviously it wasn't.'

'No, it wasn't ... and he's still a fuckwit,' Lottie added.

'You have to remember what he went through, though,' Hannah said. 'At fifteen, he did something in a moment of blind anger that changed his whole life. It was all downhill from there.'

'Especially for Ash,' Lottie said, before apologising to Eliza. 'Sorry, that just came out.'

Hannah continued, 'Perhaps if his dad had been a better role model or if he'd simply buggered off once and for all and given Scott a chance, things would've been different. My anger is directed far more at that bloated twat Fergus, to be honest.' She shook her head. 'What he did to that boy was manipulation.'

'I know. I'm angry with him too. But it's all over now. He'll soon be back on the Isle of Wight, and I can rest easy, thanks to you.' Eliza patted Hannah on the back.

'Will you be okay on your own?' Hannah asked.

'Uh huh. I have to get back to living again. I'll lock the back door and I got the lock on the front door changed today. So ...'

'You feel safe?'

'Yes. It's strange, but I really do. In a funny way I feel less anxious than I have for a long time. Maybe for years. I know you probably think I'm mad, but it's the truth. The only person who might come and visit me tonight is Scott ... and I'd actually quite like that. I want him to know that I understand and that I don't blame him.'

'He's lucky to have you,' Lottie said.

Eliza shrugged. 'We're family!'

'What are you going to do now you've solved Eliza's case?' Lottie asked Hannah.

'There's always something else to do. You know Sandlin PI, I investigate everything. Knowledge is power.' Hannah laughed. 'In fact, Dave may have found us a potential new client just this morning.'

'Oh, exciting,' Lottie squeaked. 'Will you tell me all about it when we get home?'

'Of course,' Hannah agreed. 'You are a shareholder, after all.'

'Hot chocolate and cookies at the kitchen table?' Lottie suggested.

'You know it,' Hannah replied.

35
ASHTON – 2022

AN OLD BLUE hatchback stopped opposite the house that once belonged to Robert, Miriam, and Ashley. The driver pulled on the handbrake and switched off the engine. The two occupants of the car, a man and a woman, sat in silence for a moment.

The woman lowered the car window to get a good look at the house. She asked her husband, 'Is it the one with the orangey fence?'

'Yes,' Ashton said. 'Although I can't believe she chose that colour. It's way too modern for her.'

'Are we going to go and knock?' His wife reached for the door handle.

Ashton stopped her. 'Hold your horses, Lainy. I know you find it hard to understand, because you're so close to your family, but I can't just walk up the path and knock on the door like the last twelve years haven't happened.'

'You *can*. I'll go with you. You could see your mum.'

'Why on earth would I want to see her?'

'To tell her about your journey.'

'My journey?' He tilted his head.

Lainy nodded.

'The one where I hitched all the way to Scotland in a lorry, at the tender age of eighteen, with nothing to my name but the daft clothes I stood up in and a thumping headache?'

'No.' Lainy shook her head gently. 'Your *other* journey.'

'Oh, the one where I became the man I always should've been. The one where I met the cutest wee woman and married her.' Ashton took Lainy's left hand and kissed her wedding ring.

'Aye. That's the one.'

He sighed. 'She wouldn't understand. I can hear her now – Oh, Ashley, so you're a lesbian.'

Lainy laughed. 'You are so far from that.'

'I know, but my mum wouldn't understand what I am or how I came to be *me*. My dad might have. If he'd lived long enough to see the world as it is today, he might just get it.'

'You still miss him, don't you?'

'Every day.'

'I remember your face when you watched the Euro final last year. You were so upset.'

'Bloody hell, Lainy, I would've given anything to watch England play that match with him.'

'I know, darling.' She gazed at him with so much love. 'Would've been even better if it had been Scotland.'

Ashton laughed. 'Not much chance of that!' Then, in a more serious tone, he said, 'Still, my dad's not been in that house for years, so there's no point knocking.'

'What about your cousins? Would you like to go and see them whilst we're in town?'

Ashton considered for a second. 'You know, I was so envious of Scottie. I watched him grow into a man before my eyes. He had the one thing I wanted.'

Lainy giggled.

'Not that *one thing*, you daft hen.' He smiled; his wife's giggle was his favourite sound. 'Before, when we were kids, he was such a weedy little lad. He was a pain in the arse. But when he got to about twelve or thirteen, he just grew into what I'd always wanted to be. To start with I didn't even realise it was what I wanted, I just knew I was jealous of him. His voice, his strength. His pure masculinity. It all came so easily to him.'

Lainy's eyes misted over. 'And you've had to fight so hard for yours.'

'Imagine the shame of realising you're jealous of someone you used to look down on. Jeez.' Ashton shook his head. 'Although, in truth, I couldn't look *down* on the bugger much after the age of about twelve!'

'But you're who you want to be now.'

'Of course. Although I'd like to be taller.'

'You're perfect as you are, and if you're finally who you want to be, let's go and find Scott and Eliza.'

'I honestly don't think I want to see them.'

'But wouldn't they like to know you're still alive?'

'No. Least said, soonest mended. I think we should let their cousin Ash rest in peace. She was horrible to that poor boy.' Ashton experienced a stab of guilt.

'You were hurting. You've regretted how you teased him for so long.'

Rubbing his temple, Ashton's fingers touched the old scar. 'I forgave Scott for what he did to me. I just hope *he* has forgiven *me*.'

'And there's nothing I can say to convince you to go and knock on the door and just see if your mum still lives there?'

'Nothing, darling.'

'So, why …?'

'I just wanted to see it. To know the house was still here. I've pictured it so many times in my mind. Honestly, it's enough. I'm glad we came. Who knows how long it'll be before we get back down to England again? I think it was worth the detour on our way home.'

'You're seriously happy to just look at the house from here?'

'Yes. My dad is in here.' Ashton pointed to his chest. 'Not there, or in the churchyard. So I'm carrying him back to Glasgow with us.'

'I wonder if Scott ever knew how jealous you were of him.'

'He didn't!' Ashton shook his head, emphatically.

'How can you be so sure?'

'Because I know how I felt when I was Ashley, and I was never going to let him find that out.'

'I think I much prefer you now.' Lainy reached out for her husband, pulling him into her arms.

'You'd be right to prefer me now. I was a total bitch.' Ashton took one last look at his mum's house over Lainy's shoulder.

Moving away from her arms and back into the driving seat, he started up the engine, pushed down on the clutch and slipped the car into first. Releasing the handbrake, he checked his mirrors and drove away. 'There's no way she lives there now, anyway. That fence is way too snazzy to be hers.'

EPILOGUE

2030

In the UK, when a person has been missing for at least seven years, and has not been heard from during that time by family members or any other interested party, there is a presumption of death.

People in the category presumed dead have been declared dead through legal process, in absence of a body. It is not definitely known whether the people in this category are actually dead, but for legal purposes their status as dead has been declared.

No one has heard from Cousin Scott for eight years. Scott is in the category presumed dead.

ACKNOWLEDGMENTS

A big thank you to all my friends and family who bought the first book in this series, especially those who asked me to sign their copies. Your encouragement and praise mean the world to me. As before, thank you to my advisor, Colin for his help with a couple of technical issues. Lastly, my thanks and love go to my husband, David for agreeing to chat to me about the characters in this book at any time of the day or night!

ABOUT THE AUTHOR

Sue Shepherd began her writing career in 2015, writing contemporary romance. Over the next couple of years, she created three novels with heart, laughs and naughtiness. *Doesn't Everyone Have a Secret?*, *Love Them and Leave Them* and *Can't Get You Out of My Head*.

Realising that one of the parts she enjoyed most about writing was deciding when to let the reader in on the secrets from her characters' past, Sue switched genres and began writing a crime series starting with *Swindled*.

Sue lives on the picturesque Isle of Wight with her husband, two sons, a standard poodle named Forrest and a Cavachon called Sky. Her passions in life are; her family, writing, the seaside and all the beautiful purple things her sons have bought her over the years. Ask Sue to plan too far in advance and you'll give her the heebie-jeebies and she'd prefer you not to mention Christmas until at least November!

SWINDLED: BOOK 1 IN THE SANDLIN PI SERIES

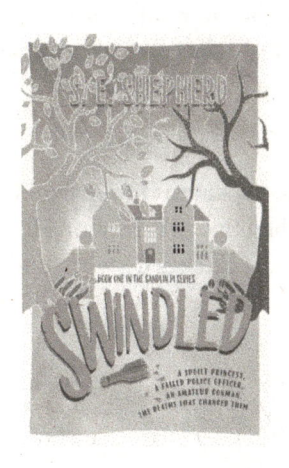

'A great debut mystery thriller with a touch of cozy.' Advance Reader

'...will definitely takes your breath away...an absolute stunner of a thriller...' Surjit's Book Blog

'Loved this book from start to finish' Nicki Williams

'He's out there somewhere. He's taken everything from me, and ... I hate him!'

Lottie
Beautiful, but a little spoilt, Lottie Thorogood leads a charmed life. Returning home from horse riding one day, she finds a stranger, drinking tea in the family drawing room – a stranger who will change her life, forever.

Hannah
After a bad decision cut short her police career, Hannah Sandlin is desperate to make her mark as a private investigator. She knows she has the skills, but why won't anyone take her seriously? She's about to become embroiled in a mystery that will finally put those skills to the test and prove her doubters wrong. It will also bring her a friend for life.

Vincent
Vincent Rocchino has spent his life charming the ladies, fleecing them and fleeing when things turn sour. How long can he keep running before his past catches up with him?

HOBECK BOOKS – THE HOME OF GREAT STORIES

We hope you've enjoyed reading this novel by the brilliant S.E. Shepherd. To find out more about the author please visit her Facebook page: **www.facebook.com/SueShepherdWrites**.

Hobeck Books offers a number of short stories and novellas, free for subscribers in the compilation *Crime Bites*.

- *Echo Rock* by Robert Daws

- *Old Dogs, Old Tricks* by AB Morgan
- *The Silence of the Rabbit* by Wendy Turbin
- *Never Mind the Baubles: An Anthology of Twisted Winter Tales* by the Hobeck Team (including many of the Hobeck authors and Hobeck's two publishers)
- *The Clarice Cliff Vase* by Linda Huber
- *Here She Lies* by Kerena Swan
- *The Macnab Principle* by R.D. Nixon
- *Fatal Beginnings* by Brian Price
- *A Defining Moment* by Lin Le Versha
- *Saviour* by Jennie Ensor
- *You Can't Trust Anyone These Days* by Maureen Myant

Also please visit the Hobeck Books website for details of our other superb authors and their books, and if you would like to get in touch, we would love to hear from you.

Hobeck Books also presents a weekly podcast, the Hobcast, where founders Adrian Hobart and Rebecca Collins discuss all things book related, key issues from each week, including the ups and downs of running a creative business. Each episode includes an interview with one of the people who make Hobeck possible: the editors, the authors, the cover designers. These are the people who help Hobeck bring great stories to life. Without them, Hobeck wouldn't exist. The Hobcast can be listened to from all the usual platforms but it can also be found on the Hobeck website: **www.hobeck.net/hobcast**.

Finally, if you enjoyed this book, please also leave a review on the site you bought it from and spread the word. Reviews are hugely important to writers and they help other readers also.

OTHER HOBECK BOOKS TO EXPLORE

Over Her Dead Body

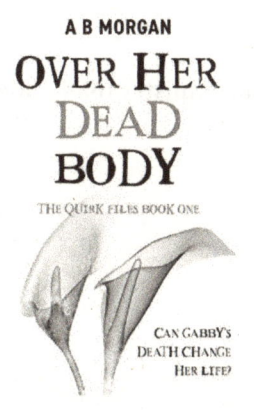

For fans of Richard Osman and Janice Hallett, introducing The Quirks in the first in a brand new crime series, OVER HER DEAD BODY - a 'what if' tale full of brilliantly drawn characters, quirky humour and dark plot twists. If you love laugh-out-loud fiction with a twist of crime then this book is for you!

'OMG WHAT A PAGE TURNER!! ... I finally turned the last page at 2am.' Peggy

Gabby Dixon is dead. That's news to her...
Recently divorced and bereaved, Gabby Dixon is trying to start a new chapter in her life.

As her new life begins, it ends. On paper at least.
But Gabby is still very much alive. As a woman who likes to be in control, this situation is deeply unsettling.

HOBECK BOOKS – THE HOME OF GREAT STORIES

She has two crucial questions: who would want her dead, and why?
Enter Peddyr and Connie Quirk. husband-and-wife private investigators. Gabby needs their help to find out who is behind her sudden death.

The truth is a lot more sinister than a simple case of stolen identity.

Throttled

Scott Fletcher is dead – his lifeless body in a pool of blood.

Sarah Holden's life is turned upside-down the day she is discovered with her fiancé's body next to the motorbike he'd been working on. She has blood on her hands, but the screams do not come.

If she didn't kill him, then who did?

The answer seems too easy. The likely culprit too obvious.

With a dead husband and now dead fiancé, is Sarah just unlucky in love?

Peddyr and Connie Quirk, husband-and-wife private investigators, are brought in to unravel the tangle, prove Sarah's innocence and find the true culprit. As they are about to discover, the truth is sometimes much more than skin deep.

Verity Vanishes

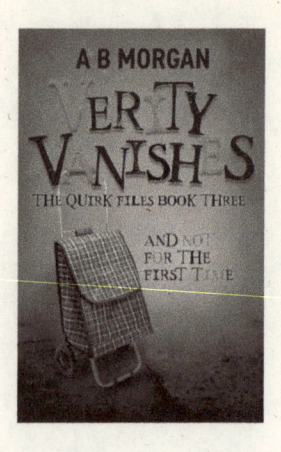

The Quirks are back and there is another crime for P. Q. Investigations.

When Verity Hudson goes missing, Peddyr Quirk – with assistance from his effervescent wife Connie – investigates a strange new case which unfolds in an unsavoury part of town. It soon becomes apparent that they are not the only ones looking for Verity.

A freelance researcher is searching for her birth mother. An influential man of power and money is desperate to find his estranged sister.

A local politician is determined to expose a hidden tragedy. A TV journalist will stop at nothing to expose the true story ... if it can be uncovered.

Where is Verity, who is Verity, and who will find her first?

Blood Loss

'...in the same league as Ian Rankin and L J Ross...' Graham Rolph

'My arms broke out in goose-bumps! Wow!' Susan Hampson, *Books From Dust Till Dawn*

Sarah
With one eye on the rear view mirror and the other on the road ahead, Sarah is desperate to get as far away from the remote Scottish cabin as she can without attracting attention. But being inconspicuous isn't easy with a black eye and clothes soaked in blood...
... and now the fuel tank is empty.

DI Paton
When a body is discovered in a remote cabin in Scotland, DI Paton feels a pang of guilt as he wonders if this is the career break he has been waiting for. But the victim is unidentifiable and the killer has left few clues.

HOBECK BOOKS – THE HOME OF GREAT STORIES

Jenna
With the death of her father and her mother's failing health, Jenna accepts her future plans must change but nothing can prepare her for the trauma yet to come.

Fleeing south to rebuild her life Sarah uncovers long-hidden family secrets. Determined to get back what she believes is rightfully hers, Sarah thinks her future looks brighter. But Paton is still pursuing her...

... and he's getting closer.

Lightning Source UK Ltd.
Milton Keynes UK
UKHW040833240722
406259UK00002B/280

9 781913 793814